THE POWERS THAT BE

ANY PRICE

HAZEL DOMAIN

ANGLERFISH PRESS

Riptide Publishing
PO Box 1537
Burnsville, NC 28714
www.riptidepublishing.com

This is a work of fiction. Names, characters, places, and incidents are either the product of the author's imagination or are used fictitiously. Any resemblance to actual persons living or dead, business establishments, events, or locales is entirely coincidental. All person(s) depicted on the cover are model(s) used for illustrative purposes only.

Any Price
Copyright © 2024 by Hazel Domain

Cover art: Simoné
Editor: Rachel Haimowitz
Layout: L.C. Chase, lcchase.com

All rights reserved. No part of this book may be reproduced or transmitted in any form or by any means, electronic or mechanical, including photocopying, recording, or by any information storage and retrieval system without the written permission of the publisher, and where permitted by law. Reviewers may quote brief passages in a review. To request permission and all other inquiries, contact Riptide Publishing at the mailing address above, at Riptidepublishing.com, or at marketing@riptidepublishing.com.

ISBN: 978-1-963773-00-2

First edition
July, 2024

Also available in ebook:
ISBN: 978-1-62649-999-7

THE POWERS THAT BE

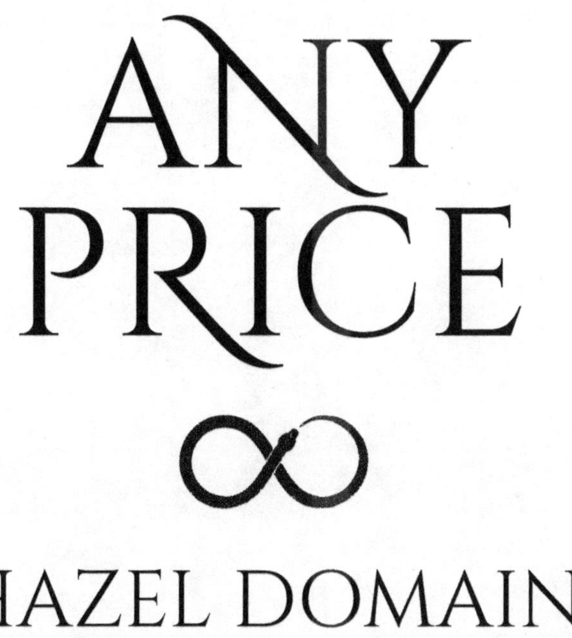

For Matt, who told me I was a writer.

TABLE OF CONTENTS

Chapter 1 1
Chapter 2 11
Chapter 3 17
Chapter 4 23
Chapter 5 29
Chapter 6 37
Chapter 7 49
Chapter 8 63
Chapter 9 67
Chapter 10 79
Chapter 11 85
Chapter 12 87
Chapter 13 93
Chapter 14 107
Chapter 15 109
Chapter 16 113
Chapter 17 117
Chapter 18 127
Chapter 19 161
Chapter 20 177
Chapter 21 185
Chapter 22 203
Chapter 23 207
Chapter 24 211
Chapter 25 231

CHAPTER ONE

On television, indent markets were all about red velvet couches and people in masks bidding on supermodels.

In reality, Dominic found himself in a cross between a car dealership and a YMCA. Large windows and white tile gave an impression of space. On the back wall, a large poster showed a woman of indeterminate age, holding a broom and smiling. *The indenturement program got me back to work,* read the caption along the bottom. *Indents move industry forward!*

There were several dozen people on the sales floor, most dressed in the black scrubs that served as a de-facto uniform for indentured employees. A young woman noticed Dominic looking and waved, though she didn't approach. Dom waved back and, for the hundredth time, wondered if he was making a huge mistake.

"See anyone you like?" said a voice at Dom's shoulder. He turned to find a salesman, grinning broadly.

"Maybe? I've actually got kind of a weird request."

The salesman's grin widened. "Doesn't everyone." He winked. "Whatever it is, I'm sure we can find someone to accommodate you."

"I work in creature control," Dom said bluntly. This was where he was going to get turned away, sent back to the job posting boards that had been failing him for the last nine months. "I need someone who isn't going to freeze when it comes to staking a feral vampire."

The salesman frowned. "That . . . is an odd one, I won't lie. Off the top of my head, I don't think we have anyone with creacon *certifications*, certainly not anyone on-hand; these are more day-labor types . . . but I can check the database?"

He didn't need to bother. If someone certified was up for hire, Dom would already have found them. "I'm not worried about the certifications. I know what I'm doing, I just need an extra pair of hands. If you've got someone with a Gift, *that'd* be really helpful."

The salesman's hum was doubtful. "I can tell you right now it's extremely rare for the Gifted to need the services of an indenturement facility. It's not unheard of for an applicant to have average magical ability, but even a little aptitude on that front raises the contract price significantly."

"I figured."

"If you don't mind my asking, do you have a budget in mind?"

Dom did, in fact. The life insurance payout had been two hundred seventy-five thousand dollars exactly, cashed out in hundreds, most of which was still in a paper bag in his trunk. But he wasn't about to tell the salesman that.

"A good assistant pays for themselves," he answered instead. "Why, did you have someone in mind?"

"I think I do." He nodded, turning toward the back, away from the windows, and gestured for Dom to follow. "Caitlyn! Over here, please!"

A tall, solidly built woman turned immediately away from a group of applicants, moving toward Dominic in what he could only describe as a march.

"Sir?"

"Caitlyn, this is . . ." the salesman paused. "Goodness, I forgot to ask your name."

"Dominic Blackburn." Dom extended his hand. Caitlyn took it, shaking once before returning her hands to her sides.

"Caitlyn was private security for seven years before joining us," the salesman said. "She's proficient in hand-to-hand combat as well as a number of close-range weapons. No magical aptitude, I'm afraid, but no one's perfect." He chuckled politely. Caitlyn didn't react. "Eight years left on her contract, eighty thousand, and you can both be out the door in an hour."

Dominic did some math. Ten thousand a year was a little low, even for a contract that someone else had given up. Even after paying the broker's fee, her insurance, and living expenses, that was *still* far less than he'd have to pay an hourly employee. He wondered uneasily why her first contract holder had decided to transfer.

"You ever done paranormal roundups before?" he asked.

Caitlyn's words were clipped, wasting no time on lingering vowels. "I did mostly household security. We had basic training on how to neutralize the more common threats, but I never dealt with any personally."

Out of the corner of his eye, Dom noticed another woman. She was dressed like a civilian and was watching him with more interest than the situation called for. He turned his attention back to Caitlyn, ignoring it for now.

This was the important question. "Could you take out something humanoid, if the situation called for it? A lot of creatures mimic humans well, or used to be human. Some people have a hard time getting past that."

"You don't have to worry about that," the salesman cut in. "We screen our applicants very carefully, Mr. Blackburn, and I assure you that we don't *have* indents with performance problems. You're guaranteed full compliance or your money back within 30 days of the purchase date."

"It's not a question of compliance," Dom said. The woman off to the side was inching closer, and it was putting him on edge. "In a life-or-death situation, most people *can* behead a zombie. I need someone who isn't going to struggle with the morality afterward."

Caitlyn frowned. "The morality of . . . what? Those were the orders, right?"

"Have you ever had an indentured assistant before?" the salesman asked. He didn't wait for a response. "Think of it like the military: having *your* judgment respected is what sets them apart from at-will employees. If your indent is struggling to follow instructions, something's gone very wrong with their training, and like I said, we screen for that."

Dominic opened his mouth to argue, but then thought better of it. Refusing their duties could get indents in *contractual* trouble, but that wasn't what he was worried about.

He'd been training to be a creature controller since he was twelve. He'd had his first successful investigation when he was seventeen, passed his exams at eighteen, and now, at twenty-eight, he'd dealt with more monsters than he could count. He knew which maladies and curses had cures, and he knew which ones didn't. But that didn't stop the nightmares, the what-ifs, the split second between the gunshot and the ectoplasm where you're certain you're about to see blood.

And if someone *did* make that mistake, contractual responsibility should be the *least* of their worries.

"I think maybe I've misunderstood what's for sale here," he said. "Nice to meet you both, but I'm gonna pass."

In his car, Dominic resisted the urge to bang his head against the steering wheel.

It wasn't like he thought he was going to find a *perfect* indent, but hell, somebody he could at least *work with* would have been great. He wasn't desperate—not yet. But the pixie den in Erie had been the third job in a month he'd had to turn down because he couldn't work it solo. Sometimes he could put feelers out to other controllers, find somebody free and nearby, but he couldn't keep that up long-term. He needed a teammate he could rely on, short notice and long-term. Somebody like—

A tap to his left startled him out of his thoughts, and he rolled his eyes. Perfect example of why he needed somebody watching his back.

Just outside the window was the woman who had been watching him earlier. His hand crept toward the gun on his hip. In his line of work, it wasn't promising when people followed you.

Sometimes they weren't people.

"Can I help you?"

"I think maybe we can help each other," she answered, giving him a wry smile. "Dominic, right? I'm Megan. I heard you're after an indent who can work security. I might have something you'd be interested in. Come with me."

She walked away before he could reply. He almost, *almost* didn't go after her. Normal conversations did not begin this way. *But then again*, he thought, pushing the car door open, *what about my life has ever been normal?*

Megan stopped behind a van and removed a padlock holding the back doors shut. They swung open, and she gestured inside. Dominic stepped up to the bumper, squinting into the darkness.

There was a man sitting in the corner, his back against the barrier behind the driver's seat. His head hung down, long dark hair falling across his features. Sparse light glinted off a chain running between his cuffed wrists and ankles.

"The . . . fuck?" Dominic muttered. The man didn't react. Dominic turned to Megan. "What the hell is this?"

"He's fit, he's healthy, he knows how to fight, and he's sixty grand." Megan counted off on her fingers. "He's got a lifetime contract. You won't find a bargain like this anywhere else."

"Yeah, right, I bet. Let me guess: I gotta pay in cash, and you've lost his paperwork."

"No, I've got his paperwork. Full training and medical records going back to the day he signed. All hard copies, plus a transfer form in duplicate. Double-check the online registry if you don't believe me. You want him, he's yours."

Dominic stared into the shadows, trying to parse what he'd just been told. He kept staring, but nothing made any more sense, so he climbed into the van, pulling out his cell phone and thumbing on the flashlight.

The indent didn't react, even when Dom knelt to get closer.

It was hot inside, and sweat beaded on the man's bare shoulders. Aside from the shackles, he was wearing nothing except plain cotton pants—dusty, like he'd been kneeling in the dirt. He looked more like a kidnapping victim than someone headed for a job interview.

He was tall. Maybe taller than Dom, but it was hard to tell with the way he was curled in on himself. Dominic would guess he was in his midtwenties, but he could have been anywhere from eighteen to thirty.

"What's your deal?" Dominic asked, and the indent raised his head, blinking slowly. Despite the light shining on his face, his pupils were huge, almost blocking out the hazel of his irises. His brow furrowed, like he wasn't sure what he was seeing.

"He can't talk." Megan's voice was defensive. "That's the catch. Take it or leave it. He's still useful, trust me."

Dominic scowled, moving the light back and forth. "I'm pretty sure he's got a concussion. Why's he in cuffs?"

"I got him that way." Megan climbed into the van, summoning a spark of witchlight with a flick of her fingers. "He was tranquilized for transport—"

"*What*?"

"Chill. It'll wear off in a couple of hours, and he'll be back to his regular self. I've known him for four years, and trust me when I tell you, he's smart and capable and all *kinds* of talented."

Dominic glanced at her. "He's got a Gift?"

"He's got *gifts* all right," Megan said, and Dominic could nearly hear her eyebrow rising.

Oh. So the indent had . . . one of *those* contracts. That explained the chains, at least. Sort of. And *maybe* the drugs? Maybe he'd allowed for them in his terms as some kind of . . . kink thing, or whatever.

Least they could have done is get the guy a fucking shirt.

"So why sell him?" Dom asked, changing the subject before she could elaborate.

Megan hesitated. "His contract's owned by the company I work for. I'm supposed to get it transferred, and I don't have time to go through consignment."

"Why do I feel like there's more to that story?"

"Because there is. But it's not your business and it has nothing to do with him. So do you want him or not?"

The man's face swung back and forth between them like he was trying to figure out who was speaking.

Dominic rubbed his face.

This was a terrible idea. An absolutely terrible idea. Paperwork or no, this was some kind of scam, and he was going to end up dead in a ditch. And what the hell was he going to do with someone who couldn't *talk*? But . . .

The indent was still staring, his eyes wide and unfocused. He looked like he hadn't taken a shower in a week, and the stifling air of the van couldn't be doing him any favors. There were lines of mud splattered across his back, and his chest had a row of markings that might have been letters. A little voice in the back of Dom's head asked where these two would go from here, if he were to simply walk away.

"Unlock him."

Megan tossed Dominic a key, and he leaned in, examining the wrist cuffs. The indent stared for a second, then turned his palms upward, exposing the keyholes. There was a barcode tattooed on the inside of his arm, so he really did have a lifetime contract. Dom made short work of the wrist shackles, wincing at the unusually loud sound of the chain on the metal floor. He held the key out, but the man made no effort to take it.

"You're sure he's not concussed? What did you give him?"

"*I* didn't give him anything."

Dom scowled. Her insistence on being cryptic wasn't doing anything to boost his confidence.

The man tilted his head toward Megan, frowning slightly, and Megan didn't meet his eye.

"It's lorazepam," she muttered. "He didn't need it, but our boss . . . It'll be out of his system in a couple hours. He'll be fine."

"I feel like he should see a doctor."

"Buy him, then," Megan said, her voice hard again. "You can play doctor whenever you want."

Her joyless grin was rife with implications. Dominic, from his place on the floor, did his best to ignore it. He unlocked the ankle cuffs and dropped the key. "All right, up you go." He stood and stepped back.

The man rose unsteadily to his feet, ducking to avoid hitting his head on the roof of the van. Megan hopped nimbly to the ground, not turning around to see how Dom fared. Dominic jumped and was a little surprised when the indent followed, leaping without hesitation and landing on his feet. He raised a hand to the sun, blinking in the sudden light.

The chains had been doing him a disservice in more ways than one. Without them, the lines of his body were straight and lithe, his stance centered and sure despite the blank expression on his face. He was closer to thirty than twenty, and standing straight, he was at least a couple inches taller than Dom. The cotton pants hung low on his hips, letting the edge of a tattoo peek out.

It was hard to tell under the dirt, but Dominic got the impression that this guy would clean up *really* well.

"Here," Dom said. He held out his hand, palm facing the other man, fingers up. "Push on this."

The indent considered for almost three full seconds before complying. He entwined his fingers unexpectedly between Dom's, before giving him an enthusiastic shove. Dom held his own, but barely.

He stuffed his hand into his pocket, addressing Megan. "Anything else I should know?"

"No. Just the voice. And like I said, he can fight. Formal training in hand-to-hand, which'll probably be useful if you're gonna have him tackling werewolves or whatever you do."

Dominic rubbed the bridge of his nose. Megan was right about one thing: a lifetime contract was a *steal* for sixty thousand, especially for someone as young and healthy as this guy appeared to be. Even if it ended up being a bad placement, he could easily get that money back. Probably more.

This was a good business decision. It *was*. He was making this decision with his *brain*, not his heart or his . . . conscience.

He pulled Megan aside, lowering his voice. "Okay. If his registry number checks out, I'll take him. Fifty K."

"I told you, sixty."

Dom crossed his arms. "If you want to clean him up, take him down to city hall, and notarize this sale, I'll get you a check for sixty. But I'm buying his contract out of the back of a van, with cash, so there's a ten thousand what-the-fuck fee."

Megan narrowed her eyes. "Fine." She retreated to the front seat of her vehicle, and he took the opportunity to retrieve the money from his. He had the cash counted out and the rest stashed before she returned with a thick manila envelope and a pen.

While she filled out the transfer sheets, he went back to the indent in question. "Can I see your arm?"

The man nodded, holding out his barcode. Dom scanned it into the Department of Indent Services website with his phone and—somewhat to his surprise—got a result.

The original indenturement had taken place pre-digitization, so the history was just a list of numbered PDFs, half of which were marked with the same date—presumably the day the files were scanned. They were labeled with his number, rather than a name. Dominic selected the most recent entry and was greeted with a photo that was clearly the man standing in front of him. His last registered contract holder was listed as A. Slate Industries.

And the contract was, as Megan had hinted, *full service*.

Dom didn't think about that too hard. "You got an ID?" he asked instead, turning to Megan. "Anything from this company?"

Megan withdrew a badge from her pocket and held it out so he could see her photo and the company name. Good enough.

Megan watched as he signed the transfer forms, more interested in the money under his thumb than the information he was writing on the papers. The ink hadn't dried when Megan snatched one from him. He handed over a bundle of folded hundreds, watching in silence as she counted it.

"Great. Up to you whether you want to register the sale. You'll probably have to visit DIS in person, sometime in the next, like, month. Show them his file. And everything I know about him is in there, so don't call me."

"What's his name?" Dominic asked.

Megan blinked. "Oh. It's Micah."

"Micah," Dominic repeated. From his place a couple of feet away, Micah perked up. His whole body seemed to focus in Dom's direction, standing at unsteady attention. "Okay. Well, Micah, let's get you out of here."

CHAPTER TWO

Dominic offered Micah a bottle of water as soon as they returned to the car. Micah, getting into the back for some reason, drank it so fast that Dominic handed him another. That vanished just as fast, and Dominic might have been imagining it, but Micah seemed a bit more alert.

"There's a pullover there if you want it," Dom said, gesturing to the jumble of stuff behind the driver's seat.

Micah dug through it while Dominic started the engine and navigated out of the parking lot.

Turning onto the road, Dominic drove toward home in what he hoped was a companionable silence. Not that he'd know how to fix an awkward silence, anyway. How do you talk to a mute man whose life contract you just bought? It wasn't like he could make small talk.

His eyes landed on the empty bottles Micah had tossed into the footwell. "It's still a while to my place from here. Do you want to get some food or anything?"

In the rearview mirror, Micah gave a single nod.

". . . Cool," Dominic said weakly, and started watching for somewhere to stop.

It didn't take long for his eyes to return to the mirror, only to dart away when he saw that Micah was staring back at him. Micah's brow was furrowed, like he was trying to figure something out.

Dom gave him what he hoped was a friendly smile. "You back in the land of the living?"

Micah nodded, once.

Dom cleared his throat. "So, uh, quick and dirty situation is: I'm in creature control, which is a fancy way of saying I make things quit bumping in the night."

Another glance in the rearview mirror. No change.

"Megan said you could fight, and that's good, because I've been doing a lot of solo gigs lately, and I'm getting my ass kicked way more regularly than I'd like. I figure I need a backup dancer, or I'm gonna end up dead."

Was that a flicker of amusement? Maybe. Dom barreled on, delivering the shitty sales pitch he'd been practicing since he'd first thought of hiring an indent. "It's a dangerous gig, I'm not gonna lie to you. And it's not easy. But the money's decent, and it's work worth doing. We think so anyway—my family's been doing it for five generations."

Thought, Dom corrected himself. The family *thought* so. Back when there *was* a family.

He forced a casual grin onto his face. "Apparently that's not a popular opinion, because there are only three controllers in the region, and the other two are a married couple, so no chance of poaching one for my team. I figured my best bet was paying to train somebody new. It'll be a lot of learning on the job, but I'll give you a cut of the fee to make up for it. What do you say? You wanna give it a try?"

Micah blinked at him, then nodded slowly. The car was silent for a long beat. Dominic didn't look away, feeling like he should say more, but unsure of what.

The car buzzed as the wheels passed over the lane-departure sigils, and Dom jerked the wheel, turning his attention back to the road. "Just give it six months. If it's not your thing, I'll transfer you to a holder that doesn't kill monsters for a living. You can be a nanny or something."

He couldn't help checking the mirror again.

Micah's jaw tensed, and agitation flickered across his face. He turned away from Dominic.

The countryside flew past, all cornfields and telephone poles. Dom checked the rearview mirror a couple more times, but Micah's hazel eyes never strayed from the window.

The gas station had a mini-mart attached to the pumps, and when Dominic went inside for munchies, Micah followed him. Dominic headed straight for the slushies and pizza racks—classic road food—but when he turned around, Micah was staring at the baskets of local produce near the door.

Dominic gestured at some stone fruit. "You want one of those?"

Micah nodded almost hesitantly, like he thought there was a right answer and he might be choosing the wrong one.

"You sure? They've got pepperoni and mushroom. Chance of food poisoning ten percent, *tops*." Dom held up a slice of pizza overflowing the edges of a paper plate. Micah shrugged and dropped his gaze to the floor.

Dom picked up a peach and placed it on the counter, along with his pizza and a six-pack of sodas. He added a couple of sticks of jerky to round out the well-balanced meal. Micah seemed hungry, watching raptly as the attendant stuffed everything into a paper bag—but it wasn't until they were back outside, eating at a table beside the parking lot, that Dom realized *how* hungry.

Dominic had eaten some delicious things in his life. Once, when he was fourteen, he'd eaten a peanut butter brownie so perfect that he'd had a wet dream about it later. In his adulthood, he'd become a connoisseur of tuna melts, and he could point out the five greatest burgers in the country on a map. He was an individual with a deep and lasting appreciation for food. Even so, he didn't think he'd ever enjoyed *anything* the way the man in front of him was enjoying that peach.

Micah held it with both hands, eyes closed, not so much eating it as making love to it with his mouth. A drop of juice ran down his face and hand, and when his tongue darted out to lap it off his palm, a piercing glinted in the light.

Dom would've been painfully aroused if he weren't so busy getting a bad feeling about how long it had clearly been since Micah had eaten. It didn't make sense. He didn't *look* starved. He couldn't put on muscle like that if he weren't getting fed on the regular. Whatever was going on with him was pretty clearly bad—but it was also *recent.*

"You want some more?"

Micah nodded, wiping his mouth with the back of his wrist.

Dominic handed him a couple of bills. "Get whatever you want. If you don't like the pizza, you won't like what I've got back at my place."

Micah eyed him and took the money slowly, like he was expecting something sudden and awful to happen once he did.

"I'll be here when you get back," Dominic said, and settled in against the picnic table to eat. He turned his attention to where a nearby couple was feeding perfectly good french fries to pigeons. He very deliberately watched the couple and the birds, not the man walking away. Micah would return or he wouldn't. If he was going to run, Dom wanted him to run now. Not when Dom was up to his neck in trolls and waiting for backup that wasn't coming.

Besides, they both knew Micah wouldn't get far if he did. He'd be caught and thrown in jail until he could be returned by the state. There were places that bought broken contracts, the military likely being the comfiest. If Micah vanished now, Dom *might* lose some money on the resale, but it was better than being eaten by monsters.

A couple of teenagers came by with a box of chocolate bars, some school fundraiser or something. Dominic bought two of them, figuring he'd eat both if his new companion's weird healthy eating preferences extended to a moratorium on chocolate.

The couple on the next bench ran out of fries and left.

No sign of Micah.

Dominic checked his watch. He'd resolved to give it five more minutes, when he heard the pneumatic door open, and Micah came out carrying a paper sack.

"Got what you need?"

Micah nodded. Dom waited, but he didn't sit back down, just stood there holding his bag.

"You . . ." *Why was he just* standing *there like that?* ". . . good to go?"

Micah inclined his head toward the car, but otherwise didn't move. Dom shrugged and headed for his car.

CHAPTER THREE

"Home sweet home," Dominic announced an hour later, pulling up the gravel drive. "It's not much, but it's mine."

The house—if you could call it that—was partially underground. Back in the fifties, Dominic's great-grandpa had decided that werewolves were less of a threat than the Russians, and had built himself a fallout shelter in the Pennsylvania Appalachians. Structurally, it was a couple of old rail cars welded against the frame of a double-wide trailer. The whole thing had been shoved up against the side of a bluff and covered with enough rocks and dirt to protect the inhabitants from The Big One. After the cold war ended, the family excavated one side and installed windows. Half-buried, the house appeared to grow from the hillside like a pyrite crystal.

Dominic had grown up here, the same as his dad and grandfather. He'd hung the drywall himself, done a fair amount of the wiring, even repainted the exterior one hot dull summer a couple of years back.

Back when his grandfather was still alive, Dominic had spent a lot of time here by himself, holding down the homestead while his father and grandfather were out on jobs. He could map the surrounding woodland as easily as his own bedroom, and more than one tree in the area bore the initials *D.B.*

Dominic realized he was daydreaming with the car door half-open. Micah hadn't moved and was staring at him with a mixture of curiosity and concern.

Dom climbed out of the car, rolling his shoulders. "Come on. Not getting any younger."

The footsteps behind him stopped as Dom reached the doorway. Micah had paused on the gravel drive, dirty and barefoot. He was holding a grocery sack containing all he had in the world, and damned if he didn't give the impression of being *small.*

Once again, Dominic felt like he should say something, but hell if he knew what. Instead, he unlocked the door and walked inside, flicking the lights on and gesturing for Micah to follow.

Without thinking, he checked the ikons carved into the wood of the doorframe. His was glowing dimly, but the others' were dark, nothing but simple scratches. Obviously.

Dom surveyed the interior. Everything was as he'd left it, all cleaned up for company. The house (or fallout shelter, or what have you) was built with an open floor plan. The front door led into a living room. Daylight streamed through the windows, illuminating the beat-up couches circling the flat-screen. The couches were secondhand. The television was the second most expensive thing in the house, after the sound system. May it never be said that the Blackburn men did not have their priorities sorted.

Dom kicked his boots off and left them on the mat, shucking off his jacket. Before he did anything else, he would have to get his new roommate some clothes. Scratch that. A shower. Then some clothes. And then an introduction to decent food. Clearly, something had gone seriously wrong in his dietary education.

A breeze blew through the room, and Dom turned back. The door still stood open, and Micah hadn't come inside.

Dom beckoned impatiently. "What are you, a vampire? Get in here."

Hazel eyes rose to meet his, then dropped. Then Micah squared his shoulders and stepped across the threshold. The door swung lazily closed behind him.

And then he grasped his borrowed pullover by the collar and stripped it over his head in one fluid motion, folding it over his arm before setting it aside.

In the daylight, Dom noticed marks on his chest, scuffed lines that could have been words, once. Dominic's confusion exceeded the time he had to process it. Before he could form a question, Micah's hands dropped to the drawstring of his pants.

"Hey, uh—"

Micah was breathing slowly and deeply. Dominic found himself distracted by the sight of Micah's stomach muscles stretching and tensing, the way his pants hung low on his hips.

There was a tattoo there, Dominic remembered. Over his right hip bone, coming into view as—

"Pants. Um. Hey. Pants stay on. Dude? Dude. Pants stay on. This isn't that kind of job."

Micah's hands stilled on the drawstring, then swiftly retied the knot. He kept his gaze focused on the far wall as he went down to one knee, maneuvering gracefully until he was sitting back on his heels.

Dominic blinked. He didn't know what to do with this development. He very carefully tried to maintain eye contact.

Micah closed his eyes, and then, very deliberately, licked his lips. He didn't close his mouth, and when he smiled, his piercing glinted on his tongue.

Dominic had been in a lot of odd situations in his life. He and his father had once exorcised a succubus. It had been an unusually quiet job, devoid of eye contact as they arranged the various *preparations*, and they'd never spoken of it again.

That had *nothing* on this.

"What are you doing?"

There was no answer. Of course there wasn't. Micah silently knelt there, hands on his knees, focusing on the wall over Dominic's shoulder.

Dom scrambled for something to say. He ducked into the kitchen, rummaging around in the scrap drawer until he found a notepad and a pen. And another pen. And finally, a pen that worked.

He went to Micah and held them out. "What are you doing?"

Micah took the pad and pen, staring at them. He grinned up at Dominic. Then, in plain print letters, he wrote, *Offering*.

Dom gave himself a few seconds to process that. As much as he *appreciated* the offer, it felt inhospitable to get down to business when Micah had only been here for, like, forty seconds.

"You want me to show you around first?" Dom gestured toward the rest of the house, an act that almost completed the tour. "You can take a shower? I'll dig out some clothes that'll fit you, until we can get you something better."

Micah's eyes flicked to Dominic's face, and then he stood up with the same fluid grace he'd used on the way down. He gestured for Dominic to go on.

Dom pointed out his own bedroom, the workshop, and his fath— the spare bedroom. He dug a clean towel out of the linen closet and tried to ignore the way Micah paused in the bathroom doorway, like he was waiting for Dominic to follow him.

Five minutes later, Micah was in the shower (alone, thanks to all of Dominic's willpower, possibly augmented by a visit from an actual shoulder angel). Dom was scrolling through creacon news feeds on his laptop and waiting for macaroni to boil. He turned his phone on and immediately got a text from Garrett, one of his dispatchers.

We got something up north dropping bodies, minus faces. Thinking it might be a shapestealer trying to cover something up. U want more details?

Dominic read it over twice, then messaged back. *Got a newbie here. You got anything easy? Don't care about the fee.*

He set his phone aside and waited. It wouldn't be long.

Garrett communicated entirely through electronic means, and he was never more than a minute away from his keyboard. There was a rumor he wasn't a man at all, but an AI put together to help keep paranormal outbreaks at bay. Dominic thought his sense of humor was too good for a robot, and it was more likely that he had a Gift for technomancy. Either way, he was trustworthy, if a little eccentric. His tips sold for a little higher than usual, mostly because his pattern recognition was unparalleled. More often than not, he knew where clients were going to be before anyone officially posted a job.

Dom's phone dinged, showing him a link to a listing on the board.

About three hours east, a poltergeist was pestering a well-to-do family, and they were *very* eager to be rid of it. They were offering more than expected, and Garrett thought it would be a cakewalk.

Water spilled onto the burner, telling Dominic that the food was ready. He'd made double and a half his usual amount. Micah didn't look starved, exactly, but Dom couldn't forget the intensity with which he'd devoured the peach.

Dom strained the macaroni, added the milk and cheese, and separated it into bowls. Sitting on the table surrounded by newspaper clippings and old books of folklore, they didn't feel much like a meal.

He dug an apple out of Micah's bag and set it next to the bowls. For some reason, it made him feel better.

CHAPTER FOUR

In the bathroom, Micah stripped off his clothes, already feeling cleaner without them. It had been a long time since he'd taken a shower. Longer since he'd taken one alone. But he was a mess, and honestly, it made sense that Dominic hadn't wanted anything to do with him.

Shame twisted in his belly. It had been his constant companion for days now, as his continued confinement made it obvious he wouldn't be getting another opportunity to prove his remorse to Slate. Now, he'd even missed the chance to make a good first impression on his *new* owner. He'd made an educated guess and gone the route of the soldier: enthusiastic and ready to follow orders. Evidently, that hadn't been what his owner was after.

When Dominic had first suggested a shower, Micah assumed he'd be joining him. *Let's get you cleaned up* was a common game that new owners liked to play. Any "cleaning" that took place was secondary to the exploration and appreciation of their new property. So when Dominic had led him to the bathroom, Micah had momentarily felt stable, like he was in familiar territory again. But then Dominic had given him some towels from a hall closet and left him standing there, alone.

He took stock of his surroundings. No cameras, or at least no obvious ones. The bathroom was used by someone else; that much was obvious by the half-empty bottle of body wash and the single toothbrush by the sink. The towels were worn at the corners, but clean and soft. Micah had originally assumed that they were castoffs, discarded by his owner and relegated to slave use, but the one on the rack was in an identical state. So either there was another slave in the house, or maybe an indent, or Dominic was letting Micah use his personal bathroom.

Alone.

Micah had never lived anywhere that didn't have slave quarters, their sparse furnishings clearly different from the materials in the main house. Slaves used different linens, ate from different plates—and certainly wore different clothes. Micah's, when he had been permitted to wear them, had been general-issue black scrubs, secured with ties to fit a wide range of body types.

The clothes Micah had been given for transport also tied shut, but had one noteworthy anomaly: they had pockets. Their purchase had obviously been a mistake, and it made sense that they would be discarded along with a departing slave. Pockets made it easier to hide things—like the money Dominic had given him to buy food.

Micah still had some of that money: paper bills wrapped tightly around the coins so they wouldn't jingle and remind his owner that he was owed change. He pulled it out and stared at it, quickly counting it again. Four dollars and fifty-two cents.

His heart beat faster just looking at it. If his new owner walked in and found that Micah had stolen it, there'd be hell to pay.

But since Slate was done with him . . . had finally gotten tired of punishing him . . .

It wasn't impossible that he'd been sent here to die.

Familiar panic clawed its way up his throat, and Micah exhaled. Willed himself still. Let it go. He just had to *trust,* same as always.

He searched the room for somewhere to hide the money. With the shower covering the sound, he opened the medicine cabinet. He cast a glance at the unlocked door. Dominic was making noise out in the kitchen, but other people might live in the house. This might even be a test.

The cabinet was incredibly well-stocked: bottles of alcohol, sterile saline, gauze pads, bandages, sutures, forceps, and even scalpels.

Dominic had said his job was dangerous. Apparently, he hadn't been lying.

Micah hid the money in the bottom of a box of Band-Aids, packing the bandages back in and placing the box exactly where he'd found it.

He closed the cabinet, avoiding the sight of himself in the mirror, then stepped into the shower. The water on his face cleared the last of the transport fog and replaced it with the beginnings of a headache.

He closed his eyes against the spray and scrubbed vigorously at his face. One of the last times he'd caught sight of himself, there had been tear tracks on his cheeks. Since then, he'd made a point of rubbing his face into his shoulder whenever he could manage. He hoped there hadn't been tracks when Dominic had first seen him, but he'd been in transport bindings for more than a day. He probably wasn't that lucky.

Micah wondered if he was allowed to use the shampoo. It wasn't *for* him, but it also wasn't . . . *not* for him.

After a moment of deliberation, he decided that being clean was worth whatever punishment he'd endure. Dominic didn't seem like the kind of owner to go overboard on discipline. If Micah was wrong, and Dominic had a hidden temper, better to provoke it with something small.

Still, Micah winced when the cap opened with a snap. His eyes flicked to the door, but there was no sound from outside.

The shampoo was blue and claimed to smell like an "ocean breeze," though Micah was almost certain it didn't. He rubbed it into his scalp, and it quickly rose into a dirty, blood-stained lather. The water carried it down his body in rivulets.

There was an uncomfortable pulling sensation in his back, where his wounds were healing into lines of scar tissue. Fortunately, most of them were weeks old and shouldn't interfere with his performance too much. He'd just have to keep Dominic from seeing them, at least for now. The scars could be removed if Dominic wanted to spend the money—but Micah didn't want to explain why he had them.

It would be bad enough if he had to explain the *writing*, though at least that would wash off. Micah soaked the washcloth and then rubbed the bar soap against it. The scent didn't match the shampoo. He wrinkled his nose. He was going to smell discordant, but there was nothing for it. Not with the state he was in. Very deliberately, he scrubbed away the block letters Slate had left printed across his chest.

DAMAGED GOODS

Micah's face burned. In his life, he'd *never* seen anyone sold with a warning like that. He was far more used to being appraised based on the Signature tattooed on his hip.

It should have helped him, but Slate had ordered it altered, the trainer's initials covered with a meaningless starburst. Micah suspected that some certifications were missing from his file too.

His fingers tangled in his hair, pulling, the feeling grounding him. Fuck it. This was a mess, but he could salvage it. He still *had* those talents, even if no one would vouch for him. He'd have to suck it up and *prove* he could do better . . . even if it *was* going to be rough.

Knowing he couldn't procrastinate any more, he knelt on the tile floor and probed the area behind his balls. It hurt, but not as bad as he'd been expecting. Slate had grown bored of punishing him weeks ago, but the others hadn't. Before Micah was bound for transport, there'd been a little goodbye party.

Micah ran soapy fingers over the area, searching for anything more serious than the soreness and bruising that accompanied such activities. The soap burned, which meant the skin was broken, but only a little, which meant he'd heal. It also meant that he'd have to be extra careful if Dominic wanted him in the next few days. Micah was good with his mouth, so he might be able to keep Dominic distracted. Then again, he might not. Most new owners spent their first night taking *everything* for a test drive.

No point in speculating, Micah thought as he shut off the water. *Just be ready.* He squeezed water out of his hair and was reaching for a towel, when someone knocked.

For a terrifying second, Micah thought he'd somehow locked the door. But no—the knob's lock was definitely set to open. Whoever it was *could* enter, they just hadn't.

Micah shook the water off his hands. He checked the mirror, making sure none of his new scars could be seen from the front.

Satisfied, he opened the door and leaned one arm against the frame.

Time to make a better impression.

Dominic blinked like he'd expected someone else. He opened his mouth as if to say something, but a drop of water fell off Micah's hair, and Dominic's eyes followed it. Micah could almost see the blood flowing out of his owner's brain as the drop landed on his chest and trickled down his wet body. It came to a halt in the hollow of one bare hip.

Dominic cleared his throat, avoiding Micah's eyes, only to focus on the piercing in his cock.

Micah recalled what he'd said: *"Not that kind of job."* He'd had owners in denial before. Micah tilted his chin, regarding Dominic with a knowing smile.

Dominic's eyes snapped back up. "Uh, so I realized you've only got the one set of clothes? You probably don't want to put them back on until they're clean, so I found these. They're mine, but they're the biggest I've got, and they'll have to do until we get to a store. Okay?"

He held a bundle out. Micah paused for a second, then took it.

Dominic cleared his throat again. "Good. So. Food's on the table when you're done. And I might have a job. If you're up for it. So. Uh. I'll be . . . out there." He gestured over his shoulder, backing away on a collision course with the far wall. He hit it and corrected, heading back toward the kitchen.

Micah closed the door, letting his forehead rest against the back. This was going to be more of a challenge than he'd thought.

CHAPTER FIVE

"Real smooth, Blackburn. Fuckin' preteen girls everywhere wish they had your charm." Dominic buried his face in the paper he'd been failing to read. "*I'll be out there*," he mimicked. "Hells."

Dominic was not a virgin. Far from it. He'd been picking up tail of all varieties since he'd been old enough to rent motel rooms—ten interesting, colorful, *imaginative* years ago.

He couldn't think of a single damn reason why he'd be thrown so out of whack by a drop of water running down Micah's chest. Probably something to do with the "come fuck me" vibe the guy had been giving him.

Dominic scowled, rubbing his face. He had to figure out the catch here. Megan had sold him cheap for a reason. But Micah wasn't an escape risk, he cleaned up *nice*, and he was certainly friendly enough. So why the hell had Megan been in such a hurry to get rid of him?

Dominic remembered the envelope with Micah's paperwork. It was still in the car. Maybe there was something in there that would solve this mystery. He stood to search for his car keys but lost his train of thought when Micah walked into the kitchen.

A beat-up table stood between them, surrounded by three mismatched chairs. Right now, it was covered with books, newspapers, Micah's macaroni, Dominic's laptop, two half-sharpened obsidian knives, and the apple. It was a pretty typical state of affairs.

"That's for you." Dominic gestured at the macaroni. "If it's cold, pop it in the microwave for about thirty seconds. Always thirty seconds at a time. She's temperamental."

Micah surveyed the space, then picked up his bowl and settled cross-legged in a corner of the living room. Dom wondered if he'd left something on the other chair but got distracted, again, by several observations. For example: Dominic's jeans were too tight on Micah, and he had to wiggle to get situated. The T-shirt was tight too.

He needs a V-neck, Dominic thought. He rolled his eyes at himself, then forced his attention back to his laptop, which was currently displaying details about the case Garrett had sent him.

"Okay, so, if you're up for it, I've got a job. There's a family a couple of hours from here getting plagued by a poltergeist. In case you never took cryptobiology, that's a violent ghost that manifests by breaking a lot of shit." He brought up a photo on his screen—a nice professional shot of a typical suburbanite family, complete with dog—then leaned back so Micah could see. "It'll be a basic exorcism, probably just a matter of laying the remains to rest. The family is pretty sure they know who it is; they just need somebody to handle it. Should be an easy first gig. You wanna give it a go? It's okay if you want to wait a couple—" Micah's bowl was empty. Dom raised an eyebrow. "Dude, did you eat that whole thing already?"

Micah's bowl spoke for itself.

"Do you want me to make some more?"

Micah opened his mouth, frowned, and then shook his head.

"Okay, then. I'm thinking we hit up a store, get you some of your own stuff, and see if we can make it to—" he checked the listing again "—Farroway, Ohio, before midnight. Sound like a plan?"

Micah nodded. Dominic closed his laptop and shoved it into the backpack that already contained a spare power cable, flash drives, and an assortment of small tools. He went down the hall to his room, chucking spare clothes, ID, and a toiletry kit in his go-bag. Packing done, he rummaged through his closet until he came up with an empty duffel.

It had been his dad's, and even empty, it was heavy with the assorted extras everybody in creature control kept sewn into the linings of their work bags: warding, or maybe lock picks, emergency cash, and the like. His father's crooked stitches paraded up and down the bag like lines of ants.

It was stupid, leaving mystery tools sewn up like that. Dominic didn't know what was in there. Even if he did, he wouldn't know where to look for them. But he hadn't been able to tear his dad's stitching out. He'd unpacked the clothes and gotten rid of them, but left the stitching to deal with later. That had been months ago, and somehow, he'd never gotten around to it.

The stupid duffel got blurry.

He shoved it under his arm, picked up his own bag, and headed out to the living room.

Micah was waiting exactly where Dom had left him.

"Oh. Almost forgot." He pulled the candy bars out of his jacket pocket and handed them to Micah. "I got these for you at the gas station."

Micah smiled.

Their first stop was the local big box store. It was one of the ones where you could buy a hunting knife, a carton of eggs, *and* a couple of joints if you talked to the right person in the parking lot.

It was here Dominic really realized that Micah had *nothing.* Wherever that great big payment for his lifetime contract had gone, it seemed Micah hadn't benefited from a penny of it.

Dominic had packed bags a thousand times, but he'd never kept track of exactly how many *things* the average person needed on a daily basis. And Micah's stuff, apparently, had been company-owned.

To make matters worse, Micah wouldn't ask for anything. They ended up going through the toiletry aisles twice after Dominic realized that every "Do you want this?" was answered with a head shake.

Dom gave up asking and tossed some basics into the cart, sticking mostly to the familiar until he caught Micah taking sidelong glances at the shampoo. Dominic always kept his hair short and washed it with the same all-in-one he used on the rest of his body. That probably wouldn't work on hair like Micah's.

He gestured at the shelf. "What do you want? Lilac? Or the one with Hannah Montana on it?"

Micah gave him a blank stare.

"I'm insulting your masculinity. It's how I show affection. Pick one."

Micah selected a nondescript white bottle off the bottom shelf, popping the cap to check the scent. Apparently it passed muster, because he dropped it in the cart. Then, hesitating, he added a similar bottle sitting next to it.

Dominic picked it up. "The hell is 'conditioner'?"

Micah pulled out his notepad. *Keeps it from tangling.*

"Yeah, okay. We'll get that until we can get you a haircut."

Micah looked like he was going to say something, but then he closed his mouth and shoved the notepad back into his pocket.

"I'm joking," Dom said awkwardly. Micah didn't respond, just kept his eyes on the floor and waited for Dom to move down the aisle.

Micah didn't know what size clothes he wore, so Dominic had to guess. He tossed packages of socks and undershirts into the cart, getting enough to match his own schedule of twice-a-month laundry.

"Boxers or briefs?"

Micah blinked.

Dominic held up the packages. "Come on, you've gotta have a preference. I can't make this call for you."

Micah retrieved his writing pad again. *I don't know.*

"How do you not know? This is *essential*, man."

Indent uniforms are 1 layer.

"Okay, but—" Dominic stopped. The logical question to ask was, *What about before?* But he caught the words as they tried to escape. *Before* was a big conversation, bigger than he wanted to have in the underwear aisle, for sure.

Lifetime contracts were the last resort of the desperate, or a sentence for something *awful*, which would've been in bold print at the top of his file and also have prevented him from working for a nongovernmental holder. And if Micah had signed his that long ago . . . How old could he have been? At least eighteen, but still. In the end, Dom took the middle ground and got a couple of packages of boxer briefs.

Shoes came next. Micah searched through the boxes for a pair of work boots that fit while Dominic tried to stretch one of the disposable sockies over his head. Micah didn't know how he liked his jeans, so Dominic picked out a couple relaxed fits and sent Micah into the dressing room with instructions to choose a favorite. While he was gone, Dominic stuck a couple of V-necks in with everything else.

The store didn't stock a jacket large enough to fit over Micah's shoulders, but it was the offseason, and Dominic decided it could wait.

After that, he couldn't think of anything else. Micah wasn't speaking up, so Dominic paid and sent him back into the dressing room to change.

In the parking lot, Dominic shoved the bags into the back seat. They were parked in the overflow area, significantly farther from the doors than the almost empty lot required. He closed the door, turning back to Micah. "Megan said you can fight?"

Micah nodded.

"Okay. I'm sure you're right, but I'd like to check for myself before I bet my life on you. Fair?"

Micah held his hands wide, presenting a target.

Dominic walked several paces from the car, rolled his neck, and gestured for Micah to come closer. "To start off, I'm going to try to hit you, okay? Right hand." Micah shifted his weight, on guard. Dominic made sure he was ready, and aimed a quick hard punch at Micah's ribs.

Micah could move quicker than his size indicated, and Dominic's fist passed harmlessly through the air.

Dominic tried again, faster, followed by a left swing into Micah's stomach. Micah blocked the first, dodged the second. Dominic redirected, went for an uppercut into the sternum, followed closely by a hook punch to the temple.

Micah caught his arm, twisted it up to deflect the second hit. With his other hand, he tapped Dominic on the side, right under his ribs.

Dominic shifted his weight forward, hooking an ankle around Micah's calf and shoving him off-balance. Micah almost went down but pivoted to drop his center of gravity. He used Dominic's hold to steady himself, then ducked and aimed a quick set of punches at Dominic's lower belly. Dominic was ready for him and caught his arms. Micah surged upward, and Dominic would have taken a forehead to the jaw if Micah hadn't paused at the last second. Instead, Micah stared up at him with a self-satisfied grin.

Dom let out a soft laugh. "You weren't kidding."

Micah's grin gained a couple of teeth. Confidence looked good on him.

"For the record," Dominic said, letting go and stepping back, "I'm going easy on you because you've had a long day and I don't want to actually hurt you."

Micah inclined his head, putting an awful lot of condescension into the silent gesture.

Dominic scowled. "I was wrong, you *do* have an attitude."

The smile vanished, and Micah dropped his eyes.

Dom changed the subject. "Anything else I should know about?"

Micah's note was slow in coming. *I've had some training with bladed weapons.*

"Okay, in the name of not going to the ER tonight, I'm going to take your word for it. Let's get out of here."

Micah paused at the car door. He'd been heading for the back seat, but it was full of bags. Dominic didn't generally put things in the trunk. He kept his tools back there, and he liked being able to get to them in a hurry.

"Do you mind sitting up front?"

Micah paused for longer than the question really called for.

"All right, come on." Dominic slid into the driver's seat, and a moment later, Micah got in on the other side.

Dominic took a breath. "I gotta ask. Is the back seat a personal preference?"

That's where we sit, Micah wrote.

"Is that why you wouldn't eat dinner at the table?"

Micah nodded.

So Micah's last holder wasn't just an asshole, he was a *bougie* asshole. Dominic sighed. "Okay, listen up. I appreciate the, like, respect or whatever. But I don't have time for that. Wherever I am, you're there with me. I need you focused on what we're doing. We're both gonna get killed if you're constantly trying to find somewhere subordinate to stand."

Micah seemed to process this information, forehead furrowed.

"Also, I hope you like Red Hot Chili Peppers because that's what we're listening to on the way to Ohio. And I'm gonna sing the whole time because I want to see how far I can push you before you rebel and slit my throat."

Micah startled, and Dom grinned, spinning the volume knob until "Breakthru" drowned out the engine.

"Gods, I'm tired." Dominic flopped down on the bed farthest from the door. He made a weak effort to kick off his shoes, realized they were still tied, and groaned as he sat up to unlace them.

Micah stood by the door, crudely stitched duffel over his shoulder.

"I'll show you how to ward the room, and then I'm going to bed," Dominic muttered, freeing himself from his shoes. Rummaging in his duffel, he withdrew two telescoping PVC tubes. "One for the window, one for the door." He tossed the shorter one to Micah. "They're filled with a combination of salt and graveyard dirt. Keeps the beasties out while we're sleeping."

Micah examined the warding burned into the tube. Dom doubted he spoke Aramaic, but he did feel a little flattered by Micah's attention to the craftsmanship. "They're usually more important *after* we've started the job, but it never hurts," he explained, setting his across the windowsill.

He only had three of them, because he and his dad had always shared a room. It was safer that way. It hadn't occurred to him until check-in that he might need to rent two rooms now. He'd asked, but Micah, somewhat predictably, hadn't had an opinion.

So, one room, Dominic thought as he set feathers and crystals on a laminated spell circle from the duffel. *Because it's safer.* He spread his hands over the circle and inhaled. Feather. Gossamer. Salt. Water. Earth. The circle glowed a pale, flickering blue. *And not because he opened the bathroom door naked.*

The glow faded out, and Dom resisted the urge to bang his head on the table. Gods, but he was tired. He needed to focus. Out of the corner of his eye, he saw Micah approach, watching the spellwork attentively.

"Dunno how much magic you know? We can get into it later." Dom summoned the glow again. This time he kept his eyes on it, willing the energies to bind. The glow flickered once, twice, then sparked into white and vanished. "That's activated. Nothing can find or bother us until the morning. Well, later in the morning. So I'm going to sleep."

He didn't wait for Micah's reaction, just went to his bed and kicked out of his pants, dropping them unceremoniously on top of his shoes. His socks and overshirt followed, and then he flopped into bed and wriggled under the blankets. Behind him, he heard Micah undressing as well.

There were two beds in the room, but Dominic was only a little surprised when he felt weight on the other side of his.

He summoned his energy and rolled over. Micah was kneeling on the edge of the mattress, eyes down, shirt and shoes discarded. His long hair tumbled over his bare shoulders, silhouetted by the dim bedside light.

Dom's cock made a valiant effort to sit up and pay attention, but it was past three in the morning. The little man up top had long since shut down all nonessential systems for the night. He almost felt bad. Who knew what kind of dry spell Micah might be coming off of? And it wasn't like the guy asked for *much*.

Unfortunately for both of them, the mind was willing, but the flesh was well on its way to becoming one with the mattress.

"Not tonight, man. I'm friggin' beat." He gestured at the other bed. "Go sleep over there."

His eyelids felt like lead weights, but he kept them open long enough to watch Micah cross the space between the beds. Micah lay down facing Dominic, the silence stretching out. Then Dom leaned over and shut off the light.

CHAPTER SIX

Micah woke up slowly, allowing himself a languid stretch across the sheets. It felt good to be on a real mattress again, even if he *was* banished to the far bed. He wasn't too worried about that—he'd earn his place before long.

He glanced at the man in the other bed. Dominic was sprawled on his back, blankets a tangled mess. One pillow was shoved under his head; the other was on the floor, several feet away.

Micah's new owner was an energetic sleeper. Good to know. Maybe *that* was why he preferred his own bed?

No. It was too early to make excuses for himself. For some reason, even cleaned up and dressed in the clothes his owner had picked, he'd been unacceptable. He needed to figure the reason out and do better. That was all.

Micah slid out from under the covers, planning his morning. Dominic hadn't given him any instructions, but he could guess. Essential duties didn't change much from place to place.

He made the bed, glancing occasionally at his sleeping owner. He needn't have worried; Dominic was dead to the world.

Micah checked the clock: 6:15. He didn't know what time Dominic was accustomed to waking up, but he wasn't going to be caught unprepared. The alarm on the clock wasn't set. Nervousness twinged in his gut. Did Dominic expect to be woken up? He hadn't said anything yesterday, so probably not?

Micah considered his options as he crept to his duffel, retrieving an apple he'd packed the day before. He ate it quickly, then set to working through his morning routine silently, in the scant glow seeping through the blackout curtains: brush his teeth, wash his face, comb his hair. He was determined to be presentable when his owner woke. At least Dominic didn't seem to have any love of makeup, so Micah would be spared that task for the time being.

He considered doing his morning exercises, then decided against it. He wasn't sure he could get through them quietly, and the last thing he needed was for Dominic to wake up and find him a sweaty mess.

Instead, he got dressed and slipped out the door. He walked barefoot down the hall, eyes down. There was no one else in the hallway, but it was better to stay in the habit.

The lobby smelled divine, the scent of baking bread and cooking eggs seeping out of the breakfast area. A few people were sitting at the scattered tables, drinking coffee and reading newspapers. There were several other indents, likely on the same errand as him. One of them wore a uniform; another was identifiable only by the barcode inked onto their arm.

Micah picked up a tray, pausing when he realized he didn't know what food his master preferred. Something greasy, probably.

Micah erred on the side of plenty, picking up a selection of everything. The paper plates were printed with simple ikons designed to keep the food at the proper temperature. He filled one with eggs, sausage, bacon, and toast, and another with granola and yogurt. Dominic almost certainly wouldn't want that, or the fresh orange Micah balanced atop it. It was cheating, pretending that he was bringing this food for anyone but himself, but sometimes, a little cheating was how the game was played. Unfortunately, plausible deniability wouldn't cover two cups of coffee, so Micah made only one. Maybe tomorrow.

When he got back to the room, Dominic was still asleep. Micah glanced at the clock: 6:30. He set the tray on the little table in the corner, then crept back to the space between the beds to wait in the typical relaxation pose: sitting back on his heels with his knees spread and his hands resting lightly on his thighs.

Micah had impeccable form, and he wanted Dominic to know it. He'd been drugged during the transfer, which had been unnecessary as well as humiliating. He knew how to present for buyers; he'd been to the market a dozen times since his original owners. Always in the primary auction. Always clean, unbound, and dressed for show.

He could have sold for a *lot* more, but Slate obviously hadn't been interested in the money. It made sense that he would sell his rebellious slave degraded, starved, beaten, and dirty, like Micah was worthless. He probably would have had Micah branded as violent if it hadn't meant admitting he'd been struck by one of his own slaves. Twice.

Micah shifted a few millimeters and wondered again whether Dominic was expecting a wakeup. Were wakeups taken for granted, like breakfast? Dominic was hoping to get a job resolved today, which probably meant an early start. Micah just wasn't sure *how* early.

He risked a glance at Dominic. He'd give it until 7:15.

At 6:45, he changed his mind and resolved to wait and take the punishment for negligence if it was the wrong call.

At 7:00, he decided that his original conclusion had been correct.

He glanced at the clock four times between 7:00 and 7:06.

At 7:08, he took his shirt off, but a minute later, he remembered Dominic's earlier discomfort at his nudity and put it back on.

At 7:11, he determined that Dominic's discomfort had been distinctly *aroused*, and took it back off.

He made it half a minute before putting it back on.

By 7:14, he was thoroughly disgusted with himself. Slate's decision to cover his Signature had been justified, because he had no idea what he was doing.

When 7:15 finally rolled around and Dominic still hadn't moved, Micah climbed into the bed. Dominic would probably have a morning hard-on. He could work with that.

He burrowed under the blankets, positioning himself alongside Dominic's legs, then nuzzled against Dominic's upper thigh, glad to find that his prediction had been correct.

Dominic stirred, making a questioning noise as he realized what was happening. He lifted the covers, looking down at Micah. "You're up early."

Micah chose not to take it as a criticism. He moved his hands up Dominic's thighs, gently pressing them further apart, asking for permission.

Dominic didn't resist, groaning when Micah mouthed against his cock through his boxers. They had a button, which Micah undid with his teeth. Dominic's cock sprang free, and Micah laid a quick kiss against the base.

Dominic's hand came to rest on his shoulder.

"You really want to do this? Not just because it's in your contract?"

Micah nodded, humming his assent against the inside of his owner's thigh. It was a standard enough question, and as always, there was only one answer: Yes, and thank you. Pretending to love it was one of the first things he'd learned.

He wet his lips, planning. The first time with a new owner was always exploratory. He licked at the frenulum, moving up and over the head before tonguing the slit. Dominic moaned, and Micah took him into his mouth, careful to cover his teeth. He sucked gently, letting the ridge pop back out. Then for good measure, he repeated the pop a few more times.

Dominic dropped the covers, running his fingers gently through Micah's hair. Micah took him all the way in, relaxing, letting Dominic's cock rest in the back of his throat. He moaned, knowing Dominic could feel it despite the lack of sound. His tongue laved up the underside, drawing a gasp out of Dominic. And then Micah sank down, taking him to the base.

Soft dark hairs prickled his nose, and pride surged even as his body fought him. He repeated this motion, in-out, gently bringing his master out of sleep and into the waking world.

Dominic's fingers tightened in his hair. "Fuck, Micah, you keep that up, I'm gonna come."

Micah kept it up, tongue darting out to flick against Dominic's tightening balls. Dominic's hips were canting up, and Micah had to hold very still to keep from choking. He half expected Dominic to hold his head down, and he breathed deep in anticipation, but then Dominic came with a groan. Micah swallowed, throat closing around Dominic's cock, drawing a strangled gasp out of him.

Then Dominic stroked Micah's hair, and Micah pulled back, waiting. Dominic's fingers slid easily out of his hair, and Micah realized he hadn't yanked, not once.

He preened in the darkness. From "not that kind of job" to a job well done in less than twenty-four hours. Not bad at all.

Dominic lifted the blankets, staring down at him. "That was fucking incredible."

Micah smiled and waited for orders.

Instead, Dom gestured toward him. "You want me to, uh, return the favor?"

Micah froze. What was the answer to *that* supposed to be? God's teeth. The whole *point* of a blowjob was that the master *finished* and then it was *over*. He hadn't expected it to go further, hadn't put any effort into getting himself hard—

But it was a question, and a hesitant one at that. And since it was a gamble either way . . . He shook his head, pulling away from Dominic with an easy shrug.

"If you're sure . . ." Dominic shrugged back, dropped the blanket, and climbed out of bed. Micah disentangled from the bedding and set to straightening the rumpled sheets. He opened the curtains with deliberate nonchalance, feeling his owner's questioning gaze on him. He didn't look back. It might be interpreted as reconsidering.

"Shit, you got *breakfast* too?" Dominic sounded surprised but not upset. Micah hoped he'd guessed right about the food.

Dominic dropped into a chair by the table, picking up a sausage link and eating half of it in one bite. Micah finished making the bed and then knelt on the floor to wait.

Dominic watched him for a long moment. "Did you already eat?"

Micah shook his head.

"Why not?"

Micah wasn't sure how to answer that. He hadn't been given any instructions; did his master think he was presumptuous enough to *take* things without permission?

His mind flicked guiltily to the money hidden in the medicine cabinet, and he dismissed the entire line of thought with a shrug.

"Even lifers get lunch breaks," Dom joked. When Micah didn't laugh, Dominic gestured awkwardly at the other chair. "You don't have to wait for me if you're hungry."

Micah rose to his feet, closing the distance to the table in two steps. Dominic ate the rest of the sausage link.

Micah picked up the orange and sat. Immediately his mind screamed at him to get down. Very deliberately, he began to peel the fruit. When it was peeled, he divided it into sections. When it was divided, he took a section and ate it. Without permission.

Dominic was utterly unfazed.

It was beginning to dawn on Micah that Dominic didn't know how this dynamic generally worked. He was treating Micah like a regular indent, rather than a trained professional. Micah's Signature was covered up, but Dominic surely had *some* idea of what he'd purchased. Right?

Dominic took a bite of toast. "So, how'd you learn to fight, anyway?"

Micah dropped a half-eaten orange segment and retrieved his notepad from the bedside table. *Trained as a bodyguard, then for competitive fights.*

"Was that your last job?"

Micah shook his head with a little smile. *Never got the chance. Switched majors.*

Dominic laughed. "What to?"

Micah peeked up at Dominic through his eyelashes, giving him his warmest smile. *Hospitality.*

"Yeah, all right. I get it, you're hot and charming." Dominic turned away, his expression suddenly unreadable. "Must've sucked, all that preparation and work and then they pull you out of it to be window dressing."

Micah's exasperation came rolling back, but he was careful to keep it off his face. What the hell did that mean? Even if Dominic didn't appreciate the finer etiquette—and judging by their conversation in the car yesterday, he didn't—he should at *least* be able to appreciate the talent in the training Micah *had* been allowed to use.

He considered his next words, pushing his ego down before it could get him in trouble. *You didn't enjoy the hospitality this morning?*

"What? Oh. Hell yeah. Best wake up I've had in . . . ever, and then breakfast on top of it." Dominic fixed him with a stare. "But that's . . . not really your *job*, though."

Micah ate his orange and didn't respond. Eventually, Dominic went to shower, leaving the granola yogurt behind as predicted. Micah considered it intently, wondering if this was some kind of test. In the end, hunger won out and he ate it anyway. He snagged the last of the toast as well, clearing the table in the hopes Dominic wouldn't notice.

Half an hour later they were ready to leave, and Dominic opened the trunk of his car. Inside were three plastic cases, each covered in neatly lettered warding. Dominic unlocked the largest one, revealing assorted weapons nestled in foam inserts.

"Normally, for a ghost, we'd do a séance and try to communicate with it, try to make it move on by itself. But this is a poltergeist, and they've been known to get handsy. So to speak." Dominic leaned forward, fingers resting on the straps holding a shotgun in position. "Know how to shoot?"

Micah shook his head. Of course he didn't know how. Nobody taught slaves to work guns.

"Yeah. I just thought maybe before, you know. You might have learned."

Micah frowned. When would he have learned? He'd been sold when he was eleven.

"Quick inventory," Dominic said, pointing. "You've got your shotguns here, handguns over there. Ammo's organized in this lockbox. It's all color-coded: red is salt and brick dust, green is iron, yellow is silver. Regular ones are black. There's glyphs carved into the tips. It doesn't hurt, might help. When in doubt, take a variety."

Micah passed him the notepad. *Which for what?*

"There's a whole system, I'll teach you later. Until then, bladed weapons are this case here. We've got gold, silver, copper, obsidian, and iron blades, which go in this rack next to the gross adjustment tools." Dominic gestured to the collection of blunt weapons. "Those are mostly iron, though I do have a trusty aluminum slugger to fall back on. Works particularly well on human monsters."

Micah snorted.

Dom raised his hands, defensive. "Hey, we get all types. I've also got some wooden stakes here. The wood type is marked on the handle, see? Sometimes it doesn't matter, sometimes it does."

Micah nodded, trying to commit everything to memory.

Dominic settled on an iron knife for Micah. He hesitated for a moment before handing it over, and Micah thought maybe Dominic didn't trust him with it.

But then Dominic spoke. "This was my dad's. Don't lose it."

Ah. Dominic must have been close with his father.

Micah had not been close with his. Gerald Sawyer had been a drifter and an alcoholic, dragging Micah around from one rented room to another for years until finally selling him or losing him in a poker game or whatever had happened. Micah remembered that his father had been broad-shouldered and strong, like Micah was now. Unlike Micah, Gerald had been aggressive and quick to violence, even with his son. Sometimes Micah was glad he'd never get the opportunity to screw up as bad as Gerald had.

Micah realized he was staring at the knife. Its leather sheath was stained with something that was probably definitely blood. Dominic was waiting expectantly. Micah crossed his heart.

"All right," Dominic said, slamming the trunk. "Let's go scare a ghost."

Micah was almost certain that the client's lawn was plastic. Or magic. Grass didn't grow that evenly by itself anywhere. The house beyond the plastic lawn was identical to the ones on either side, across the road, and for a quarter mile in every direction.

"Gives me the creeps," Dominic muttered as the car purred past streets named after trees. In alphabetical order.

The woman who opened the door stared at them in surprise. She quickly caught herself and put on a wide smile. "Madeline Carmichael," she said, graciously extending a hand.

Micah had seen that smile before, lots of times. He grinned back at her while Dominic made the introductions. Dominic paused when he gestured to Micah, stumbling over the realization that Micah, like all lifers, had no last name. At least, not one that could be read out loud. His official paperwork would list his surname as his barcode number.

The woman looked at him a little differently after that.

"So, ma'am, you say you've got a poltergeist?"

"Yes." Her gaze moved from Micah to Dominic. "On the second floor. We haven't been upstairs in days. Try to go up and it starts screaming and throwing things."

Something shattered upstairs, followed by an earsplitting shriek.

"That was the bathroom mirror, I suppose." Madeline sighed. "It's been slowing down recently, but I think it's just running out of things to break."

"And she never comes downstairs?"

"No. Never."

"Anything that might be binding her to the house? A lock of hair, something with blood on it?"

"No, nothing like that."

Micah listened to the questions carefully, trying to remember anything he knew about ghosts. Mostly, he tried to keep himself physically between the stairs and his owner.

"All right, then. Like I said on the phone, you probably just need a purification ritual to set the spirit to rest. Where's she buried?"

"That's the problem. She was cremated."

Dominic frowned. "In the report you said your sister died several months ago and was buried here in town. Did something change?"

"Well, Mrs. Garcia down the street, *she* had a ghost, after her dog died? And *she* said that when she told creacon that the body had been cremated, they didn't want to take the job. So, obviously I wasn't going to say so."

Dominic sighed. "Mrs. Carmichael, do you know why ghosts appear on this plane?"

"To break my bathroom mirrors, apparently."

"Because something binds them here. Usually, it's their body. If not that, it's something else, something they valued even more. Without knowing the deceased, the best we can do is start purifying things they touched and hope we hit on the right mark."

Madeline blinked. "That's not very helpful at all."

"That's why we don't take the job."

She sighed. "Can you at least go take a look? Maybe you can kill it."

"She's already dead. The best we can hope for is some hint as to why she's still here."

"Please? I'm desperate."

Dominic glanced at Micah. Micah shrugged. He'd never seen a ghost, or a purification for that matter. He was pretty confident he wasn't going to panic; it couldn't be *that* scary.

Dominic rubbed his face. "I promise nothing."

Madeline gestured helplessly toward the stairway. They took a couple of minutes to make a plan and raid the trunk, and then Dominic headed up first, with Micah following close behind.

The staircase opened into a hallway with cream carpet, doors all tightly shut. Screaming and the distinctive sound of things breaking could be heard emanating from the room at the end.

They crept toward the door, Dominic with his shotgun and Micah with his knife. Dominic silently leveled the gun, gesturing for Micah to take the side.

Carefully, silently, Micah twisted the handle and pushed the door open.

The sounds stopped instantly. The door swung open to reveal a guest bedroom that would have been very tastefully decorated if everything inside hadn't been utterly trashed.

Standing in the middle of the mess was a man in a suit, a tie, and a fairly even layer of dirt and blood.

He stared at them.

They stared at him.

And then he unhinged his bloody jaw and shrieked.

Dominic fired the shotgun, hitting the thing dead in the center of the chest. Micah expected it to vanish, maybe turn to smoke and float away, like ghosts on TV. Instead, the round hit the creature with a meaty smack, and a geyser of blood spurted from the wound.

It charged.

Micah ducked in front of Dominic, slamming the door just in time for the creature to crash, shrieking, against the other side. The door splintered but Micah didn't move, planting himself between the danger and his master. That was his place; he would hold.

Turns out he didn't need to—the howling resumed, but the monster left the door alone.

"That's not a ghost," Dominic said. "Come on." He turned and stomped back down the stairs to where Madeline was waiting. Micah followed, keeping an eye on the hallway behind them.

CHAPTER SEVEN

"You said it was the ghost of your sister!"

"Well, who else could it be?" Madeline sputtered.

"Have you *been* upstairs?"

"No. Like I said, that creature keeps throwing things anytime we get close."

"But have you *seen* it?" Dom pressed.

Madeline pursed her lips. "Of course. It's disgusting and leaves mud on everything."

Dominic took a quick stock of his face. He felt like it was about to make an expression that would get him in trouble. "Madeline, is there any particular reason you thought your sister would manifest in the form of a man in a suit?"

"*I* don't know!" she huffed. "Aren't *you* supposed to be the one who knows about all this paranormal stuff?"

Dominic gritted his teeth. "I can only work with the information I have. Which, so far? Hasn't been great."

"Is it *my* fault it's so hard to get you guys to do your job?"

There it was. The troublemaking expression. Dominic could feel it spreading over his face.

Micah snapped his fingers repeatedly, drawing their attention. When Dominic didn't say anything, Micah pointed toward the ceiling. Dominic glanced up.

It was quiet.

"Oh thank god," Madeline breathed. "Finally."

Dominic rounded on her. "Okay. While we have a moment of peace: How long has that thing *actually* been up there?"

"A little under two weeks."

"And did it start slow?"

"No. It just . . . showed up."

"Could it be attached to something you bought recently? Something for the guest room, like an antique or some artwork?"

Madeline paused. "We got some boxes of things from my sister's house. The real estate agent wanted it emptied out fast, so we didn't have time to go through all of it. Maybe there was something in there?"

Dominic rubbed his temples. Great. Time to go dodge a monster to dig through boxes of a dead lady's shit to see if anything in there was cursed. For the thousandth time, Dominic wished he'd been born into a family of lawyers or doctors. But no. Had to be a family that specialized in paranormal pest control.

Micah pushed the notepad at him. *How did her sister die?*

Dominic blinked. "That's . . . actually a good question. Madeline, what happened to your sister?"

"She died in a car accident. On vacation, actually. Tampa."

"Were any of her possessions brought back? Anything that was in the car when it crashed?"

"No." She considered. "Well. Just my nephew."

Dominic carefully held his face very still. "Your nephew was in the accident? Where is he now?"

"At school. He's been living here since his mother died."

"In the guest room?" Dominic guessed.

Madeline nodded. "Until all this started, yes." Her eyes widened. "Oh! Do you think that's relevant?"

"It might be," Dominic said, keeping his voice level. From the corner of his eye, he could see the edge of Micah's mouth twitching.

Micah scribbled at his notepad again. *Where's his father?*

Madeline shrugged. "No one knows who he was. My sister never told." She leaned in conspiratorially, whispering even though they were alone in the room. "She was only sixteen. Scandal, you know. My guess? He was married." She clearly expected them to share her disapproval.

Dominic responded with a clipped smile. "Right. Well. Let us know if you remember anything else. I'm gonna go get my plan B out of the car."

Micah was right on his heels as he marched out the front door. Epsom salt was great for dispelling ghosts and bringing the odd curse victim to their senses, but it wasn't going to do anything against what was, apparently, some kind of zombie.

"So much for a simple exorcism," he groused, unloading the shotgun and placing it back into its slot. He rummaged through the trunk, searching for the gold knife. He had it in here somewhere, he was sure of it.

Micah was bent over beside him, watching with interest, and Dominic realized he should probably be narrating. "Theoretically, something in this little arsenal of mine should put that noisy bitch in the ground. It's corporeal, which means we can kill it. The question is, with what?"

Micah scribbled at the pad. *It's quiet now. Look around while it's gone?*

Dominic saw a yellow glint and pulled the knife from under a sack of flares. "Yeah. You ready?"

Micah nodded, and Dominic slammed the trunk shut. With some trepidation, the two of them made their way back inside and up the stairs. The creature was quiet, but that didn't mean it was gone. Dominic crept down the hall with a pistol full of assorted specialty rounds, and Micah was armed with the iron knife and a nice solid oak stake for good measure.

Dominic covered the door while Micah pushed it open, keeping out of range.

The room was empty.

Well, no, the room was filled with cardboard boxes, toys, and children's clothing, all covered with a fluffy layer of what might once have been a mattress. The bed frame was on its side, shoved into a corner with enough force to punch through the drywall.

A number of the boxes were marked *Josh's stuff*, and Dominic ignored them for now, focusing on the ones marked *Annie*.

"Ready for the fun part?" Micah gave him a blank look. "Sarcasm. This is actually boring as shit. Here's what you do." He hefted a box off the stack and placed it in Micah's arms. The tape was already cut, which was probably a clue. "Go through here and see if anything gives off a general vibe of fucked-upness. You got any kind of Sight?"

Micah shook his head, which Dominic had expected. The ability to see metaphysical power wasn't rare enough to be considered a Gift, but it wasn't exactly common, either.

"Me neither. But, usually, if something's messed up enough that they need to call us, the power can be felt by regular folks. Eight out of ten, it's just plain spooky looking. Worst-case scenario, I can call in a specialist, but I don't think it'll come to that."

Micah nodded.

Dominic pulled down a box of his own. "Right. Let's do it, then."

They spent four solid hours sorting through perfectly normal household goods: yarn skeins, knitting needles, and half-finished hats and scarves. Nothing felt particularly paranormal, as far as they could tell. The clothing and assorted dishware were equally benign.

But then, pay dirt.

Dominic whistled. "Mom was a *witch*."

The box was packed to the brim with grimoires, charms, and spell-working tools. Micah pulled out a book (*Incantations, Moon Phases, and You*) and flipped through it. A couple of passages were highlighted but otherwise it seemed unremarkable. Trust Mrs. Madeline "Helpful Information" Carmichael to completely neglect to mention the box of fucking *witchcraft supplies*.

Micah gestured with his notebook. *Something cursed?*

"Possibly. Sometimes witches use self-preservation spells that can interfere with the veil, particularly when they die unexpectedly. Whatever the problem is, I'd bet anything the source is in this box. Only one way to tell for sure: torch it."

A bloodcurdling shriek erupted from directly behind Dominic, and he almost dropped the box in shock. Micah was on his feet in a second, shoving Dominic out of the way and sinking his knife deep into the creature's eye socket. Blood geysered out, splattering across the side of Micah's face.

It seemed impossible, but the screams increased in volume. The eye socket smoked and hissed around the iron. The thing reached out, its fingers digging into Micah's upper arms. Micah twisted the knife, then withdrew and slashed it across the monster's throat. More blood, impossible amounts of blood, poured down the creature's chest.

The shrieking turned into a choked gurgle and it collapsed, crumbling into a waxy, flaky pile of gray dust.

"I guess it's vulnerable to iron," Dominic deadpanned.

He ignored it for a moment, watching as Micah cleaned the knife blade methodically, almost absently, with a scrap of torn bedding. It made Dominic wonder just what experience with blades Micah *had*, exactly. It didn't seem like he was about to have a panic attack, at least not right now, which made Dom wonder even more. But given how clearly Micah was using his powers for good (or at least to protect Dom), Dom figured now wasn't the time to ask.

He turned back to the dissolved ghoul, retrieved some gloves from his bag, and knelt to touch the waxy remnants. The powder was cold under his fingers and had no smell that he could detect. He brushed his hands through it, hoping for an object or talisman that might have held it together. Nothing. Just gray powder, all the way through.

He stood up, resisting the urge to wipe his hands on his jeans. "I'm not gonna lie. I have no idea what this is."

Micah passed him the notepad. *Dead now.*

The letters were slightly shaky. There was a smear of blood across the bottom of the page. Dominic glanced at Micah. He wasn't as nonchalant as he was trying to appear, arms crossed and hair falling in dark, blood-wet spikes across his features.

Fucking hell. So much for easing him into it. This was supposed to be a quick and easy purification, a test run to see if Micah even *wanted* the job. Having him take out a corporeal humanoid on the first day was just . . . irresponsible.

"You okay?"

Micah's eyes snapped up, bright with adrenaline. He nodded quickly.

Dom watched him closely, trying to play it cool. "Never stabbed anybody in the eye before?"

Micah shook his head, beginning to grin. He might even have laughed, but with his silence, it was hard to tell. Dominic relaxed a little. The tremor in his hand wasn't trauma—it was excitement.

"You get used to it. I gotta say though, man, I dunno why they didn't have you go competitive," Dom joked. "You would have killed it out there."

Micah shrugged, his smile faltering, eyes dropping back to the floor.

Dominic handed the notepad back, but it seemed Micah had nothing to say.

Downstairs, Madeline had left a note explaining that she'd gone to pick the kids up from school.

Dominic led the way to the kitchen, pulling a fistful of paper towels off the roll and running them under the kitchen faucet. "You've got a little something on your face," he said, handing them over. The white towels turned a dirty salmon-pink as Micah scrubbed at his skin. The hair was probably a lost cause, but thankfully the spurt had managed to miss his clothes.

"C'mere," Dominic said, gesturing him over. "Probably unnecessary, but better to be safe . . ." Using a small grease pencil, he drew a preservation ikon on Micah's skin, to the side of his eye. "There's probably nothing to worry about, but it'll keep you whole, in case the blood had anything infectious."

Micah reached up, stopping short of touching the mark. Then he went for his notebook. *Do you need one?*

"Ha, no." Dominic pulled his collar down, showing the lines of glyphs along the back of his left shoulder. The black ink had faded to a dark blue in the decade since he'd gotten them, but the ink had its own magic, keeping it from getting blurry and negating the meaning. "I'm immune to everything but the common cold."

The front door slammed open. The sound of raucous screaming had the two of them reaching for their weapons again, until a pack of tiny, brightly dressed humans burst into the room. There were three of them, and they barely seemed to notice the two controllers as they scrambled toward the kitchen cupboards.

"Not until after dinner!" Madeline shouted from the entryway. The children let out a single simultaneous groan of disappointment before clambering as a unit into the living room.

Micah and Dominic exchanged a look.

"Kids, right?" Madeline laughed as she entered the kitchen. Her arms were full of jackets and backpacks that the children had dropped between the door and the kitchen. Some kind of hellish, high-pitched singing began to echo out of the living room. Dominic wanted very much to be literally anywhere else.

Madeline dropped the garments into an unceremonious pile and asked Dominic, "Got any of your own?"

"No, ma'am. Not me."

"Probably makes sense. With your line of work."

"Yeah. Right. So, which one is your nephew?"

"Oh, those three are all mine. Josh is still out in the yard. He's a little more subdued than his cousins. The counselor says that's perfectly normal, after, you know. What he's been through."

"Well, at least his room's not haunted anymore. I'm not sure what exactly was up there, but it's dead n—"

The shrieking from upstairs was matched by an equally earsplitting cacophony from the living room.

"Are you *fucking* kidding me?" Dominic snapped.

The living room exploded into giggles and *awws*. Madeline narrowed her eyes at Dominic, but he was busy gawking at the creature at the top of the stairs. It was the bloody man in the suit, and he looked *pissed*.

It wasn't fair. "That thing was fuckin' *dead*."

"Mr. Blackburn. Language, please."

"It was dead, wasn't it?" Dominic turned to Micah for verification. Micah nodded. The monster's blood was still in his hair, so Dominic couldn't have imagined it. He turned back to Madeline. "That thing disintegrated into dust. We both saw it. Micah damn near cut its fuckin' head off."

"Mr. Blackburn! *Language*!"

Madeline was staring at him, aghast, and Dominic realized that "Mr. Blackburn" was *him*. "Oh. Sorry." Something ceramic hurled past Dominic's head and shattered on the wall. "*Shit*!"

He and Micah dropped, taking cover behind the counter. Madeline darted into the living room, out of range of the creature now taking potshots from the top of the stairs. The children's giddy shrieks turned into sobs, but Dominic could barely hear them over the keening of the monster pelting them from above.

"Break for the front door," Dominic said, but Micah was way ahead of him, scrambling out from behind the counter and staying low. Something knocked him in the hip, bouncing off and spinning across the linoleum. Some kind of stuffed animal, by the feel of it. Whatever this thing was, it was bound to the upstairs, and it was clearly running out of projectiles.

A piggy bank smashed into the counter above Dominic's head, raining pottery shards and loose change down over him. He launched himself across the kitchen entry, taking a paperback to the shoulder on his way past.

Madeline and the children had escaped out a side door and were waiting for them by the car when they got outside. Irritation was written on her features.

"What did you do?" she demanded. "You were supposed to kill it, not make it worse!"

"Well, Micah stabbed it in the eye, and it crumbled into dust, so we were pretty sure it was dead."

"So now it's, what, undead?"

"Maybe? Honestly, I didn't know what it was to begin with, and I've only got *slightly* more to work with now."

"How can you *not know*?"

"I dunno," Dom griped. "How did you forget to mention that your sister was a witch?" He froze, then groaned, mentally kicking himself. The box of witchcraft supplies was still in the kitchen. If there was any clue about this thing, it would be in there.

Micah quirked an eyebrow at him.

Dom gestured back toward the house. "We forgot the box. We've gotta go back in."

Micah nodded and, without further preamble, strode back inside.

Something shattered.

"I didn't mean *alone*!" Dominic shouted after him.

Micah, of course, didn't answer. There were no more crashes. Dominic paused, waiting.

"Has he been working for you long?" Madeline asked.

Dominic looked between her and the now-silent house, trying to draw a connection between her words and their current situation. "What? No, like . . . two days. Why?"

"He's very loyal," she said simply, and before he could reply, Micah came back out of the house with the box in his hands. He set it on the ground near the trunk, and when he bent, sparkling shards of glass fell from his hair and clothes.

"I didn't mean you had to go in by *yourself*," Dominic repeated.

Micah shrugged, gesturing to the box.

Dominic peered into it. There were at least a dozen spell books in there, plus the charms and talismans. "It's gonna take all day for us to go through all this. I say we go back to the hotel and set up shop there."

"What about us?" Madeline sputtered. "We can't go back in there! What are we supposed to do while you're figuring this out?"

Dom shrugged helplessly. "Stay with a friend? Or get a hotel room."

"My husband's going to be home in forty minutes, and I'm supposed to tell him that this isn't handled and we can't go back in the house?"

"That or lie to him." Dominic shoved the box into the back seat and slammed the door. "Either way, we've got your number. We'll call you when we know something."

When they got back to the hotel, Micah insisted on carrying the box. He followed Dominic two steps behind and one to the left, all the way up to the room. Dominic stopped short a couple of times, or took corners too tight, trying to knock him loose, but Micah was persistent.

Dominic unlocked their door and collapsed into the seat where he'd eaten breakfast. Micah set the box on the bed, and Dominic was up again, pulling items out and arranging them onto the bedspread. The largest pile was things he knew for sure were garbage. Healing crystals, energy focusing pyramids, lucky penny talismans, and the other pseudo-magic crap every middle-class housewife kept right next to the shake weights.

Dominic pulled out a stack of books and dumped them to the side, then went back to the talismans.

Micah was kneeling on the floor again.

Dominic paused, taking in the sight. The way he was kneeling seemed weirdly formal, sitting back on his feet with his spine straight and his head bowed. It suddenly occurred to Dominic that he still had blood in his hair.

"Hey, did you want to shower while I get started on this?"

Micah's posture visibly relaxed, and he nodded at the ground.

"Micah."

He stiffened again, hands tight over the tops of his thighs.

"Hey. Look at me."

Micah raised his eyes, head still down.

"You're acting weird. Something bothering you?"

Micah shook his head.

"You sure?" He wracked his mind for an explanation. "Is it about killing that thing? 'Cause that was a *lot* of blood. It's okay to . . . not be okay."

Micah scratched out a quick note. *This is how we wait.*

Dominic read it over three times, trying to find some kind of actual meaning. "What?"

For a moment Micah looked almost exasperated, but then he scribbled down another line and pushed the paper back. *I'm not being weird.*

Dominic took in the tableau; Micah was still kneeling with his back tense and straight, fingers splayed across his knees. "Okay, fine. Not weird at all. Whatever. Go take a shower."

Micah nodded, then rose to his feet.

"Dude, in the bathroom!" Dominic said a moment later when Micah, predictably, began pulling his clothes off. Micah stopped dead, his jeans half-open. He hiked them up and dutifully went into the other room, *almost* closing the door behind him.

Fuck.

Dominic stared at the open door for longer than he should have, remembering the interlude they'd had that morning. He had work to do, but he *would* actually like to return the favor, at some point. And it wasn't like the guy wasn't inviting, but . . . Dom couldn't shake the feeling that something was *off* about Micah.

It was with no small amount of willpower that he turned his attention back to the box.

The first book was some mumbo-jumbo about communing with your guardian angel. It was the biggest load of bullshit Dominic had ever seen, and he still flipped through it three times before realizing he didn't remember a single word. He tossed it aside with the crystals and the pennies and picked up another book. Shoving some pillows behind his back, he settled against the headboard to read. This one was some kind of *The Secret* rip-off, all about the mystic power of visualizing things into reality through sheer force of will.

Dominic spent a minute visualizing a partner who wasn't a *fucking weirdo*, but Micah didn't come out of the bathroom to explain himself. Made sense. Dominic had always been particularly terrible with magic, anyway.

He tossed the book to the side.

The one after that was about fairies. Fairies who granted wishes if they were appeased with certain varieties of fruit juices and baked confections. Dominic was pretty sure it was bullshit, but the fae folk weren't really his specialty. In any case, the fairies seemed inclined to offer boons, not curse people with loud-ass monstrosities that destroyed guest rooms and threw things. Maybe she'd summoned a genie instead? It was an easy mistake, until the wish went horribly wrong.

Dominic set the book aside for possible later inspection.

The water in the bathroom shut off.

The next book was old, and in Latin. Those two things alone gave it an air of authenticity, but Dominic's Latin could best be described as *passable* and so, after thumbing through it for diagrams, he set it aside as well.

Micah came out of the bathroom shirtless and toweling his damp hair down, but at least he was wearing jeans. Dominic counted that as a win.

Micah draped the towel over the back of one of the chairs and then settled onto the floor again. Same as before, sitting back on his heels, knees spread, spine straight.

Dominic sighed. "What are you doing?"

The notepad was on the dresser. Micah retrieved it, writing a single word under his earlier message. *Waiting.*

"For what?"

Instructions.

"Why like that, though? You keep doing that."

Micah's head was still lowered, but his eyes flicked quickly up to Dominic. *This is how we wait.*

Bullshit. Dominic pointed at him. "Nah, 'cause, see, I've dealt with indents tons of times, and I've never met one who acts like you."

Dominic swore the expression that flickered across Micah's face was *smug*. Micah passed the paper back to him. *I told you I was in hospitality. We're trained a little better.*

Dominic panned back in his memory, all the pieces slotting into a pattern: sitting in the back seat, in the corner of the living room, the kneeling—somebody had *taught* him all that? To hold himself a certain way *all* the time?

Dominic remembered the manila envelope, still out in the car, with Micah's whole story written out in twice-signed forms printed in triplicate. He should read it.

Or he could be normal about it and just *ask*.

And Micah would answer, because he wasn't just indentured, he'd been *trained*.

"So," he started, "when you said they 'trained you for hospitality,' that's what you're talking about? It's not just a euphemism for being, uh, 'full service'?"

Micah looked confused. He started to nod, then shook his head. This time when he wrote, he did it slowly, deliberately choosing the words. *In part. The etiquette is a big part. Presentation. But being hospitable is more like a mindset than a skillset.* He started to write more, then seemed to think better of it.

Something tickled at the back of Dom's mind, some suspicion he wasn't sure he wanted to chase. He didn't know much about indents, but he knew they weren't particularly specialized. Lots of them chose to be indentured in lieu of jail time, or signed on to repay a debt, or were too old or unruly for anything but general labor or housework. To get an indent like Micah: young, handsome, intelligent, *skilled*—it was already almost too good to be true. But for him to have that level of formal training? That was the sundae under the cherry.

Something was very wrong with this picture.

"So why wasn't your contract sold into the industry? Seems like it would go for a hell of a lot more with all those skills."

If anything, Micah's head dropped lower. *I was disobedient.*

"What did you do?" Dominic asked slowly. *Disobedient* was an odd word choice, and it opened a door Dom wasn't sure he wanted to walk through.

Micah's eyes clenched shut. His pen hovered over the paper, making tiny dots each time he tried to start. Finally, he scribbled out a short line and handed the paper over. *I made a mistake I will not repeat.*

Dominic read the words over and over, trying to figure out how to respond. Whatever had happened, it bothered Micah a lot. It had apparently bothered his previous holder a lot too.

Dominic was thinking he should go get that envelope.

It felt like cheating, though. Dominic held Micah's contract, but that didn't mean the guy's entire personal life was Dom's to dig through. If Micah had done something really serious—arson or assault or something—he'd be in jail, or a work camp, same as anybody else. Whatever it was that Micah didn't want to talk about, it was personal, not dangerous.

He'd deal with it later. Micah had already had a long day, and whatever Dom was scratching at here, this wasn't the time. The mystery of his weird new partner would have to wait. Right now, they had work to do.

"Fair enough," Dom said, handing the notebook back. "You can tell me about it when you're up to it. Here's what I need you to do now. See these talismans? I need you to figure out what they are. Don't touch them with your bare hands; get some gloves out of my bag if you need to handle them. If anything gives you a weird vibe, tell me. How's your Latin?"

Micah did that silent laugh of his. Some of the tension lifted off his shoulders. *Not great.*

"I figured. That's fine. Google Translate can help, or just leave it for me."

Micah nodded and rose up off the floor, going to inspect the small pile of trinkets.

Several hours later, Garrett texted to ask how the job had gone, and Dominic filled him in on the details of Madeline's spectacularly inaccurate report. Garrett commiserated and made a note on her file, in case she requested help again in the future. He didn't have any good ideas on what kind of creature was immune to salt and could return from being disintegrated. He suggested a phoenix, since they were known to rise from ashes, but nobody had ever seen one that appeared as a screaming man in a suit. Garrett said he'd ask around, and Dominic got back to the books.

Micah agreed to sit in a chair to use the laptop. After Dominic showed him the bookmarks for the different paranormal research sites, Micah actually made good progress with the talismans. As Dominic had suspected, most of them were hokey garbage.

So far, they had a great big pile of nothing.

"I need a beer," Dominic mumbled. Micah immediately stood, but Dominic waved him back down. "I don't mean you need to get me one. I mean, it's late and this crap isn't giving me any clues, let's go to dinner."

Micah nodded, staying on his feet. Dominic grabbed his keys.

"I know a place about forty minutes from here with a tuna melt to die for. You okay going that far?"

Micah gestured to the door.

CHAPTER EIGHT

For some reason, it seemed very important to Dominic that Micah eat a sandwich. It was probably one of the easiest tasks Micah could've possibly been given, but he still didn't understand why Dominic seemed outright bothered by his preference for natural foods. He understood why Dominic didn't share those preferences: Dominic didn't know what it was like to live on white bread and stolen gas station chips. He didn't know about supplement shakes that let your body build muscle but never fat. He didn't know about show diets. He didn't know the safety in the unbroken skin of an apple.

Dominic knew none of this, and Micah had no plans to tell him.

Micah knew the bitter-sour taste of an additive that meant Slate had something intense planned. He remembered the confused, heavy sensation that would settle over him and leave him pliable in his master's hands. He'd been drugged when they did the piercings, hands pinning his mouth and legs open, too confused to even think of struggling. They had pierced him a dozen times that day, for entertainment, to see if they liked the look. Micah had been blindfolded, never knowing where the needle would penetrate him next. For days afterward his mouth had tasted of blood, and even gentle caresses had been agony.

Still, the drugs were the worst of it. If his master had simply *told* him to open his mouth and spread his legs and *allow* himself to be pierced, Micah could, and would, have done it for him.

Micah didn't need the drugs to get through difficult scenes. He could *always* hold still when his masters worked him over. He'd *earned* his Signature. He was silent when told to shut up, came when instructed to, and usually cried only when he was allowed. His masters had been proud of him, and with good reason. He would give them what no one else could, and they would praise him and stroke his hair and feed him sweets straight from their fingers. Sometimes they let him stay the night in their bed, sleeping late on soft sheets.

But Adam Slate had been different from the others. Drugs before a difficult task were for Slate's benefit, not the slaves'. Slate liked that from the first taste of bitter-sour, they knew he was going to hurt them, and they didn't know how.

Micah had done his best, but the uncertainty and fear were a blanket that coated Slate's entire household. The slaves never knew how he would come for them, or when. More than once, Micah had been roused in the middle of the night, summoned by a bored guest. He was normally safe in Slate's bed—normally. But there was never certainty, never forewarning, never time to prepare, and seemingly no excuse for not having done so anyway.

Micah knew he'd been set up to fail there, that failing was the *point*, but the knowledge didn't help. The anxiety had soaked into his body along with the pain, and over the years it ate away at his will. He hadn't just *failed* to follow orders—he'd deliberately chosen *not* to. It was a mistake he hadn't made since the first of his father's rages, and one he never planned to make again.

So if Dominic wanted him to eat a sandwich?

Micah had been asked for harder things.

The restaurant was busy, so they sat at the bar. Micah paused when Dominic took a seat, but before he could decide his place, Dominic grabbed his shirt sleeve and guided him into the seat next to him.

There were several other indents here, marked by uniforms, barcodes, or subservient positioning. With his sleeves covering his arms, he had none of these. To the outside observer, it would seem as though he and Dominic were friends, or family, or coworkers.

It struck Micah as deeply inappropriate. He didn't know what was expected of him here. It couldn't last. The waitress would come to take their order and Micah wouldn't be able to speak to her and he'd have to write it down and it would be obvious he'd never done it before and she'd just *know* that he was a slave and he didn't belong here sitting next to Dominic like he—

"Dude, you okay?"

Dominic was watching him with concern on his face, and Micah realized he was breathing very fast. He tamped it all down, bringing the cool, composed mask over his features. Of course the waitress wouldn't know, and even if she did, so what? Micah was exactly where his owner wanted him to be. If Dominic wanted to buy a disgraced hospitality slave, dress him up, and take him out for tuna melts, that was his right.

Micah relaxed and gave Dominic a small smile. Dominic studied him for another couple of seconds, then gave up with a shrug.

It turned out that Micah didn't need to worry about writing down his order, because Dominic had a whole list of things he was adamant that Micah try and ended up ordering for both of them. He insisted that the tuna melts were fantastic, that the locally-brewed beer was a good pair. Micah preferred iced tea but didn't mention it. He let Dominic put ketchup on the massive pile of fries, rather than gesturing for the malt vinegar.

There was no reason his owner needed to know that Micah's preferences differed from his own. Micah kept these minor disagreements stored away down somewhere deep, where they belonged. It was good practice.

Dominic knew what he liked, and he clearly wanted Micah to like them too. His excitement had a higher payoff than any condiment ever could. Dominic laughed with his whole body, and Micah thought he'd like to make his owner do it more often.

Dominic clearly liked that Micah liked french fries. Micah thought that maybe he liked Dominic.

It was dumb. He'd met him a day ago and knew close to nothing about him.

But still.

Micah wasn't stupid. He knew his time with this owner was limited; a hospitality slave could generally expect less than half a year of servitude in any given house. After that, the novelty would wear off and he'd be traded for something new.

And Dominic wasn't dumb either. He was piecing together the clues about what he'd actually bought. Once he realized what Micah was worth—*really* worth—he'd turn around and sell him again. Or maybe he'd have Micah start doing fights, make his money that way.

Micah wasn't sure which prospect sounded worse, but it didn't matter because it wasn't up to him. Dominic would do what Dominic wanted to do.

When they got back in the car, the manila envelope with his paperwork was sitting on the dashboard, seemingly surrounded by blinking neon lights spelling READ ME. Neither man acknowledged it, and when they got back to the hotel, Dominic left it in the car.

CHAPTER NINE

The next morning was uneventful. When Micah woke up, Dominic was already dressed and working. He glanced at the clock; it was almost eight. Shit. How had he slept in that late? Why hadn't Dominic woken him?

He didn't get a clue from his owner, just a neutral "good morning" while Micah made the bed. Dominic didn't send him to fetch breakfast, so that opportunity had clearly been missed.

He washed and dressed quickly, then went to watch what Dominic was doing. Each item in Annie's box had to be tested for a handful of different energetic sympathies. Dominic explained the process and gestured to a pile for him to work on. It wasn't difficult, but it was time-consuming.

By the afternoon, Micah had finished. To the best of his knowledge, the entire pile of trinkets was inert. Even setting aside the obvious "made in China" stamps on most of them, the power they were meant to invoke wasn't real. By the looks of it, Madeline's late sister had gone in for every magic fad that popped up on her television. If these spells could do half of what they promised, the spiritual energy in that house would have been focused enough to burn ants.

He tossed the last charm across the room, where it clattered into the box along with the rest of the discarded items. Dominic glanced up at the sound, then turned back to the stack of books he was searching.

Micah picked one up, flipping through it and pausing when he got to highlighted sections.

The spells were real enough; Annie had just been a terrible witch. She seemed almost pathologically disinclined to follow directions, and spell after spell was marked with revisions and substitutions.

Doesn't work on a half-moon, was scribbled in ballpoint next to one clearly calling for a full moon. *Does not work with skim milk*, read another note. *Do not use gluten-free flour!*

Micah scoffed and rolled his eyes, turning the page toward Dominic.

Dom clicked his tongue. "Yeah, they're all full of crap like that. But she was interested in general wellness spells. These are all about bringing peace and tranquility and that shit. There's a couple love spells, but it's more the 'find your soulmate' kind, instead of the rapey ones. Definitely nothing about summoning a howling monster to trash your sister's house."

Dominic tossed his book to the side, stretching out on the bed. His T-shirt pulled up, revealing an inch of skin along his lower belly.

Micah wanted to put his mouth on it, but he wasn't sure if that came from inside him or if he was just abstractly aware that the skin there was a secondary erogenous zone, so *Dominic* would probably like it.

It was difficult to tell, sometimes, where his impulses came from.

Dominic noticed the attention. "See something you like?"

Micah nodded before realizing that the question was rhetorical. But Dominic was laughing again, and that was good.

"You're such a perv. Is that what happened at the last place? They couldn't get you to quit jumping people's bones?"

Dominic presumably meant it as a joke, but Micah's blood ran cold. He set his gaze back on the floor, where it belonged. *Please don't make me tell*, he thought desperately. *Please.*

Micah was too high up. He couldn't be here, sitting in a chair and staring at Dominic like they were on equal footing. He slid off the chair, melting easily into the supplicant's pose. Knees together, palms flat on the floor, forehead pressed to the backs of his hands.

"Hey, man. I'm not . . ." Dominic sighed. "We probably need to talk about this."

"*Please*," he whispered, but of course there was no sound. Slate hadn't wanted to hear him beg. He'd wanted Micah to bear his punishments in silence. It wasn't enough to order that he be silent, because sometimes sounds had slipped through anyway. Slate had wanted Micah *incapable* of begging, and so one day there had been the sour-bitter taste and a bright white room and a mask that turned everything black. He'd woken up to fire in his throat and sobs that made no sound.

The doctor had been kind to him, Slate told him later. The tone had been conversational, as though he hadn't had a hand fisted in Micah's hair to hold him still while he'd used Micah's mouth. He'd planned to have Micah's tongue cut out, but the doctor had argued strongly in favor of devocalization. The recovery time was faster, and it didn't interfere with the slave's ability to suck cock.

"He was very persuasive," Slate had said, and Micah had closed his eyes and swallowed through the fire in his throat. The late mornings in his owner's bed were long gone by then.

And Dominic wanted to know what he'd done to deserve it.

Micah's face burned with shame. A snide little voice reminded him that he was supposed to be in the *chair,* Dominic didn't *like* it when he knelt on the floor, that he wasn't obeying, he was *hiding*.

"I'm serious, man. Something isn't matching up here, and I need to know why. Whatever happened, it pissed your last holder off a *lot*, and right now I'm just wondering if you're planning to shiv me in my sleep and make a run for it."

He said it like a joke, but Micah shook his head vehemently. He would never. Not to an owner a hundred times worse than Slate, and certainly not to Dominic.

"Okay, so what, then? I gotta know. And look, if you can't talk about it, I get it. I can read it in your file. But I'd like your side, if you can give it to me."

Micah clenched his jaw, then reached for the pad of paper. He was responsible for his own actions, no matter how much he'd come to regret them. The pen was heavy in his hand. He didn't know how to start.

Bracing himself, he closed his eyes and forced himself to remember.

In the years that Micah lived with Slate, he learned to work through the effects of the drugs. They made him slow, and confused, and tired, but despite all that, he had a job to do. He wanted to think he was able to do it well, but his memories weren't clear.

That evening, it seemed, Slate was visiting someone. Several of his favorite slaves were summoned from the barracks, blindfolded, shackled, and loaded into a van. As soon as they recognized each other, it became clear what kind of night they were in for. These weren't the kitchen workers or chauffeurs or maids—those for whom *indent* was an actual title, rather than a euphemism to be used in polite company. No, that night, Slate had called for his *slaves*.

The drive wasn't long, maybe forty minutes or an hour. Micah let the drugs and the rocking of the van lull him into a sense of calm. By the time they arrived, he was relaxed, pliant. It was a good way to begin the evening. Too much fear interfered with his performance.

The blindfolds and shackles were removed in a garage, and the slaves were hustled inside with the others. This gathering had quite a few attendees, all of whom had traveled with their own entourage. Micah recognized a few faces, but knew better than to greet them.

They undressed in silence, donning the clothes that their host had provided. The theme, as close as Micah could tell, had to do with forest spirits. All the slaves were given skirts in earthen tones, artfully torn and dyed to mimic the aesthetics of age. Attendants flitted through the throng, brushing iridescent powders onto cheekbones and eyelids and nipples and navels. To one side, two slaves were facing the wall as terrifically intricate wings were painted onto their shoulders and backs. Gold rings and bangles and piercings accentuated the interlocking gold circles painted carefully on each wing.

Micah staggered slightly while dressing. He had to sit down in order to don the soft buckskin boots he'd been given. Beside him, another slave was struggling. Micah checked himself, making sure he was presentable, and then knelt before the other slave. The man's fingers were shaking as he struggled with the laces on the high boots. Without speaking, Micah pushed his hands away, working the laces until they were snug but not tight. He ran his hand up the slave's calf, smoothing the leather. The man gave him a thankful smile, and Micah smiled back.

A chime sounded, signaling the beginning of the event, and Micah rejoined the slaves from his own household. They were directed through the corridors toward the main gathering. At the door, one of the ushers gave Micah a tray of drinks. The room was dim, but Micah was used to that. In the center was a raised dais, which he ignored. He scanned the crowd, quickly locating his master.

Slate was reclining on a dark couch, listening to another man speak. Micah approached him silently and from the left, taking a knee and presenting the tray.

Slate took his drink without looking, too engrossed in his conversation to acknowledge his slave. Micah was used to this, and he turned slightly, offering the tray to the man speaking.

There were seven people in Slate's group, four women and three men. They listened to the speaker with rapt attention while Micah went around the circle, presenting his tray.

When it was empty and an usher had collected it, Micah returned to his master's side, kneeling silently beside him.

One of the women gave him a sly grin, and he returned it before leaning his head against his master's thigh. Slate's hand came to rest on his shoulder, fingers stroking the nape of his neck. It was a gentle reward, and he accepted it contentedly.

"What I don't understand," Slate was saying, "is why they think we'll be limited to one creature. Especially now that the door is stable."

"Maybe they're trying to drive up the price of their stock," said the woman who had smiled at Micah. He had no idea what they were talking about, but he simpered at her as though she'd said something clever.

"Rarity is the lifeblood of value," commented the man who'd been speaking earlier.

A scattering of applause rippled through the crowd, and attention turned to the dais. The two slaves with painted wings were standing in the center, while a man in a suit bowed.

Micah felt fingers hook through his collar. The woman was tugging at him. He glanced to Slate for permission. His master distractedly waved him off.

The woman pulled him onto the couch and climbed, a little unsteadily, onto his lap. Her dress was embroidered with small beads and gems that scratched against Micah's thighs, but he didn't let his discomfort show. Instead, he made a performance of reacting to the woman's hands as they traveled over his body.

The man on the dais was doing some sort of magic show. The slaves with painted wings were subjected to a number of death-defying stunts—impaled with swords, bisected, even beheaded—before emerging unscathed.

With other masters, Micah might have paid more attention. Maybe speculated as to how the tricks were performed, if they were illusions or just real magic. Now, it was all he could do to stay focused on his own tasks.

"I wish they'd skip the theatrics and get to it," the other woman remarked.

Micah's guest rolled her eyes. "*I'm* enjoying myself. What's the point of acquisition if you can't stop and sample what you've earned?"

She cupped Micah's jaw, pulling him up for a rough kiss. She tasted like wine. "Where *do* you find such gems, Slate?" she asked when they broke apart. "I'd give my husband's left ball for a pet like this."

The group laughed, but Slate only shrugged. "Rarity is the lifeblood of value," he quipped, winking.

Micah preened at his master's praise.

The woman's fingers traced over his belly, the black outline of his signature. "Maybe someday, I'll learn your secret," she lamented. Her fingers slipped beneath Micah's waistband, heading south. From the corner of his eye, Micah could see Slate watching. It was his master's prerogative to protest; if Slate said nothing, then Micah was to give her what she wanted.

Micah focused his attention on the feel of her hand, encouraging his body to respond. He didn't want to offend her by appearing uninterested. Her fingernails scratched over the short hair above his cock, and the lights dimmed. A single spotlight appeared over the dais.

There were twelve people there now, Micah realized. They were draped in heavy cloaks, and they stood in a circle around a heavy metal frame. The male slave was being cuffed to this frame, spread-eagled so that the elaborate wings were fully on display.

"This is it," the woman whispered. Her eyes were fixed on the platform. Micah checked his master, but even Slate seemed engrossed.

"A little heavy on the drama, aren't they?" Slate asked, but the woman shushed him.

"Once again gathers the Esoteric Order of Dagon," the man in the suit announced, and laughter rippled through the crowd. "After months of preparation, we feel confident that we have something to offer you tonight. Something . . . *new*."

He stepped to the side, where a slave offered him a heavy cloak. He donned it and joined the circle, partially blocking Micah's view.

The woman on his lap was utterly disinterested in him now, but Micah kept his attention on her. He wasn't in the business of being caught unprepared.

The hall filled with the sounds of chanting, words so low that Micah wasn't sure they were words at all. They grew in volume, reverberating until his teeth ached. The pressure in the room seemed to change, but it might have been the drugs confusing him.

And that was when the screaming started.

Micah kept his head down, tried to focus on his own work. He was used to screaming. Begging, sobbing, all the myriad expressions of the powerless. What he heard now was something more, and his attention snapped to the dais.

As the chanting continued, the painted wings began to bulge, pushing at the man's skin from the inside. It might have been another trick, except for the noises that the slave was making as he struggled to escape.

The painted wings were light, gossamer, but the ones that burst free were thick and heavy. Rather than clear and sparkling, these were defined by twisting, knotted veins, black beneath the skin.

Blood trickled across the floor, too much, streaming in dark rivulets from the misshapen appendages. They collapsed under their own weight, the man's abortive attempt to hold them up failing spectacularly.

The chanting stopped, and the slave let out one last scream before sagging in his bonds.

The room was absolutely silent. Micah scanned the faces of the crowd, the other slaves . . . everyone was still, staring wordlessly at the dais.

Within a few seconds, two slaves appeared from the shadows and freed the chained man. They were dressed in dark coveralls, and with a start, Micah realized that the ritual's failure had been anticipated, even planned for. As the man was bundled into a dark tarp, Micah realized he wasn't just unconscious.

He was *dead.*

Micah's stomach twisted.

Slaves expected a certain amount of pain, even *injury*, in the course of serving their masters. The trick was to keep your mouth shut, to complete the assignments given to *you*, to trust that it would be over soon and be grateful when it wasn't your turn. But this was the first time Micah had ever seen anyone *die*. It happened, everyone knew it happened, but *irresponsibly*, by *accident*, and not to the caliber of slaves that cost what Micah and his ilk did.

"That's why they bring a spare," Slate said. He looked around the group, gauging the reactions of his companions. Micah was confused for a moment, until a ruckus erupted from the direction of the dais.

The woman with painted wings was being dragged onto the stage. She was struggling and shouting, though she'd been gagged since the last time Micah had seen her.

The audience almost seemed to relax, turning to each other and murmuring. Micah waited for someone to stand, to protest. If nothing else, the woman's *owner* should object to their slave being wasted this way?

Nothing.

Micah looked to Slate, hoping to see some concern there, some disgust, but Slate was flagging down a nearby waiter for another drink.

The woman on Micah's lap had him by the chin; he'd let his mind wander and that was dangerous. He tried to focus on her, tried to arrange his features into the sly smile that would satisfy her.

The slave on the stage screamed again, dragging Micah's attention away. The cuffs were still wet with the other slave's blood, and before Micah realized what he was doing, he'd pushed the woman off his lap and stood. Immediately he was dizzy, vertigo hitting him like a hammer.

"They can't—" he started to say, but his words were lost under the other slave's protests. Someone grabbed his collar and yanked him down. He lost his balance and crumpled, head spinning. The collar cut into his throat, and he choked.

"The fuck do you think you're doing?" Slate snapped at him.

"What are *you* doing?" Micah heard himself say. The words seemed far away. He'd have been horrified at his own impertinence if he'd had the capacity to think beyond the woman on the dais. Slate slapped him, leaving his ears ringing. He couldn't breathe. A hand was around his throat, pulling him onto the couch, his back to Slate's chest.

"Shut *up*," his owner hissed into his ear. His fingers tightened, and Micah's vision darkened. For a moment, Micah was relieved. This was familiar. He was making bad choices and his owner was helping him. Slate would take him to that place, that deep-down place where there were no thoughts, only faraway sensations and the warmth of his master's body. A few more seconds and he would be there. All he had to do was *nothing*, and this would all be over soon.

Instead, the chanting began again, and that wild screaming, and Micah found himself driving his elbow into Slate's ribs, on his feet before either of them knew what was happening. He turned toward the dais, but his vision was doubling, brightly lit wings splitting and spinning like a kaleidoscope.

Something sharp bit into his thigh and he looked down, watching his master's face vanish behind the image of a syringe, doubling, two, then four.

"What are you doing?" he heard again. He didn't know who was speaking.

An usher appeared, and Micah was half escorted, half dragged back to the slave quarters, away from the crowded ballroom. Distantly, he could hear Slate apologizing to the woman Micah had pushed.

He never found out what happened to the other slave.

Back in Dominic's hotel room, Micah stared at the single line he'd managed to write.

I saw something that

Micah frowned at it. What word could possibly describe his reaction to what he'd seen? *Confused*? *Shocked*? *Disgusted*? *Frightened*?

No. Micah was frequently frightened; he could follow orders that frightened him. That was just part of being a slave. The winged man's death hadn't *frightened* him, but he didn't have another word, something to describe the stomach-twisting *wrongness* of the way the splintered, bloody appendages had torn themselves from underneath the man's skin, the *sound*—

The tip of the pencil hovered over the paper. Every second he delayed was another second before he was forced to face Dominic's disappointment. Dominic was kind, but he wasn't stupid; he wouldn't leave his life in the hands of a slave who couldn't obey when he was *frightened*.

Micah wished he were weak enough to blame the drugs, but he knew it would be an excuse. He'd only been drugged at the beginning, and if he were being honest, his disobedience hadn't come from what he'd seen. Micah had a deeper flaw, a failing that had already changed his life once.

No matter how hard he tried, he knew the miserable truth: it wouldn't be long until he failed again.

The next day, someone had come and tattooed over Micah's Signature. His training, Slate said, had clearly been incomplete. He didn't have the *temperament* to be a Signed slave. Micah was prideful. He thought he knew better than his owners. He had an exaggerated sense of his own importance, and the importance of other slaves.

Slaves, Micah had failed to learn, were *property*.

It was a word Micah repeated many times before he lost his voice. Every time Slate struck him, he asked what Micah was. What the other slaves were. What their bodies were. What their lives were. Micah woke up from nightmares, alone in his cell, screaming that he would obey.

But no matter what Slate did, or had his men do, Micah couldn't stop being prideful. He knew the answers they wanted. He could perform any task, no matter how debased, but he couldn't learn to *truly* submit. Couldn't just accept that they knew best.

He put on a good show. He was even able to lie to himself, tell himself he had learned. That he *believed* again, the way he always had before. He listened to Slate speaking and agreed vehemently. Slaves didn't make decisions. They were property. Owners had rights and were to be obeyed. Always.

It made perfect sense.

Until the day that Slate gave him a flogger, gestured to another slave, and told Micah to prove what he'd learned. Micah had seen the metal wires braided through the leather. He knew what those wires could do. He had the scars on his own back as testament.

He'd stared at it until his owner got impatient. Slate snatched the flogger back, and Micah braced himself for the pain of the impact; he'd bought another slave's safety with his own skin, not for the first time, and the trade wouldn't come cheap. Suddenly he was fifteen again, about to lose his last fight because even with everything on the table, he *couldn't—*

But then Slate brought the flogger down, hard, on the other slave's back. Thin lines of blood appeared instantly, and Slate raised it again.

Micah snatched it out of his hand.

The two of them stared at each other, wide-eyed, frozen. Micah was disobeying. Micah didn't *disobey.*

The sound of the wings, tearing through skin—

And that was when he struck his master in the temple, turned tail, and ran.

He didn't get far.

I saw something that upset me. An indent was killed during a performance.

I lost my composure and embarrassed my holder. I was disciplined appropriately, but afterward I was unable to perform my duties as ordered.

He turned the paper to Dominic, who scanned it and handed it back.

"Seriously. I'm going to need a little more than that."

Micah began writing in short, objective sentences. He tried not to sound defensive, though it probably came off that way. He wanted to explain—he'd been shocked by what he'd seen, he was reluctant to inflict pain he'd experienced—but it would come off as making excuses. He'd disobeyed, and it wasn't his place to do so.

Above all, he tried not to show how afraid he was. Afraid of Dominic's reaction, but also afraid he'd fail if Dominic decided to test him.

He tried to be good, he really did. He hoped Dominic could see that. See that he was *trying* to be someone with value. Slate had seen it in him once, had kept him on for four years while others came and went around him. Micah could be that to someone again, he was sure of it. He just needed a chance.

Dominic read the lines as Micah wrote them, the set of his jaw growing more and more severe with each new page. He didn't look at Micah. For that, at least, Micah was grateful. He didn't think he could bear Dominic's disappointment.

Micah hid his face and waited.

CHAPTER TEN

∞

The last words on the last page were a promise to do better.

Dominic felt sick.

This should be impossible. There were laws. Indents had strict legal obligations, but they were still *people*, were still protected by all the same rights and laws everyone else was, you couldn't just *beat* them. You couldn't just . . .

Couldn't just what?

Drug them? Slice their vocal cords?

Kill them?

Obviously it wasn't unheard of for an indent to get killed. They often did dangerous jobs and tended, honestly, to be dangerous people. The system had been designed to help the criminal, chronically unemployed, and drug-addled find steady work. It wasn't exactly populated with *angels*. Things happened. And those rare instances were investigated, weren't they? Someone noticed and made sure that it had been an accident, or self-defense. The cops or something.

. . . Right?

And now this. Micah on the floor, again, doing some cross between a bow and the fetal position, apologizing for something that Dominic still didn't fully understand.

It was dawning on him that no one was watching out for Micah. Dominic had bought his contract with cash in a parking lot where any other occupant would deny having seen either of them. Megan had made it more than clear she didn't care whether Dom even registered the sale.

It must have been terrifying, being brought to that place, drugged and shackled, and having his contract sold to whoever wandered by, knowing full well no one was coming to find him.

Can indents refuse a transfer? They must be able to . . . right?

He didn't know. He'd never thought about it.

Dominic ground the heels of his hands into his eyes, suddenly unable to shake the image of Micah's blade driving into the zombie. All Micah had suffered to get away from his last holder's violence, only to end up *here*.

"Micah, get off the floor. Please, man."

Micah's fingers twitched, and he rose slightly, keeping his back arched and his head down.

Dominic realized Micah was hiding from him.

Micah was scared.

Of him.

"Okay. Ah, fuck. I'm not mad at you. What about that thing you were doing before? The kneel. Can you at least do that?"

Micah's shoulders relaxed and, after a moment, he rose up into the kneeling position. He still didn't look at Dominic.

Dom let out a slow breath. "I'm not gonna lie, dude, that's a fucked up story. Not 'cause of you. I get that you tried to do whatever he wanted, but it's fucked up of him to want it in the first place. Wanting to hurt people like that is *fucked up*. Even if he was your holder, that's *way* beyond what your contract covers. And man, I gotta say, I'm glad you couldn't do it."

Micah's face stayed blank.

Dominic carried on slowly. "I'm starting to kinda get a picture of the place you came from. You talked about training, and I thought they just taught you how to *do* stuff. But it's more than that, isn't it."

It wasn't a question. Micah agreed anyway.

Dominic got off the bed and sat cross-legged across from his indent. Micah was more comfortable on the ground, but this needed to be said eye-to-eye.

"I need you to look at me for this one. Because this is important and you gotta believe me when I say it. I don't want that from you. I'm not a . . . a trainer or whatever. I'm not gonna hit you, I'm not gonna have, like, sex parties. I just need somebody to watch my back. Got it?"

Micah's hands tightened on his thighs, and Dominic knew he'd said the wrong thing again, but fuck if he had any idea why.

"*What*?" he said, exasperated. "What now?"

Micah let out a breath, the emotion falling from his face and leaving a blank, absent stare, and oh *fuck* no, they weren't doing that again.

"Tell me why that upset you. I don't give a shit if you don't think it's your place. You want instructions or whatever? Tell me what I said wrong."

Micah picked up the pad again and wrote, *I can do more. You're not getting the most out of me.*

Dom pushed the paper back. "Yeah, so? You're a person, not a stock portfolio."

Micah paused before writing another line. *You could sell me. You'd get more than you think.*

"I know your contract is worth more than I paid. I don't care. I'm not sending you back to that."

Micah passed him a number. It was seven digits, and it took Dominic too long to realize it was a sale price.

Dominic gaped. His *house* wasn't worth that much. "You're shitting me."

Micah smiled, and Dominic didn't miss the touch of pride.

He whistled. "You must be one fantastic piece of ass."

Micah rolled his eyes, though the smile didn't fade. He snatched the paper back. *It's more than that.*

"Like what? The kneeling thing?"

The relaxation pose. For when an indent is not in use and expects to wait awhile.

"They literally taught you how to sit and wait?"

Very specifically. There are twenty-six positions which a Signed indent is expected to know.

Dominic couldn't imagine. It was all he could do to avoid talking to himself out loud, or absently tapping on the tabletop, or any of a hundred other little things that used to drive his dad crazy.

"So, at any given point you've got an exact way you're supposed to be standing or sitting or whatever and you're supposed to remember to do that all the time? And you're . . . okay with that?"

Micah nodded. *And I'm very good at it.*

"Cocky fucker, aren't you?"

That got Micah to grin. Dom was glad. For the first time since this conversation had started, he didn't feel like someone was sitting on his chest.

"What does 'Signed' mean?" Dom asked, tapping the paper.

Micah's smile vanished, and he seemed almost offended. He gestured to the tattoo on his hip. *It means my trainer is confident enough to vouch for me unreservedly.*

Dom blinked, sure he was misunderstanding. "So you mean literally *signed*? That tattoo is someone's actual signature?"

That has *to be illegal,* Dominic thought. But then again, there was the barcode.

Micah shook his head, letting his hair fall across his face. *It was a Signature. "A" for my trainer, Arabelle. But my last holder had it covered up. I'm not sure whether I'll be able to get it back.*

Dominic glanced at the circular black mark. Beneath the starburst, he could see slight variations in line width, and he realized there *had* been an *A* underneath.

His stomach twisted. Someone had stamped their approval right onto Micah's body. And Micah was *proud* of that.

"You're way over my head with that, Mic," he said helplessly. "I don't know how any of this crap is supposed to work. I'm just an exterminator; the closest I've ever gotten to 'formal' was when my grandpa took me to Olive Garden for my birthday."

That got Micah to laugh—strange and silent, but genuine. Dominic relaxed. He'd been worried that this job wasn't for Micah, but it hadn't occurred to him that Micah would have a *different* job, one he took pride in and would rather go *back* to. Not just a different job, but a whole different *world*, one that Dominic had always thought was made up for pornos.

"Yeah, so, sorry your sadist holder decided to punish you by selling your contract to a dumb hick. And, really, I shouldn't have taken you on the job today. I should have explained better, and as soon as I've got the Carmichaels settled, we'll find you someone who can better appreciate . . . this." He gestured to all of Micah. "Promise. You don't even have to go back with me tomorrow."

Micah bit his lip. *Can I go with you? Just to finish this job.*

Dominic read it twice. That . . . wasn't what he'd been expecting. "Yeah, I mean, if you want to. It's gonna be more blood and guts, though. You might have to stab something else."

Micah shrugged, but he didn't write any more.

Dom ran a hand through his hair. "Honestly, you can keep coming with me as long as you want to."

I'd like to. Please. If I'm not in the way.

Dom wasn't prepared for the rush of relief that brought. Micah glanced up at him with a grin, then returned his eyes to the ground.

"I like it when you look at me," Dominic realized out loud, and then kicked himself because who the fuck said stuff like that? Maybe next he could write some fucking poetry about how Micah's eyes were the color of the ocean or some shit.

No, they were darker than that. Micah was meeting his gaze again, and there were flecks of gold and brown in there. They were dark under the cheap motel lights, but Dominic thought that out in the sun they would be a brilliant green, not like the ocean at all.

And then Micah was leaning forward, his hands on Dominic's thighs, and Dom pulled back because this was wrong. Micah was vulnerable and asking him for *instructions*, and Dom was pretty sure there was a special circle of hell waiting for him if he took advantage of that.

"I'm sorry," he stammered. "It's not you. That's just a hell of a story and I'm . . . I'm not good at, like, being reassuring or whatever. Sorry. Um. I'm gonna make a phone call. You okay here on your own?"

Micah nodded, his eyes on the floor again.

Dominic stood a little shakily. His left foot had gone to sleep, and it gave him a considerable limp as he grabbed his phone and headed out the door.

It was time he took a good look at Micah's file.

CHAPTER ELEVEN

Ian Soulton was working late.

He worked late a lot.

It was one of the downsides of having a job primarily on behalf of second-class citizens. Too many cases, not enough cooperation, not nearly enough resources.

A call came to his desk just after eight. He should've been home by six.

"Detective Soulton, Indent Services."

"Hey. It's Dominic. Blackburn." The voice was hesitant, like he wasn't sure what he was supposed to say. "We did some fae abduction cases like two years ago?"

"Dom! Yeah, I remember. What's up?"

"I think I might have something to report?"

It ended as a question, but with an undercurrent of stone that Ian had heard far too often in his line of work. He picked up a pen, rummaging for a blank report form. "How can I help you today, Dominic?"

"So I bought this contract a couple days ago, and this guy, uh . . . he's got some stories. I don't have any proof or anything, but I think he's telling the truth. And I'm not a lawyer, but I'm pretty sure the stuff he's describing is illegal."

"Can you give me an example?"

"The most obvious thing? He can't talk. Says his last holder had his vocal cords cut."

Ian sat up in his chair, leaning over his desk and digging for a file in a stack. He tried in vain to keep the rest of them from toppling over and cursed when he failed.

He transferred the phone to his shoulder to search the pile with both hands. "Can you give me any names? Does he know who did it?"

"He says his last contract holder was a guy named Adam Slate, but I'm not sure that's accurate."

"Why not?"

"Well, I bought his contract with cash, and I haven't gotten him registered yet, but apparently he's valuable? He's got a tattoo that he says is a Signature. Anyway, all his other transfers were done by estate agents and signed and witnessed and all that shit. And according to the dates that are marked down on his paperwork here, he's been an indent for just over sixteen years."

"So what's the problem?"

"He says he's twenty-seven."

Ian whistled.

"Yeah, I get that people fudge their ages sometimes, but there's no margin of error where that's even close to right."

Ian found the file he'd been searching for. Murder case from a few months ago. Body found in the woods, excessive mutilations, including a missing face. Trachea and vocal cords ablated and healed.

"Dominic, can you send me a copy of that file? I'd very much like to see it."

CHAPTER TWELVE

The front desk had a fax machine, which Dominic was grateful for, but seriously, a fax machine? What fucking year was it? Who faxed things anymore?

Apparently he did, because here he was, pulling pages out of an envelope and sending them one at a time to the police department in Selina, Pennsylvania. As the ancient scanner copied them, Dominic read. The number Micah had given him wasn't an approximation. It was the exact dollar amount for the sale to Slate over four years prior.

Dominic's stomach turned when he realized Micah had been with that fucknut for that long. The story Micah told him had put him on edge, put a tenseness under his skin like he needed to *do something*, but he had no idea what. He wasn't a "plans" man, he knew that. He'd gotten through high school, gone straight for his creacon certifications, and spent his life getting rid of shit that needed getting rid of. He wasn't going to storm out, find Slate, and chop his head off, and unfortunately, that kind of exhausted his arsenal of coping mechanisms.

The fax machine groaned, hauling the ancient scanner bar back to the starting location, and Dominic laid down another bill of sale. Slightly less money, dated six months prior. And another, eight months before that. Two months. A year. Names Dominic didn't know, signatures on a receipt. Sometimes there was a description attached, written in a medical professional's objective language, detailing Micah's condition and marked with a hurried signature.

There were photos too—glossy black and whites taken as addendums to the forms. They documented Micah's body in impartial detail, wide shots from the front and back, defined shadows accentuating impressive musculature. Then there were close-ups, the predictable erotic shots, the tattoo, and then, in the back, one of Micah's face. The colorless photos left his eyes looking dark, but more than that, empty. The face in the photo was handsome, and utterly expressionless. Maybe it was the greyscale, but it felt worse than what Dominic had seen from him in person. Dominic wondered if they'd drugged him for these, or if it was possible for a person to disassociate that fully.

He checked the date on the photos. They'd been taken right before Slate had bought him. Four years earlier.

The Micah in the photos was easily fifteen pounds heavier than the version currently waiting for Dominic in the hotel room. His hip was adorned with a stylized *A* rather than the starburst.

The scanner bar wheezed back to the starting position, and Dominic realized the clerk was watching him, probably because he'd been staring at photos of a naked indent in the lobby of a hotel for the last several minutes.

He shoved the photos back into the envelope. Ian didn't need those.

Well, not all of them. He took the one of Micah's face back out and laid it softly on the glass.

The last page in the pile was Micah's title. It would have been written up when Micah first agreed to be an indent and would contain his personal information from before he was indentured.

Micah's title contained a small grainy photo of a man who wasn't Micah. The resemblance was there, but this man was older than Micah was now, his face covered in rough dark stubble. The eyes that glared out were tired, angry.

The name on the title wasn't Micah's. It was "Gerald Sawyer," and the birth date listed was forty-eight years ago. Dominic did some quick mental arithmetic. Gerald Sawyer would have been thirty-two when the title was drawn up. The man in the photo could be thirty-two, if the years had been hard.

Micah's title had been contracted in exchange for the forgiveness of four hundred thousand dollars in unspecified debt. The debt holder was not named. Dominic flipped the paper over. There were no further details. Just a rubber stamp at the bottom of the page where some faceless government clerk had witnessed the document.

Dominic replaced the photograph with the anomalous title, studying the headshot for another moment before returning it to the envelope.

He pulled his phone back out, swiping to redial the last number. "You getting these, Detective?"

"Yeah, the title is coming through now. I'm assuming the information on it isn't accurate."

"The name, the photo, and the date of birth are all wrong. I don't know about the rest of it. It looks like it was authorized, so I'm guessing the sale date is right."

"And the description. If there is such a person as Gerald Sawyer, he's tall and broad shouldered, just like Micah. Might be a family member? I'll do some digging. Will you be available at this number if I have questions?"

"Yeah."

"And I'd like to talk to Micah, if you'll allow it."

"Yeah, yeah of course. We're out of town on a job, but I can bring him in later this week. He doesn't, you know, *talk*, but he writes. If you make him. He, uh . . . doesn't really seem like he wants to talk about it."

The voice that came over the phone was far too tired, even for the hour. "Would *you*?"

"Yeah, probably not."

There was silence on the line. Then Ian spoke.

"There's one other thing. I wouldn't bring it up, but it's a requirement. You have a legal right to know."

"Shoot."

"If this leads to an investigation, Micah's title may be seized as evidence. You might get it back, you might not. If his paperwork's forged, your chances aren't great."

Dominic rubbed his temples. "Yeah, I know."

"No good deed, right?"

"Right. Look, Detective, it's late and I've had a hell of a day. Can we pick this up in the morning?"

"Sure. I'll call you when I know something. And Dominic?"

"Yeah?"

"Call me Ian."

"Yeah. Right."

Dominic stared at the phone until the screen flicked black. Then he gathered up the paperwork and trudged back to the hotel room.

The far bed was covered in books, and the near bed was covered in Micah. He was half-under the covers, curled on his side with one of the pillows clutched close to his chest. He'd switched his jeans for a borrowed pair of Dominic's sleeping pants and had predictably forgotten to add a shirt to the ensemble. The room was cool, and his skin was pebbled with goose bumps, fine hairs standing on end.

Dominic moved silently to pull the comforter up over Micah's sleeping form. He paused, too close. His mind said *move back*, but his hand reached out and brushed a lock of hair away from Micah's face. Micah's features were calm, serene, and Dominic couldn't help comparing them to the face in the photograph.

That face had been expressionless, *empty*. This one was content. The little furrow between Micah's eyebrows was gone, and his jaw had lost the hard set that meant he was trying to hold his composure.

Dominic was probably imagining it, but he thought that Micah could feel safe here. He smiled, but it died on his face when Micah opened his eyes. Dom knew how this looked: he was crouching a foot away from Micah, frozen in the act of stroking his hair. He withdrew quickly, searching for an excuse and not finding one—but Micah just smiled that little grin of his, and lifted the corner of the blanket in invitation.

Do not go over there, Dominic thought as his legs carried him closer.

You are taking advantage of him on so many levels, he admonished himself as he climbed into the bed.

This is completely the wrong way to do this, he thought as Micah snuggled up close to him, hands skirting over his sides.

Micah lifted his head, pressing his lips softly against Dominic's. Dom opened his mouth, letting him in, and Micah's tongue was hot where it flicked across his skin. Micah's hands delved under the waistband of his pants—and that snapped him out of it.

"I can't do this," Dom muttered, closing his eyes before the sight of stubble on that strong jaw could shatter his convictions completely. "I can't handle you thinking you're *supposed* to."

Micah's grin turned flirty and dark. He ground his hips against Dominic's body, and *fuck* he was big. Micah's mouth was on his again, hot and wet, teeth nipping, his hands pulling Dominic's thigh up over him, and all Dominic wanted was to push against that lithe, firm body until—

"Wait, wait," Dominic gasped, pulling away and pressing his hands to Micah's chest. "Do you want to do this? Do you really, really want to do this? Not because you think I want to do it. Do *you* want this?"

Micah stared at him, hazel eyes flicking back and forth across Dominic's face. And then, very slowly, he shook his head. His gaze dropped.

"Hey, look at me."

Micah struggled, but he met Dominic's eyes.

"It's okay that you don't want to. You don't have to. It's okay. Really. I'll clean off the other bed and—"

Micah's hands shot out, bunching in Dominic's shirt. And then panic crossed Micah's face, and he drew back like he'd been burned.

"Hey, it's cool. Do you want me to stay here? We don't have to do anything else, it's fine. I can just be here, and you do whatever, okay?"

Micah looked lost, torn, and confused, and it was breaking Dominic's heart. Dom didn't know what to do. He was afraid that if he moved, Micah's fragile stand of self-determination would crumble and he'd end up having seven-figure sex with someone who didn't want it.

Micah seemingly came to some kind of conclusion and pulled away, settling in the middle of the bed. He rolled onto his side, reaching out for Dominic, and Dominic went. Micah pulled at his shoulder, putting Dominic where he wanted him, which turned out to be the little spoon. Not what Dominic would have guessed, but not bad. Micah's body felt impossibly warm and solid pressed up against his back, one strong arm over his waist, holding him close.

Within a few minutes, Micah had fallen asleep again.

Dominic couldn't sleep. This was definitely the frontrunner for top ten most comfortable sleeping positions he'd ever been in, but he couldn't stop going over his conversation with Ian.

"I'd like to talk to Micah, if you'll allow it."

If he'd allow it.

Micah had been beaten, abused, and mutilated, and it had been going on since he'd been a child, but he needed Dominic's permission to talk to the police.

Dominic had bought the contract, but even when he'd handed over the money, he hadn't realized what, *exactly*, he was buying. What he now owned. It was more than having a roommate he could boss around, or someone he needed to buy stuff for, or a partner to work with. He owned something that should never, ever belong to anyone but Micah.

It was terrifying in its importance, and only slightly more terrifying was the prospect of having to give it up.

When Dominic woke up in the morning, the bed was empty. He smelled bacon and coffee, and that was enough to rouse him. He'd gone to sleep in his clothes, and he felt sticky.

When he opened his eyes, he half expected to find Micah naked on the floor, kneeling and waiting, but the space between the beds was empty. Micah was fully dressed for once, bent over the other bed and studying the collection of books with his brow furrowed in concentration.

"You're up early," Dominic remarked, voice rough with sleep.

Micah startled. He wavered, and Dominic could *see* him shifting back and forth on some decision.

"What's up?"

Micah tossed his notepad to Dominic, letting him read the sentence already written there.

There's a book missing.

CHAPTER THIRTEEN

Dominic blinked at him. His hair was messy, and Micah could see this was a bit too much information to process this early in the morning. He retrieved a mug of coffee from the table and set it gently on the nightstand.

Dominic pulled himself into a sitting position, rubbing at his temples. After a moment, he reached for the coffee and downed half of it in one swig. "Ah," he rasped a second later. "Okay. Yeah. So, book?"

Micah nodded, turning to the other bed where he'd arranged the books. In between the self-help advice and the paperbacks with Borders price tags still attached, there were a number of hardcovers, older and plain. The covers featured nothing but a simple engraving of a flower or a tree, and the last name of the author, Sikora.

These were recipe books for spells, skipping over the typical introduction of light vs. dark magic and the great joys of communing with Gaia and getting straight to the methodology. And these spells were specific. They weren't about positive energy or magnetism healing or aligning ions in the body.

The first one Micah had found dealt with creating wells on land without water. The one after that was to banish vermin from a home. Whole chapters regarded specific plants: make wheat grow in damp soil, bring a sunflower to blossom, kill dandelions and milk thistle in a field. There were spells on how to make a person or animal catch pregnant. Simple, practical magic, presented without embellishment or flourish.

"So, why do you think one's missing?"

Micah snatched up his notepad. *There's a pattern. Botany, biology, metaphysics.* He gestured to where the books were laid out in columns by type. *The set's one short. Three botany, three biology, two metaphysics. Checked the publishing dates. One of the metaphysics is missing. Botany in 1953, biology in 1954, botany again in 1956. 1955 is missing.*

"Think we might have left it in the house?"

Micah shrugged.

Dom frowned. "That, or the kid's got it. I'll call Madeline." He grabbed his phone off the side table, then paused. "You eat yet?"

Micah shook his head.

"You get food for yourself?"

Micah nodded. He had, a reward for waking up on time. An orange and a big cup of granola with yogurt, like before, and another coffee, with soy milk and sugar. This he had hesitated on, because there was no way he would be able to pretend he had gotten it for Dominic. He'd eventually decided to risk it, and now he was glad he had.

"Good. You eat, this might take a bit." Dominic flopped back onto the bed, listening to the phone ring and flipping through one of Sikora's books. "Hey, Madeline. It's Dominic. Hey look, we're looking for— Yeah, sure, I'll talk to your husband."

The voice from the phone was so loud Micah could hear it from where he was sitting. Dominic jerked it away from his ear and waited for a pause before replying. "Yeah, I know what hotels cost. I'm in one right now."

More shouting.

"It's not my fault your house is haunted. My partner shanked the thing in the eye, and it came back. Not sure what else you want us to do."

The shouting was faster now.

Dominic rolled his eyes. "Okay, well how about you come over here, I'll give you some of the sharp shit I keep in my trunk, and you can try your luck. I won't even charge you a rental fee."

The line went quiet.

"Yeah, I thought so. So, like I was telling Madeline, we're looking for a book. Green, hardcover, old. Author's named Sikora. Might have a tree or something on the cover. We think Josh might know where it is. Take a peek for us?"

Loud mumbling.

"Thanks, you're a real champ." Dominic hung up and tossed the phone onto the bedspread. "What a douche."

Micah snorted, laughing silently around a slice of orange. Dominic smiled at him. Maybe Dominic liked it when he laughed. Some owners got annoyed when their slaves had opinions. Laughing at their jokes was a relatively safe way to test the water.

"Good catch on the book. Not sure I would have got that on my own."

Micah kept his eyes on his orange.

Dominic downed the rest of the coffee and hauled himself to his feet. Once he was up, he blinked a couple of times, like he'd forgotten what he was doing. After a second, he shuffled into the bathroom.

Micah finished his orange and picked up Dominic's bag. He didn't know if Dominic planned out his wardrobe, but he doubted it. He made an educated guess on what to lay out.

Out of Dominic's eyeshot, he reached his hands above his head, stretching. It brought him equal parts pain and pleasure, the cuts and bruises on his back still mildly protesting. He ignored them.

The shower kicked on, and Micah glanced at the bathroom door. Dominic had left it open a crack—not just unlocked, but *open*. With a normal owner, that meant he'd be expecting Micah to join him.

But Dominic wasn't a normal owner, so maybe he hadn't thought of that.

But he'd left the door open, so maybe that was supposed to be a hint?

Maybe Dominic didn't *expect* him, but was just *hoping*.

Or he'd just left the door open, and he didn't care what Micah did at all.

Micah wished he could ask. Just knock on the door and offer an invitation. But he'd done that yesterday, and Dominic had pressed him on it. Dominic had questions whose answers were more complicated than Micah could explain to him: Micah didn't want to have sex. He *did* want to be such a good lay that Dominic would be left breathless and with no further thoughts of selling him.

The water shut off before Micah could decide, which was a decision in and of itself, if he were being honest. It occurred to him that if Dominic *had* been waiting, then Micah had screwed up, and Dominic would be angry when he emerged.

Micah glanced around the room, hoping for something to placate or distract Dominic with if necessary. Nothing jumped to mind. Normally, he'd wait on the bed and turn their attention, but Dominic didn't want him to do that, that much Micah was sure about. So, he was at a loss.

He was too high up.

He settled on the floor between the two beds, his back to the nightstand. It felt better being low, being surrounded. It focused him. Anything that came at him would come from one direction.

He was being ridiculous. He'd upset masters before. It was a learning opportunity, that was all. There would be punishment, and afterward, he'd know what was expected of him. He'd survived Slate's punishments; he was sure he could withstand Dominic's with the dignity and grace required.

He folded his legs underneath him, sitting back on his heels, but he kept his knees together, placing his hands on the floor to either side of them. Leaning forward, he put his weight on his palms, keeping his arms straight.

Dominic came out of the bathroom just as Micah realized he should have taken his shirt off. Leaving it on contradicted the purpose of the position, and he hoped Dominic didn't take it as a challenge.

He heard Dominic cross the room and sit at the table. Micah kept his eyes down. It was killing him not to know what Dominic was thinking, but he knew better than to raise his eyes on an angry master.

"This is new." Dominic didn't sound angry. Maybe a bit amused. Micah didn't react. "Is this one of the twenty-six?"

Micah nodded once.

"But this isn't the 'sitting and waiting for orders' one, so what's this?"

Micah didn't know how to explain. His notepad was on the bed, and he didn't dare stand up to retrieve it. But he'd been asked a question; he couldn't just refuse to answer. He shook his head.

"Seriously, man. What are you doing?"

This was a nightmare and getting worse by the minute. Dominic stood and came closer, and Micah braced his shoulders. He wished he could respond, but he couldn't, so he'd take the punishment and explain his failure later.

But Dominic sat on the floor next to him, his back to the bed, and held the notebook out. "I'm gonna have to find a list of all this somewhere. In the meantime, would you humor me and tell me what the hell's happening with you?"

Micah took the notepad, keeping his head down. *There are things I haven't done. It might have upset you.*

"So this is, what, the 'sorry I fucked up' pose?"

Yes. Anticipation of punishment.

Dominic was silent, and then—"You think I'm gonna *punish* you?"

If you thought I needed it.

"For *what*?"

You left the door open. I wasn't sure if it was an instruction.

"Oh, for god's sakes, man, I left the door open because we've got *one bathroom*." Dominic's hands were on his shoulders, pulling him up and pushing him back against the nightstand. "Look at me. I want you here and understanding this. I don't know these rules, and I don't play these games. I am literally not smart enough. So I'm not gonna hit you, and I'm not gonna *punish* you. I'm probably not even gonna get to *keep* you."

Micah nodded. He'd thought as much. After he'd told Dominic his last sale price, the man had gone outside to make some calls. He was gone a long time, and Micah was more than smart enough to connect those dots. So what if Dominic had said Micah could stay? Dominic had won the lottery; it was stupid to hope he wouldn't collect.

Dominic sighed. "I made a police report yesterday."

Micah frowned. He'd messed up by hitting his previous owner, but it would have been *Slate's* prerogative, surely—

"After what you said, I felt like . . . I needed to do *something*. It crawled under my skin, the idea that this guy was out there doing this shit, and no one even noticed. You were with him for *years*, and no one knew. And then your file . . ."

There was actual concern on Dominic's face. "Have you really been indentured for sixteen years?"

Micah counted off in his head. He knew the year he'd been sold, and he knew what year it was now, and yes, it had been sixteen years. Seemed like longer. He nodded, then shrugged. *All my life* seemed a better description than anything he could count off in years.

"So how did they do it? How did they get an eleven-year-old registered as Gerald Sawyer?"

Micah blinked at him, frowning. He supposed his father's name would be on his paperwork somewhere. After all, he was the one who had sold him originally. But registered? That didn't make sense. Micah should be registered under his own name. He'd never seen his documentation, but he knew that much, at least.

Dominic rose and returned with the manila envelope. Flicking through the contents, he found a piece of paper and passed it to Micah.

His father's picture hit him like a hammer. He hadn't seen the man since he was child, and even still, the grainy photo was enough to make his stomach drop. This was the man who had broken two of his fingers and then pinned him to a wall and choked him until the crying stopped.

Gerald hadn't liked the excuses any more than Micah's other owners.

He'd long since lost the ability to picture the man clearly, but the photo brought it all back, and Micah was disgusted to see himself in those features. They had the same mouth, the same angular jaw, the same eyes.

Gerald Sawyer. And he had been Micah Sawyer. Back when he'd had a last name.

Micah scanned the rest of the document. It didn't make sense. It was his father's photo, his father's face, his father's description, his father's birthdate. Or so he assumed. The year seemed right.

What is this? he wrote.

"It's your title."

That's not me.

"Yeah, I thought that was weird too. You've never seen this before?"

Micah shook his head.

"But the year is right? This is when you were sold?"

Micah nodded.

"And you were eleven?"

He nodded again.

Dominic buried his face in his palm, rubbing at the bridge of his nose. "Gods, that's fucked up. Micah, you can't *sell* an *eleven-year-old*. Whatever bait and switch they pulled to make this happen . . . someone's going to jail over this, man."

Micah blinked. This was news to him. *Why?*

"Because you have to agree to it! They set it up to get people out of prison and debt and shit, not to fucking *trade kids*!"

Micah closed his eyes, picturing the place where he'd lived when he was first sold. There had definitely been other children there, outcasts like him who were too much trouble to keep. Most of them were like him in other ways too—happy to be there, to be *anywhere* except where they'd come from. They lived in the barracks together, training for the various roles that would eventually, if they worked hard enough, make them worth something.

Training that was currently failing him. Dominic was upset, and Micah didn't know how to make it better. If Dominic wasn't going to take his frustrations out on Micah's body, there wasn't much else he had to offer. He wracked his brain, trying to stave off the shrill little voice telling him *you're fucking up again*. He should have lied, said he already knew, anything to stop Dominic from being so irrationally upset on *his* behalf.

Dominic threw the envelope across the room, but it only made it a couple of feet before fluttering unsatisfyingly onto the bed.

"*Fuck*!" The phone buzzed on the nightstand, and Dominic snatched it up. "What?" he snapped. Muffled murmuring from the speaker. "Yeah, all right. We'll be there in an hour." He tossed the phone back onto the nightstand without further discussion. "Kid's got the book."

Micah didn't know what to do with that information, so he waited for Dominic to tell him.

"Okay. Fuck. I gotta get these people back in their house. Finish eating and pack your shit, we're getting out of here and meeting up with the Carmichaels at their hotel. The kid's got the book, and hopefully that'll tell us what the fuck this thing is. We kill it, we head back home, and then tomorrow I'm taking you to meet a very nice police officer who's going to help us put some *motherfuckers* in a *fucking cell*."

Micah nodded and began packing his clothes. He didn't want to talk to the police. Never in his life had people spoken positively about them. Usually when a police officer showed up to talk to his dad, it meant they were moving. Sometimes they'd wanted to talk to Micah, like when he'd gone to the ER for the broken fingers. Micah knew better than to tattle.

Bad things happened when cops figured out the truth.

On the drive to Ohio, Dominic had changed the CD no fewer than six times. He'd sung along with every single song in a deep baritone. Micah suspected Dominic spent a lot of time singing to his dashboard.

Dominic was not singing now.

The radio was on, turned down low, the lyrics to "Don't Stop Me Now" barely audible over the engine. Dominic had to know the song—everybody knew this song—but he wasn't even tapping his fingers on the wheel.

Micah wished he knew how to fix this. Who cared if his paperwork was wrong? Or if he'd been sold too early? He was here now. That should be enough, right? It wasn't like *Dominic* was the one who'd been sold.

He couldn't even say anything. He had his notepad in his pocket, but he didn't know what to write. And anyway, Dominic was driving. Driving and fuming.

The phone buzzed. Dominic picked it up with one hand, the other still clenched on the steering wheel. "Yeah?" A pause. "We're five minutes out." Another pause. This one longer. "Well just *stay away* from it. You got that book? Good. We'll need it." He hung up the phone. "Our boogeyman's at the hotel."

Micah waited for him to elaborate, and when he didn't, Micah made the "go on" gesture.

Dominic rolled his eyes. "Boogeyman's at the hotel, it's breaking shit, they're gonna lose their deposit, and the dad's pissed at us for not handling this yesterday. That's all I know. But it does tell us one thing: whatever it is, it's connected to the kid. And the kid has the book. Out of all the shit he left in his bedroom to get ruined, he *still has that book*." He knocked Micah lightly on the shoulder. "Your hunch paid off."

He took the exit ramp too fast and rolled the stop sign. The hotel could be seen from the highway, but it was five more turns through a divided thoroughfare before they pulled into the parking lot. The Carmichaels were waiting by the lobby doors in their pajamas.

There were, in fact, kind of a *lot* of people waiting by the lobby doors. Probably something about a bloody screaming specter camping out in one of the rooms.

Dominic was out of his seat and stalking toward the building before Micah could get his seatbelt off. He scrambled out of the car, following Dominic to where Madeline was sitting miserably on a stone wall surrounding a topiary.

"Got the book?"

She handed it over. She looked like she could use a cup of coffee. Maybe Irish coffee.

Micah waited behind Dominic, watching as he paged through the book, searching for anything obvious. It wasn't hard; a Percy Jackson bookmark was sticking out a quarter of the way through. Dominic scanned the page and rolled his eyes. He flipped the book over to Micah.

To Reclaim a Wandering Lover

> *-for the return of a philandering husband or father to his rightful house and home.*

Dominic pinched the bridge of his nose. "You keep a lot of clove oil in the house, Madeline?"

"What's clove oil?"

"Yeah, that's what I thought. Where's Josh?"

"With my husband, why?"

"Because he's a shitty witch, that's why." Dom grabbed the book back from Micah, pausing to wave it at Madeline. "With Mom gone, Josh decided to make a go at finding his dad. But he's doing the spell with something other than clove oil, and also, the spell is supposed to work on 'philandering,' not 'dead.' So, we're gonna kill that thing again, and if Josh doesn't *summon him back*, you should be all set."

Madeline blinked at him.

Micah turned back to the car. He had a feeling he was going to need his knife again.

The hotel was nicer than the one they'd been staying at, if you ignored the haunting. The lights in the hallway were flickering and erratic, plunging them into periodic darkness that finely accentuated the earsplitting shrieks coming from the room at the end.

Micah had a distinct feeling of déjà vu.

He felt like this scenario should not give him déjà vu.

Dominic's shotgun was filled with iron birdshot, so with any luck, Micah wouldn't be taking another bloodbath. He kept the knife ready anyway. They'd been wrong about this once before.

They reached the Carmichael's door, not bothering to stay quiet. Places like this had warding in the walls to help soundproof the rooms, but even without the sigils, there was no way that thing could hear them over its own din.

Micah took point. He dropped the key card into the slot, shoving the door in when the lights turned green.

The room was a maelstrom of torn bedding and pottery shards. In the center stood the man in the suit, covered in blood and grave dirt. He stared them down with his one remaining eye, then unhinged his jaw in a horrific scream and barreled toward the door, arms outstretched. Dominic fired. Micah almost winced at the sound, but managed to keep still.

Just inside the doorway, the corpse burst into a cloud as it fell to the carpet, once more dissolving into waxy powder. Dominic kicked the pile, then turned and stomped down the hallway. By the time Micah caught up, Dominic was calling Garrett and telling him the job was done.

Mr. Carmichael approached from the direction of the topiary, pulling along a kid that Micah assumed was Josh. "Well done, boys.

Absolutely fantastic detective work, there. That's why I told Madeline we needed to hire professionals. If it were up to us, we never would have figured out that one of Annie's books was haunted. What a freak coincidence, am I right? But that's the world we live in nowadays."

Micah deferred to Dominic, who rolled his eyes but said nothing. People were staring at them.

Very quietly, Josh started crying. "Am I in trouble?"

Dominic sighed. "Nah, kid. Just . . . no more magic, okay? Maybe when you're older. And as a general rule, never do a summoning unless you know for sure what's gonna show up."

Micah felt like he should add something or do something, but he didn't know what, so he knelt down and ruffled the kid's hair. Josh smiled shyly.

Mr. Carmichael's expression indicated that he was going to revisit the "not in trouble" ruling after they left, but for now, he fixed Dominic with a big smile. "Can I speak to you privately for a moment? Your man can wait for you down by the car."

Micah knew when he was being dismissed and left them alone without further hinting. Madeline gave him a little wave as he passed, and he waved back. Her children were climbing onto the topiary and laughing. Micah wondered if Josh was ever going to be like that. Probably not.

It didn't take Dominic long to meet him in the car. He slammed the door and twisted the key in the ignition, punching the radio knob to shut off the music. Micah gave him a look, but Dominic ignored him, pulling back onto the thoroughfare and taking the on-ramp at ten miles over the limit.

Dominic seemed to be settling in for a nice long silent sulk, but the car ruined it after five minutes with a cheery *ding* that meant they were low on gas. Dominic slammed on the brakes, veering onto the shoulder, and threw the car into park. And then for good measure, he punched the steering wheel.

Micah raised an eyebrow, a silent *What's wrong?* that he didn't really expect an answer to.

Dominic reached into his pocket and pulled out a fifty, eyeing it like it offended him. "Here." He handed it to Micah. "This is yours. I'll get you a cut of the total fee once Garrett transfers it."

Micah stared at it. He'd never held so much money in his life.

He offered it back to Dominic, who didn't take it. He tried putting it in Dominic's pocket, but Dominic pushed him away.

"Don't. Just, fucking don't. That fucking tool gave it to me as a *tip*, on account of what a *good thing* I was doing, taking on an indent with a disability. Like I was doing you a *favor*, like you're some kind of *charity case*, and . . . Ugh!"

Micah looked down at the fifty. He looked at Dominic. Dominic glowered at the windshield.

Micah leaned over and kissed him. He didn't know how else to fix this.

It was chaste and a little off-center, but then Dominic turned toward him. Micah leaned forward, and they melted together like they were made for it.

And then Dominic pushed him away again, saying something like, "You don't have to," but he didn't get to finish because Micah grabbed him by the lapels and pulled him back in. It was hot and insistent, and Dominic's protests were buried when Micah's tongue slipped into his mouth. Dominic's fingers tangled in his hair, and that was better. That was how it was supposed to be.

Micah let go of Dominic's jacket and let his hands travel up Dominic's throat, cupping his jaw and running a thumb over one high cheekbone. He kissed Dominic slowly, pulling back after each one, setting a rhythm that Dominic picked right up. His kisses were soft, calming, and the tension drained out of Dominic until, finally, he leaned into Micah and stayed there, foreheads pressed together.

"It's fucked up."

Micah stroked his thumb along Dominic's cheek. It was a silent acknowledgment, the best he could do.

A semi blew past them, laying on the horn, and it seemed to shock Dominic back to his senses. He pulled away from Micah, put the car into drive, and merged smoothly back onto the road. "Sorry. This is just getting to me. It's stupid. You're the one who's living through it, and I'm the one who's reacting like a crybaby."

His voice was calmer. Good. Micah grinned down at his hands, his own mind settling.

The old methods *were* the best.

The gas station sold CDs, but nothing Micah recognized, so he didn't know what to buy. Dominic had been so insistent that he take the money, he was pretty sure he was expected to *do* something with it now.

Dominic bought a cup of coffee, so Micah bought one too. He put sugar in it, and cream. Dominic, to Micah's surprise, also liked milk. Micah's guess of black had been wrong, another mistake his owner had allowed to pass without comment.

Once Micah had made his coffee how he wanted, he paid for it with his own money, then put his change into his pocket.

Dominic kept watching him, and Micah realized he was smiling. Maybe that's what made Dominic start smiling too.

When they got back in the car, Dominic turned the music back on. The radio served up Metallica's "Stone Cold Crazy," and after a while, Dominic started singing.

Micah thought he could listen to Dominic sing forever.

He wished he could sing too.

CHAPTER FOURTEEN

Ian shuffled through the growing pile of paperwork on his desk. He'd checked up on "Gerald Sawyer" and found that the official records matched Dominic's file exactly. Sale dates, purchase prices, everything—all registered and authorized, neat as you please. Anyone interested enough to read it would find a story about a down-on-his-luck man who traded his freedom for four hundred grand and went on to make something of himself as an indent.

Micah Sawyer, on the other hand, was a kid who'd been bounced between twenty school districts before vanishing just before his twelfth birthday. The last district filed a token truancy report, but everyone assumed he'd simply moved on.

After that, there was no record of him until he was sixteen, at which point he'd gotten a driver's license and started accumulating speeding tickets, DUIs, and defaulted payday loans from a colorful assortment of states. Ian picked a city at random—Atlanta—and called the police department to have them send over the arrest record.

The booking photo was the man on Micah's title. Ten years more haggard, but definitely the same man.

He called Atlanta back. The officer who answered double-checked the case file and confirmed that yes, the man in the photo had been booked under the name of Micah Sawyer and yes, his official identification did list him as twenty-one at the time of booking.

"He look a little old for twenty-one?" Ian asked.

"We've got a lot of meth out here," the officer answered. "And honestly? Read the file. We booked him for drunk and disorderly. He slept it off, paid his fine, and left town. The situation didn't exactly need a detective."

That raised the question of why the Selina police department was looking into a six-year-old DnD in Atlanta. Ian thanked him and hung up. The most recent record of Micah Sawyer was in Alabama, where he'd been brought in three weeks earlier on a vagrancy charge.

The officer who answered the phone in Birmingham was having a much better day than Ian was. Ian told her that Micah Sawyer was wanted for questioning in a possible case of identity theft. She seemed pretty confident that he'd turn up again before long, and promised to have her guys keep an eye out.

All that was left was convincing a judge to issue an arrest warrant. Oh, and the troubling issue of Micah's last owner.

Ian dug out the bill of sale. It didn't give him a lot of information. Name, address, sale price. Dated four years ago. Depending on what Micah told him, there might be enough evidence for a search warrant. There might not. A lot rested on the judge. It was an election year, not a good time to make enemies of wealthy taxpayers. Indent rights were a touchy issue, and careers had been made and broken on the subject of sex work and acceptable discipline.

Ian reached for his mug of coffee.

Empty. Again.

Technology could put the full wealth of human knowledge onto a six-inch phone, but somehow hadn't managed to create an ikon to keep coffee from running out. Ian cursed the unreliability of his mug and headed for the break room.

His phone buzzed. Dominic.

Headed back from the case. You got a time tomorrow?

He texted back.

ASAP.

CHAPTER FIFTEEN

They got back to Dominic's house late—late enough that Dominic pointed him toward an empty bedroom and retired.

The new room was huge. Huge and empty. Micah was used to sharing a bed with at least one other person. Even when he'd had his own cot, he'd always been able to hear the other slaves in the dormitory, breathing easy and talking in low voices.

This room was silent.

And the bed was too big.

Micah pushed it into the corner and lay with his back to the wall, clutching a pillow to his chest and trying to sleep.

The stillness was oppressive. Without the sleeping breaths or gentle murmuring of other people, there were only the sounds of the walls.

There was no one to wake him if there was danger. If he was called and didn't hear, there was no one to find him or repeat the request. No one to cover for him.

He finally gave up and crept out into the hallway with a blanket.

Dominic's bedroom door was open a crack, but Micah didn't dare go in. Instead, he settled down outside and leaned his head against the doorframe. He couldn't hear Dominic, but he knew he was there, and that was enough.

Micah would have to get up and go back to his own room before Dominic found out. He had a feeling his owner would be upset to find him sleeping in the hallway.

Dominic didn't need to know.

When Micah opened his eyes, sunlight was streaming through the windows. He could hear Dominic moving in the kitchen and he kicked himself. He should have woken up. Why hadn't he woken up?

He got to his feet uncertainly. His left leg was asleep all the way from his foot to the back of his ass. Shaking it, he grimaced at the pins and needles, before limping his way to the kitchen.

"Morning, princess!"

Micah dropped his eyes.

"What's the issue? Pea under your mattress?"

Micah shook his head. In the daylight, it seemed impossible to say something like *I can't sleep by myself.*

Dominic watched him a minute, but when Micah didn't elaborate, he carried on. "So, Ian wants us down this morning as soon as possible. It's about an hour's drive, and we'll probably be there awhile, so eat up."

Dominic was making eggs. Micah wasn't hungry. It was one thing to tell Dominic what had happened. It was a different matter to tell the police. For the first time in years, Micah wondered where his father was. What it would mean to see him again.

If the police tracked Gerald down, Micah would have to stand up and condemn him for all this. And if he argued, Micah would have nothing to say because he'd done it willingly. He'd done it *all* willingly. He could have tried to run, like some of the others. In his place, that was what his father would have done. Run, been caught, and ended up in a work camp or a battlefield. Anything to avoid the life that Micah had chosen.

Micah remembered drunken rants about prettyboys and cocksuckers and how if Micah ever turned out like that, he'd strap him straight. What Gerald would think of him now. If he knew his son had pleasured so many men he'd long since lost count.

Micah's eyes burned. He stared at the floor.

And Slate. Micah had been Slate's *favorite*. How was Micah supposed to face him and tell him how to treat his slaves? He'd done it once and been punished. He'd learned his lesson, he *had*, he didn't need to learn it again.

Micah rubbed his hand over the barcode tattooed on his forearm. They'd done it when he was sixteen, so it wouldn't be distorted when he grew. Or so they said. The code was his number, he was registered, so he could always be returned to his owner. It identified him as property, as goods. Yet Dominic wanted him to stand up and tell his owners they *couldn't*, that they were wrong and they'd owed Micah better. And Micah would do it because that was what his owner was asking of him. Because that was what it would take to dispel Dominic's anger, his sadness. And when it was over . . .

Micah decided, right then, that nothing would come of it.

That was all.

They'd talk to Ian, and Micah would go through the whole humiliating story, and Ian would nod and understand. He'd explain to Dominic that Slate could do whatever he wanted with Micah, he had the right, he *owned* him. Wasn't that the whole point? And Dominic would be upset, but Micah could fix that, show him it was all right.

Micah would tell Ian that he didn't mind being sold early. It'd given him a head start on his training and had made him more valuable. There was no need to find his father or his original owners, because they hadn't really done anything wrong. Ian would see the confusion, and he'd be able to explain it to Dominic.

It would all be fine.

Micah had no appetite, but he ate what Dominic gave him because Dominic wanted him to eat it. He did the dishes and stayed out of the bathroom while Dominic showered, and then he took his own turn. He turned the water to cold—jarring cold—and it kept his mind focused. By the time he finished he was shivering, but his stomach was settled, and he wasn't so worried.

Ian was going to be disgusted with him, but he wouldn't punish him. Not while Dominic was there. And Dominic wouldn't punish him. If Dominic was disappointed, Micah could make it up to him. Micah could learn what Dominic liked and go right back to being the exemplary obedient slave he'd been before Slate.

It was all going to be fine.

He dressed in the clothes that Dominic had bought him and crept back out to the living room.

Dominic was waiting.

It was all going to be fine.

CHAPTER SIXTEEN

Never in his life had Ian seen such a large man look so small. The resemblance between Micah and Gerald was even more obvious in person, but where Gerald had stared into the camera with his eyes narrowed and his chin raised, Micah kept his eyes on the floor. Ian had been dealing with indents for years, and for him, the evidence of classical training was so obvious it could have been written across Micah's forehead. That was good. Trained indents were predictable. Easier to work with.

He offered them a cup of the shitty break-room coffee, which they declined, and then led them into a conference room. He didn't do these types of interviews in the interrogation rooms; they got better responses elsewhere. The framed drawings of police cars that they'd gotten from the local elementary school put people at ease.

He set up the tape recorder. Micah raised an eyebrow.

"It's to record the questions, anything I say, anything Dominic says, things like that," Ian explained. "As your holder, Dominic has the right to stay through the duration of this interview; the law gives contract holders the right to hear and refute accusations brought by indentured persons. If you think it would be easier to answer questions without him here, you may say so, and he will have the option to leave. Do you understand?"

Micah withdrew a pad of paper and a pencil. He scratched down a single line. *Yes. I'd like him to stay. This isn't about him.*

"Understood. Would you please sit down?"

Micah took the seat across from him. His back was straight, his eyes down, his hands palm up on the table. Ian guessed that under the table, Micah's knees were exactly at shoulder width.

"You can relax, Micah." They both knew he wouldn't, but Ian liked to offer anyway. He slid over the small stack of photocopies, with the title on the top. "What can you tell me about these?"

Micah tapped the title. *This is my father. The information's right, as far as I know.*

"Does the sale date match your original sale date?"

Micah nodded.

"Do you remember your social security number, birth date, mother's name, or any other identifying information we can use to look up your records?"

Micah wrote down a date, followed by the name *Hannah*. He didn't know his social.

"Thank you. Can you go through the rest of the sales documents and tell me if they're accurate to the best of your knowledge?"

Micah examined them one at a time, nodding at each. Slate's was at the bottom of the pile. Micah swallowed, then nodded once again. He pushed the pile back to Ian.

"This is correct? You were sold on this date? Four years ago?"

Micah wrote the date, followed by a *Yes*. He was starting to get a tenseness in his jaw that Ian wasn't sure he liked. "Micah, could you talk when Slate bought you?"

Micah tapped the *Yes*.

"Can you tell me how you lost that ability?"

Micah picked up the pen, but turned to Dominic.

"Tell him," Dominic instructed.

Micah started to write. *We got sedatives sometimes in the food. It helped us stay calm during more demanding duties. One of these times I was taken to a room with bright lights, and I was given a mask to breathe into. Afterward there was pain in my throat, and I couldn't talk.*

"Was it a surgery?"

I think so.

"Can you tell me how you know?"

Micah hesitated. *Slate talked about it afterward. He had specific punishments he preferred for disobedient indents. Devocalization was one.*

"Were there any other indents in Slate's home that were devocalized?"

Micah shrugged.

"I'd like to show you some pictures. Do you recognize these tattoos?"

Ian slid some photos across the table. They were a cropped version of the original, leaving only the identifying marks visible. The people in the photos could have been sleeping. Ian knew better. Micah likely knew better, too.

Micah studied them for a moment, then pointed at one. *This is my trainer's Signature. But I don't know on who.*

Ian hummed. "You said there were specific punishments Slate used. Can you tell me some of them?"

Micah swallowed, his fingers tightening on the pen. *The usual. Flogging, whipping, caning. Sometimes electricity. He used restraints if he needed them. Sometimes it was painful because they were very tight or restrictive. Sometimes there was a little bit of nerve damage afterward, because of how he'd tighten them. Sometimes*

Micah paused. He wrote a line, then crossed it off, going over it several times. Finally, he tore the page off, crumpled it up, and put it into his pocket. He started again on the next page.

Sometimes he'd burn us. A lot of indents were branded, but the punishment burning was different. And sometimes the floggers had knots with wire. Not very often. It left scars, put indents out of commission for a while.

"Jesus fuck," Dominic breathed.

Ian shot him a reproachful glare. It wasn't helpful to react like that. Indents like Micah had an arsenal of defense mechanisms against *any* perceived source of conflict. More than anything, they wanted to avoid the consequences of causing it. They'd go silent in a heartbeat if they got the idea that their words were upsetting people.

"Anything else that involved a doctor or medical professional?"

Micah looked unsure. *Slate said that other indents who spoke out had their tongues removed. He said I was lucky to keep mine. He might have been lying. One woman was blind. Might have been an accident. Someone else was missing part of his ring finger, but he wouldn't say what happened. We didn't tell stories.* Micah stopped writing, returning his hands to the waiting position and staring down at the paper.

Ian took a breath, trying to keep his voice calm and reassuring. "Micah, we have a nurse who works here, and I'd like to have him take some pictures of you. It might be several months before we see any progress, and you'll have healed by then. Would you be willing to let him photograph you?"

Micah checked with Dominic again.

Dominic raised his eyebrows. "What are you looking at me for? I'm not going first."

Micah smiled at that. The hand closest to Dominic twitched before returning to its original position. Micah was still watching Dominic. Dominic didn't notice.

"He's asking your permission," Ian told him flatly.

Dominic blinked, turned back to Micah. "Don't ask me. Can they take your picture?"

Micah's eyes widened for a second, then he nodded. *Sorry, but it might not be the proof you're hoping for. We usually got a descarring every few months. More if it was something big.*

Ian shut off the tape recorder. "I'll call Booth."

CHAPTER SEVENTEEN

Ronald "call me Ronnie" Booth was a great sport about the whole thing.

It took Dominic about five minutes to see through the wide smile and laughing blue eyes and realize that Ronnie saw this sort of shit a *lot*.

The first thing he did was offer Micah a soda. "Dominic can go get us a round from the vending machine," he said amiably. "My treat."

Micah looked at Ronnie, then at Dom, then at the open door. He shook his head.

Ronnie nodded. "All right then. Straight to business. Gonna do your chest and back first, 'kay?"

Micah pulled his shirt over his head without further preamble.

Dominic had looked Micah over when he'd first bought him, but he'd been checking for functional injuries. At the time, Micah had looked like he'd fought a mud puddle and lost. Here, he was clean and the room was well-lit, and Dominic realized that the marks he'd taken for dirt smudges were far, far, worse than that. They were still there, red and angry across Micah's shoulders and back. Some of them had broken skin.

And he hadn't realized.

He'd seen Micah naked, and all he'd thought was *fuck that's hot* because it had been from the *front* and Micah was gorgeous and pristine from the *front*.

He hadn't been paying attention.

And Micah hadn't said anything because of *course* he hadn't.

Dominic realized that Micah was staring at him, so he smiled in a way that he hoped was reassuring but probably wasn't.

"You okay?" Ronnie asked, and after a second, Dominic realized that the nurse was talking to him, not Micah.

"Yeah. I just . . . I didn't know."

Ronnie stared at him a moment longer, then turned his attention back to Micah. Micah obediently opened his mouth so Ronnie could photograph the stud through his tongue.

Why was he still wearing that? He could have taken it out. Whenever he wanted. Except Dominic hadn't told him he could. Hadn't thought of it. "You don't have to keep that," he blurted.

Micah's eyes flicked in his direction, but otherwise, no reaction.

Ronnie had Micah stand so he could photograph the marks on his back. Micah raised his arms, and for the first time, Dom saw the way the scars pulled taut. Micah lifted his hair out of Ronnie's way, and Dominic saw an even line of small round burns across the nape of his neck.

"Anything below the belt I should know about?" Ronnie asked.

Micah shook his head, dropping his hands.

Ronnie leveled his gaze at him. "Nothing? No injuries, nothing meddled with, nothing?"

Micah glanced at Dominic before answering. *Nothing out of line.*

"What does 'out of line' mean?" Dominic asked. His voice was hollow, and he could've kicked himself. Micah needed him to keep his shit together, and instead he was sitting here clutching his fucking pearls.

Micah doodled on the paper for a second, then wrote, *Expected wear and tear?*

"I think you should let Ronnie look," Dominic said, and Micah shrugged and promptly dropped his pants.

Ronnie took photos of the piercing in his cock, and the ladder of scars along the underside where Micah said he'd been pierced half a dozen times. He showed Ronnie the scar where they'd made the incision to sterilize him. Dominic stayed across the room.

Micah was utterly calm, answering Ronnie's questions like he wasn't sitting naked in a police station letting a dude photograph the scars on his junk. Dominic didn't think he could do it if their positions were reversed.

Ronnie asked when Micah had last had anal sex—not *if* but *when*—and Micah answered that it was the day before he was sold. Ronnie asked how many partners, and Micah wrote that he didn't know because he'd been blindfolded and Dominic couldn't do it anymore and had to go stand in the hall.

The hallway was tight and stuffy and he had to move, so he went off in search of the coffee that Ian had talked about earlier.

He found Ian before he found the coffee.

"He okay?"

"Micah? Yeah, yeah, he's taking it like a champ." Dominic stared at the ceiling. He couldn't face Ian. "How do you do this job all day, man?"

"Honestly? Sometimes I don't know."

"I've seen some shit. I mean. I kill shit for a living. I've seen dead people. I've been involved in bloodbaths. But those were *monsters*. This . . . What happened to Micah was because of *people*."

Ian sighed. "Sometimes I'm not sure there's a difference."

Dominic stared at him. "Tell me this is gonna end well, Ian. Tell me these bastards are going to jail."

Ian smiled wanly. "Sometimes. Sometimes not. If we can get a search warrant based on Micah's testimony, we might be able to take some other indents into custody. If they're as beat up as Micah says they are, we'll be able to charge Slate, or the doctor Slate hired, but if it'll stick? Who knows." Ian eyed Dominic. "One thing I do know? He's lucky you found him."

Dominic rolled his eyes. "Yeah, right. I bought him off the books and I've been nothing but horrible to him since then. I don't think he understands half of what I'm trying to tell him. He's always worried I'm mad. I think I scare the shit out of him."

"You called me. It's more than most people would have done." Ian gestured with his coffee. "You gotta understand, most of the time when these cases come across my desk, it's too late to help anyone. The best I can do is try to punish the holder, and most of the time, that doesn't happen either. So to get a live one in here, who's in a safe place and can communicate with us? It's a godsend. And you? You're the best thing that could have happened to him."

Ian's phone chirped, and he glanced at it. "Ronnie says they need you back."

Dominic rubbed his eyes. "I just wanna take him home."

Ian clapped him on the shoulder, but said nothing.

Dominic didn't make it back to Ronnie. He met Micah in the hallway, redressed and in handcuffs, being led along by another officer. The officer's fingers dug hard into his arm, but Micah was making no effort to pull away. His eyes were on the ground, his face pale.

"'Scuse me? He's with me," Dominic said, not at all defensively. Micah didn't look up at him.

"Not according to the report I got," the officer answered. "You got a registration?"

Dominic's blood ran cold. "Not yet. There should be a transfer record on file."

"Nnnnope," the officer replied. "Last transfer for this barcode was four years ago, to a guy named Slate. And he says this indent's been stolen."

Technically, the report said runaway.

Slate had decided to send Micah to an associate of his and had tasked the transport to an indent named Megan. That was the last anyone had seen of either of them. Slate's report speculated that they had probably made a break for freedom together.

When Ian ran Micah's barcode, a flag had gone off and he was taken into custody.

Dominic worked this information out of the front desk officer over the course of half an hour. She wasn't supposed to give it to him, since Micah apparently wasn't *his*, but Dominic was both persuasive and charming when he needed to be.

And for this, he needed to be.

In the meantime, they had Micah locked up somewhere in the back and they wouldn't let Dominic see him. The officer said it was protocol. Dominic told them where they could stick their protocols, and the officer informed him that if he didn't settle down, she'd start asking hard questions about harboring fugitives.

Which left Dom pacing the front lobby, texting Ian every twenty minutes and hoping to the gods that Slate didn't actually show up to claim Micah.

Ian wasn't responding, and every unanswered text made Dominic's stomach drop further.

"Isn't possession supposed to be nine-tenths of the law?"

The officer rolled her eyes. "The registered contract holder will be here in an hour, Mr. Blackburn. You can work it out with him then."

An hour. Fuck.

Dominic was getting really sick of people calling him *Mister*.

He texted Ian again.

It was actually closer to three hours before Slate moseyed his ugly ass into the station. He was even more of a smarmy douchebag than Dominic had pictured; he was one of those guys who left the top three buttons of his shirt open so everyone could see his straggly stupid chest hair. He was accompanied by a tall thin man in a suit, who Dominic assumed was either a lawyer or a pet demon. Could go either way, honestly.

Slate walked right past him, because why wouldn't he? He didn't know Dominic from Adam.

"I'm here to pick up a runaway," he told the officer at the desk.

"He's not a runaway," Dominic said in a tone he definitely hadn't been practicing all afternoon. "I bought him from someone who had his title. Last week."

Slate turned very slowly, looking Dominic up and down before letting out a disbelieving, "*Did* you now?"

"Yes. I bought him off a brunette who gave me his title. You can't have him."

Slate quirked an eyebrow.

"I don't *want* him," Slate said, leaving the *you filthy peasant* unsaid but strongly implied. "He's utterly worthless. I was having him sent to one of my work camps when he ran."

"He's not a runaway."

"So you've said. But that title is still registered to *me*, so that's something I'll have to determine for myself." Slate waved a hand at

Dominic, signifying the conversation was over. "You can have him back when I'm done with him."

"Like hell. You're not taking him." The last phrase came out as a growl, and Dominic was a little surprised at himself.

Slate was not impressed. He turned to the officer at the desk. "I'd like him bound for transport. My agent can negotiate the necessary fees and paperwork."

"You're *not* taking him," Dominic said again. This time there was an edge of desperation in his voice, because the officer was handing forms to the lawyer and no one was paying any attention to him at all.

"Mr. Slate! I'm glad you made it."

Dominic scowled. Sure, *now* Ian was making an appearance. The detective breezed past Dominic, extending a hand toward Slate.

"I just need you to verify a few small details and we'll be able to get you on your way." Ian brought out the file folder with the photocopies Dominic had sent him. The top page was the photo of Micah's face, grainy and gray and terrifyingly empty. "Can you verify that this is the record of the indent you reported as a runaway?"

Slate flipped through the file. Ian glanced at Dominic. Dominic mouthed the word *traitor*. Ian shrugged.

"That looks right," Slate said, passing the file back to Ian.

"Excellent. Then you'll be happy to know that local authorities just picked him up in Alabama."

Dominic blinked.

"Alabama? I was told he was here," Slate snapped.

"We had a mix-up. An indent showed up here with the barcode number you reported, but there must be some sort of mistake, because he's clearly not the man described by the title you just verified."

The blood began to drain out of Slate's face. His pet demon took a half step toward Ian, who carried on. "*That* man is in Birmingham, being processed for transport. If you can get these forms filled out, we'll have him delivered to your estate by the end of the week."

Ian winked at Dominic. "If you'll come with me, Mr. Blackburn, I think we have some more details to discuss regarding *your* case."

Micah was waiting in Ian's office, rubbing the cuff marks on his wrists and acting entirely too calm for someone who had narrowly escaped hell.

Dominic pulled him into a bear hug. He didn't care how it looked. He didn't care that he was ridiculously attached to someone he'd met less than a week ago.

Slate wasn't taking Micah.

Everything else was just details.

"Has anyone ever accused you of being the most impatient person on the planet?" Ian asked from behind him.

"Not for a while," Dominic said, still not ready to let go of Micah. "Anybody ever tell you that you should answer your fucking phone?"

"I was talking with a magistrate; it's considered bad form."

Micah's head was leaning against Dominic's shoulder; he wasn't reciprocating, but he wasn't pushing him away, either. Dom had to focus very hard on what Ian was saying.

"Mr. Slate is going to be very distressed when he gets home and finds his estate's been raided," Ian explained. "When I called to tell him we'd picked up his runaway, he had no reason to think that Micah had *told* us anything. And I may have mentioned that he'd need to conduct the handoff in person. I assumed he might want to rush the timeline on that."

"So he just showed up and handed you a confession for title fraud," Dominic realized. He could feel Micah grinning against his shoulder.

"And gave me time to get a search warrant. Ronnie's photos helped convince the magistrate that it was worth a look. She signed off on it forty minutes ago. Local authorities are conducting the search as we speak." Ian leveled his eyes at Micah. "If the others are half as bad as you, it's likely that Slate will be arrested when he gets home."

Micah wriggled out of Dominic's grip, retrieving his notepad.

They are.

"Well, as much as I don't want to say 'good,' that's helpful."

Dominic frowned, confused. "So what was that about Micah being in Alabama?"

"Micah's not. Gerald is."

Micah's eyes widened. Ian gestured to the file. "This situation is an absolute clusterfuck, and I don't envy the battle you're going to fight to get it sorted out. But the short version is, Micah's never had a valid contract. The title you have here is for his father, and Gerald's been using fake identities to avoid anyone knowing. One of those identities happens to be Micah's. 'Micah Sawyer' has quite the record. The Birmingham police department was happy to shake a couple trees once I explained the situation. Fortunately for us, Gerald fell out of one, so we've got someone to hand over to Slate."

Micah had gone very pale.

"So . . . he can't touch Micah," Dominic said slowly, wanting to make sure he was completely clear on the situation.

"No one can touch Micah," Ian replied. "Micah's a free man."

Dominic spent the next two hours on the police station floor, because Micah was sitting on the floor and Dominic thought it might help to have someone down there with him. Dominic's primary reaction was relief, but Micah's dial seemed set dead-center in the middle of "panic." He wasn't writing, so Dominic just sat with him, back to the wall, and talked to Ian.

Dominic had a lot of questions, most of which Ian wasn't able to answer. They had *weeks* of work ahead of them.

The primary targets in Micah's case were, of course, his first and last holders. Micah's treatment under Slate was well documented. Dominic still had the black-and-white portraits of Micah taken right before Slate bought him. The difference between them and Ronnie's shots was obvious. Ian was of the opinion that that was their best hope for turning a jury.

The owners in the interim would be harder to nail down. Micah's first contract holders, the ones who had trained him, had no chance of claiming ignorance. They'd registered a man in his early thirties and then taken custody of a child. And, Ian explained, if they did it to Micah, they might have done it to others, as well. An indent who was young, healthy, *and* trained was an expensive rarity. And there was no shortage of children available for cheap. Turning one into the other was risky, but the payoff was high.

By the time Micah's trainers had sold him, he'd been a teenager who could, arguably, have passed for an adult. His new holders had mostly worked through agents or agencies, and could claim plausible deniability when confronted with the obvious discrepancies in Micah's title. Ian explained that for them, criminal prosecution would be unlikely. Title fraud was too easy to dismiss as an accident, and crimes like battery and sexual assault were very difficult to prove without documentation at the time. Which, of course, they did not have.

So Ian's task now was to track Micah's sale back to whoever had taken possession of him originally. They'd used fake names, of course, but Micah's trainer had been real. Ian thought they could probably pressure Arabelle to give up her business partners. She was a professional, but the threat of life in prison tended to loosen people's professional ethics just a tad.

If she wouldn't tell them anything, they'd subpoena Gerald and see what *he* could tell them.

Micah let out a choked sob at that, silent but obvious from the heave of his chest and the tendons of his throat.

Dominic laid a hand on his shoulder, making little circles, bringing him back into the room. "Hey. You're gonna be fine."

Micah's hair fell across his face as he shook his head.

"Yeah, you are. Hard part's over."

Micah did one of his silent little laughs. He still didn't write anything.

Dominic glanced at the clock. It was nearly six thirty in the evening. "God and earth, what a day," he said, hanging his head. Then, to Ian, "Can I buy you a beer?"

Ian waved him off. "I've got more work to do here. There's a lot of leads to follow up on."

"Aw, come on. I need one. Micah for sure needs one. All work and no play—"

"Puts the scum of the earth in prison where they belong," Ian finished firmly.

Dominic let it drop.

CHAPTER EIGHTEEN

Dominic wasn't really hungry, but he went through the motions anyway, finding a local pub and ordering the special when the waitress mentioned it. By the time she left, he couldn't remember what it was.

They sat in silence, nursing a pair of craft ales until the food arrived (chicken fried steak, as it turned out), and while Dominic made a half-hearted attempt to eat, Micah just pushed his food around his plate.

Finally, he pulled out his notebook.

I don't know where to go.

"Wherever you want, dude, that's kinda the point."

Tonight. I don't know where to go.

Dominic leaned his head against the vinyl seatback. "Ugh. I don't think I'm going anywhere tonight except home."

Micah wrote something, pushed it toward Dom, then yanked the paper back and kept writing.

By the time he handed it over, he'd crossed off a page's worth of starts.

Can I come with you? Just for one night. I'll give you the best lay of your life and be gone in the morning. I just need one night.

And under that: *Please.*

Dominic read it over three times. "Of course you're coming home with me, stupid. I still owe you your cut from the Carmichael case, so you've gotta stay at least until the money clears. Then you can run off to wherever you're going." He paused. "If you want, you can pick up some more gigs with me. Just, you know, until you get situated. I've got the extra bedroom, and I could still use the help." He paused again. "If you want."

Micah nodded vehemently, giving him a grin that lasted through the rest of dinner.

Dom tried not to read too much into the enthusiasm. It probably had nothing to do with him at all; Micah was just happy to have a place to stay.

The drive home would have been silent if not for the Sound Garden playlist whispering through the speakers. Dom felt like he should say something reassuring. He thought of telling Micah he could stay for as long as he wanted, however he wanted—coworkers, or hey, maybe even collect on that BJ Dom owed him—but in his head it sounded like babbling. He shut up before opening his mouth. Micah was staring out the window, his notepad lying forgotten on the dashboard. Dominic couldn't even imagine what he was thinking. This was a man whose talents people had paid a *million* dollars for, and now he was crashing in the spare room of a fallout shelter.

It's not much, Dom thought, turning into the driveway, *but it beats the shit out of literally nothing.*

Inside, Dominic kicked his shoes off and announced he was going to bed. Micah moved, slightly, like he was going to follow. Dominic didn't wait, didn't make the eye contact that would start a conversation he didn't feel up to having . . . but he did leave his bedroom door open.

When he woke up the next morning, Micah was sleeping in the hallway again.

There was absolutely no schedule, and Micah was dying.

His placements *always* had a schedule; it was a necessity of living in shared housing. He knew when it was his turn to eat, his turn to sleep, his turn to use the washrooms. He knew when he'd be needed for a party or a show, and some owners were even thoughtful enough to plan the use of bed slaves in advance. Micah always knew where he was supposed to be, and the consequences of failing to be there.

Not here. Here, the nothingness stretched out so long that Micah almost wished for a punishment, just to break the tedium.

He sat in his doorway, doing the breathing exercises Arabelle had taught him, absolutely certain that he was supposed to be doing *something* but unable to figure out what. There were no other slaves to learn from. No overseer. No master.

The closest thing he had was Dominic, and Dominic didn't even schedule his *own* days. He'd be eating lunch and then suddenly get up and walk outside and not wander back in for hours.

Micah *ached* to go with him, but every time he resolved to stand up, he'd be struck with the undeniable fact that he *did not have permission.*

If Dominic wanted his help, or even his company, he would have *said so.*

And right now, Micah needed to be useful in exactly the way Dominic needed. If he fucked this up, Dominic wouldn't sell him. Oh no. Micah was free now. Dominic would tell him to *leave*, and then he'd *really* get the opportunity to put his decision-making to the test.

Micah bit the inside of his lip, hard. *Stupid.* He knew what he was here for: to be a tool, to help Dominic with work. But when Dominic wasn't using his tools, he packed them away in their places, ready for when he'd need them.

So Micah would just have to stay put. He'd attend to his basic needs, *quietly*, and be ready in case Dominic thought of any extra tasks. If Dominic didn't, then Micah would do his best not to draw attention, not to do anything without permission, not to be annoying.

Except, Micah realized, he wasn't like other tools. He couldn't be oiled and cleaned and put away. If he was going to stay useful, he'd have to keep his body tuned up.

This was a *practical* requirement, he insisted to himself. He wasn't just making excuses because he was desperate to move. He wasn't. He *wasn't.*

He compromised, working through his flexibility stretches the next time Dominic turned the television on. In his mind, he practiced the louder exercises that had been part of his daily routine, before. Just imagining them wouldn't keep his body strong, but counting off the sets at least gave him something to think about.

He wished Dominic would give him an order.

After four days, Dominic started to realize he was in over his head.

If *he'd* just been freed, he'd be having the kind of party they used to turn into mosaics. He'd get into his car and drive everywhere he'd ever heard of, just to say he'd been there. And when he got there, he'd eat *everything*.

So he'd been prepared to spend the next couple of days (weeks?) doing everything he could to facilitate whatever it was that Micah decided he wanted to do.

Except, as it turned out, Micah wanted to stay in the spare room. During the day, at least.

During the day, Micah would sit with the door open, cross-legged on the floor, and watch Dominic go about his business. Dom had taken to luring him out with promises of food, like Micah was a stray cat that Dominic was trying to befriend. He'd come if Dominic asked him to, but afterward, he'd return to the doorway to watch.

At night, though, Micah ventured into the hallway.

At first Dominic thought the problem was him, that Micah was afraid to come out if he was there. But he spent four hours outside working on his car, and when he came back in, Micah was exactly where he'd left him.

And anyway, if Dominic were the reason Micah wasn't venturing beyond his room, then it made no sense that morning after morning, Dominic found him sleeping outside his door.

Adjusting to Dominic's preferences proved easier said than done. Not just because of his obvious distaste for several of Micah's expectations, but for his general obliviousness regarding some of the others. Micah was used to waiting, perched on his knees, meditating, ready for his owner to need him. Trained slaves were ornamentation, something lovely for their owners to admire while they attended to other business. But for their part, owners understood that holding a position indefinitely was impossible, and would periodically give their slaves small tasks as an excuse to attend to bodily needs.

The waiting was a relatively easy skill to transfer, except that Dominic didn't realize what was happening. He didn't see fit to send Micah on errands or dismiss him. It was against everything that Micah had learned to simply stand up and walk out of the room *unexcused*, but his mind's ability to override his body's needs was not absolute.

He began to watch Dominic closely while he waited, trying to anticipate something Dominic might need. Even if Micah couldn't identify anything obvious, he made a point never to return from an unexcused absence without some token: a glass of water, a book, a jacket, a tool.

The way he offered these to Dominic must have raised flags in the other man's mind, because Dominic would accept them hesitantly, searching Micah's face for something that Micah made very sure was not there.

After a couple days of being waited on, Dominic dug out a bunch of textbooks from when he'd taken his creacon exams. He gave them to Micah, saying he should read them if he was "bored or something." Micah chose to interpret that as an order, in no small part because he was deeply curious about what the books said. They were quite a bit more interesting than being ornamental, and Micah enjoyed the challenge of reading while still attending his master and, critically, not letting Dominic know he was being attended to.

If Micah was too obvious, Dominic would tell him to "go outside or something." After a few days of that, Micah started taking runs. At first he was afraid to go too far, in case he was called and couldn't hear to respond. Once he got out of earshot, he had trouble shaking the suspicion that he wasn't allowed to be where he was. On the rare occasions that he encountered other people, he had a tendency to run his fingers over his barcode, lest someone see it and wonder what he was doing out alone.

If they did notice, they didn't mention anything, and he started making it a point to go a little farther every day. He'd come back pleasantly exhausted and clear-headed, and it helped him to keep from fidgeting when he settled back on the floor again.

Sometimes after Dominic sent him away, Micah tried to learn to cook.

Dominic didn't eat on a regular schedule, instead wandering into the kitchen when he felt like it. Occasionally he cooked up a large meal whose components might or might not correspond to the meal typically eaten at that time of day. He'd told Micah early on that the kitchen was free game, and that he should help himself whenever he was hungry.

Micah amended it to twice daily, once at midday and once in the evening. If Dominic was up and cooking in the morning, he'd eat then too, but only if Dominic offered. He'd have three meals when he figured out a way to be useful.

Dominic didn't know what to do except keep telling Micah to go outside. Micah wouldn't, unless he was told, but it did genuinely seem like he *wanted* to.

One time, he didn't come back for three hours. His knees were muddy and he had a scratch above one eyebrow, but he still looked . . . *better*. He kicked off his shoes and disappeared into the laundry room, and Dominic debated the ethical considerations of whether to avert his eyes when he came back out. His dry spell won out over his caretaker instincts, and when Micah walked across the house in his boxers, Dominic did in fact ogle him shamelessly. Micah smiled.

The next time Dominic saw him, Micah was dressed in loose jeans and a sweater, and he was sitting in his doorway again.

"You don't need to wait for me to tell you, you know," Dominic said.

Micah nodded.

Later, Dominic pushed the couch to the side so Micah could see the TV from his room.

And he started talking while he worked. At first it was stupid little comments to himself or the items he was working with.

Anything to break up the silence. He'd ask rhetorical questions like "Where did the pen go" or "How did I mess that up?" But then he'd look over and Micah would be listening, and so he started talking to Micah instead.

He told Micah that the comics were the best part of the newspaper, and afterward Micah took the paper back to his room and read it. If he laughed, it was silent.

He told Micah that the car needed an oil change and it was gonna be a pain in the ass because he'd have to get her up on blocks.

He told Micah that there was a call out for the expulsion of a coven of witches, but they weren't taking the job because Dominic was pretty sure that the client was just a busybody looking to irritate her neighbors.

He told Micah that the best way to make eggs was to make bacon first, because then the pan was hot and slick and it made the eggs taste delicious. Micah nodded sagely and ate his breakfast.

He told Micah that *Die Hard* was the best Solstice movie and that when Solstice rolled around he'd get a copy and they'd watch it.

Micah retreated back into his room after that, and Dominic realized he'd made a pretty big assumption.

The nights were the worst. Every night Micah would swear that he was going to be good, that he would stay in his place and not bother Dominic.

And then every night, he lay in his bed, surrounded by silence and darkness and memories. He'd reach the cusp of sleep and then bolt awake, sure that he'd been summoned and hadn't heard. No one was standing guard, no one would tell him—

Every night he lost the battle, giving up the fight against the emptiness and creeping out into the hall. It was weak, and needy, and disobedient, and it was no wonder that Dominic would rather sleep *alone* than put up with him.

Micah sat there in the darkness and considered, not for the first time, becoming indentured again. There was no reason he *couldn't* get another contract. It wouldn't be with Dominic, but it wouldn't be with Slate, either. He could go back to his life, the way it had been before all of this started.

He ground his palms into his eyes, tipping back into the same spiral of desperation that had been consuming him for days.

Becoming indentured again would mean leaving Dominic. He was almost sure of it. And he didn't want to do that.

But this was unsustainable. Dominic wasn't going to tell him what to do. If he was going to stay here, if he was going to be free, he was going to *have* to make his own choices.

Micah hugged his knees to his chest, hyperventilating in a way that might have been sobs if he could make sound.

He *couldn't do it*; he was too stupid and too ignorant and he always had been. That was why they'd made him an indent in the first place, so he wouldn't get the opportunity to *fuck everything up* like he inevitably would.

Every indent he'd ever met had the same story: mistake after mistake, wasting the goodwill of people like Dominic and Ian and Ronnie until finally running out of options and getting a contract. He should save everyone the trouble and just *go*.

Micah opened his mouth and screamed, screamed until his throat burned and tears were running down his face.

He didn't sleep, just ran through the same set of pros and cons, the same circle of reasoning, until the sun came up and it was time to return to his own room.

Once again, he swore *this* night would be different.

On the sixth night, Dominic heard Micah shuffling outside the door. He rolled over, watching Micah in the moonlight.

"What's wrong with your bed, man?"

Micah startled, but didn't answer.

"You gotta quit sleeping in the hallway. If you don't like your bed, fine, you don't have to sleep on it. But at least sleep on the couch or *something*."

Micah stood in the doorway for a very long time, watching him.

And then he pulled his blanket around his shoulders and crossed over the threshold.

He climbed onto the other side of Dominic's bed, above the covers. He didn't make a move to touch Dominic, not even when Dominic rolled over to face him. Micah just lay there, his blanket wrapped around him like armor.

"Thanks," Dominic said. That was . . . probably progress. On some level.

He didn't think he'd be able to sleep, but he did.

The next night Micah joined him in bed again, and Dominic said, "You can get under the covers if you want," and Micah did.

That was when Dominic started to realize that Micah didn't know how to ask for things. Not out loud because, obviously not out loud. But not on paper, either, because he saw himself as an imposition.

But Dominic started to think it went deeper than that. Maybe Micah didn't ask for things because Micah didn't know how to *want* things.

He could prefer things. Or be afraid of things. But he didn't know how to pick something, out of all the world, and *want* it.

What should really happen, Dominic thought, was that Micah should go see a therapist. Unfortunately, Dominic came from a long line of men who swore by the Jim, Jack, and Jose school of psychoanalysis, and after several frustrating hours on the internet trying to figure out where to even *begin* looking for a shrink, Dominic gave up.

Instead, he started giving Micah choices.

Closed questions worked better than open ones. "Pizza or chili?" got an answer, while "What do you want for dinner?" got only a shrug. Movie titles were met with blank stares, but Micah definitely liked action more than comedy. He liked horror movies too, the cheesier the better.

They weren't Dominic's favorites, but he played them anyway, everything from *Cabin in the Woods* to *Tucker and Dale vs. Evil.*

Sometimes, if Dominic looked over at exactly the right moment, he could catch Micah laughing.

It wasn't enough. He needed more than the things Dom could think to tell him. So Dominic sat Micah down in front of the computer, got him an email address, and showed him how to run searches. Micah found sign language tutorials on YouTube.

Turned out, he wanted that a *lot*.

Micah stood at the front door, looking out into the yard. Around the corner of the house, he could hear Dominic swearing good-naturedly, in between impacts of something heavy.

Micah was preparing to misbehave. His stomach was twisting into knots, but this was, technically, an order. Well, a request. It was, at the very least, something Dominic had liked *before*, so—

He took another step, standing fully *outside the house* without asking permission.

Nothing happened. The sounds of impacts continued undisrupted.

Of course, he wouldn't *really* have misbehaved until Dominic *knew* he'd done it. *That* was what Dominic liked. Like yesterday, when Dominic had made fried rice and tried to put teriyaki sauce on Micah's and Micah had signed no. Actually shook his head. To Dominic's *face*.

Dominic loved it. He loved it so much that Micah tried again later. Dominic had put him on the couch to watch a movie, and Micah had *moved*, putting a pillow on the floor so he could do his stretches.

But that was different. This was *outside*. Impertinence might have earned him a slap to the mouth, disobedience a few days in solitary, but *this*. This was something else.

Micah took a step, and then another, toward the edge of the house. With each one, he ran the risk of stepping into Dominic's sight, and was granted the opportunity to change his mind. To go back inside, like nothing had happened.

He came to the corner to see Dominic swing a maul, splitting a chunk of wood in half.

Dominic saw Micah and grinned, wide and genuinely *happy*. "Hey, look who's out and about!"

Micah signed hello, smiling when Dominic signed it back.

"You wanna help?"

Micah nodded, and Dominic ducked into the shed to find an extra pair of safety goggles. There was a pile of wood that needed splitting and stacking, and by the time they were done, Micah was sore from head to toe. It felt amazing.

One thing a day, he decided. He would take one chance per day.

After a week, Dom decided that the weather was absolutely perfect for a bonfire, and he and Micah spent the afternoon building a brush pile. They dragged chairs outside and sat by the flames, moving in and out and left and right as the heat shifted and smoke changed direction.

Dominic stripped a couple of pine branches, and they cooked hot dogs and marshmallows over the coals. Micah had never done it before and didn't know how to keep the marshmallows from burning. Fortunately, he turned out to be one of that crazy minority who *preferred* his food burned to a crisp and still cold in the center.

Dominic chalked it up to another fundamental shortcoming in his upbringing and didn't make a comment. He'd tried not to comment ever since he'd realized that Micah was adjusting his preferences to fit what Dominic found acceptable.

Dominic kept telling him not to, but he was pretty sure Micah was still doing it anyway. There was some kind of fucked-up catch-22 there.

The firelight made Micah's face bright in the darkness, and he was eating his black marshmallow with such a childish look of happiness that Dominic didn't even realize he was staring until Micah met his gaze.

The light in his eyes didn't dim.

There was a smear of marshmallow on the corner of his mouth, and Dominic insisted that he was *not* going to lean over and wipe it off, because that would be *far* too intimate. Micah was beautiful and wonderful and struggling, and he didn't need Dominic making moves on him.

Dominic didn't get the chance to test his resolve, though, because Micah leaned over and kissed him.

His lips tasted like caramelized sugar and burned marshmallow, and Dominic suddenly understood the appeal.

Micah pulled back, searching his face, looking for permission, and Dominic gave it to him, pressing their lips together and licking at the burned-sugar taste of Micah's mouth. It didn't go further than that. Dominic kept his hands to himself and barely noticed when his own marshmallow caught fire.

Later that night, Micah climbed under the covers of Dominic's bed, and Dominic said, "You can come closer if you want," and Micah studied him in the dark. He reached out, laying an arm across Dominic's body, just below the rib cage. He didn't come closer, but when Dominic woke up in the morning, Micah's fingers were twisted in the fabric of his shirt.

On the eighth day, Garrett messaged to let him know the Carmichael funds had cleared. Dominic told Micah that he'd need a way to cash checks, which meant government identification and bank accounts and a social security card and a driver's license would probably be a good idea. Micah nodded and then vanished back in his room and closed the door and didn't come out for a very long time.

"Oh, *fuck*, Micah."

Just like that morning at the hotel, Micah had wriggled his way under the covers while Dominic was sleeping. And just like that morning, Dominic was drawn slowly out of a dream by the feeling of being stroked and sucked and tongued and *gods*, Micah was good at that.

Dominic pulled the blankets back, drinking in the sight. Micah looked up through his eyelashes, never taking Dominic out of his mouth, and *fuck*, those eyes. His hair fell across his face, tickling against Dom's hips as Micah stroked the base of his shaft, and Dom reached out for him, wanting his hands on Micah's skin. Micah took his hand, lacing their fingers together.

He pulled off then, planting a line of little kisses up the inside of Dom's thigh, making him squirm.

"Tickles," Dom protested, and Micah smiled, pushing himself onto his elbows. His tongue laved across the head of Dom's cock, over and over, until Dom was desperate for more.

"Quit teasing me, man," Dom groaned, and then dropped his head back onto the pillow because Micah was taking him deep, going from zero to a hundred in point three seconds flat. Dom had to fight the urge to fuck up into his mouth. Micah could probably handle it, though; he was a *professional*, taking Dom all the way into the back of his throat and still managing to *suck*.

"You're gonna make me come," Dominic breathed, and Micah did a little silent hum, and *fuck* did Dom come.

When he caught his breath, Micah was still looking up at him.

"Mmm, c'mere," Dominic said, laying out his arm. Micah obediently climbed up next to him, lying with his head on Dominic's shoulder, their legs tangled together under the blankets. Dominic leaned down, kissing Micah and tasting himself on the other man's mouth. The length of Micah's body was pressed up against his, Micah's erection obvious against Dominic's hip. Dominic pulled him close, rubbing against him, and Micah's fingers tightened on him.

Dominic slipped one leg between Micah's, pressing up gently and rolling his body against Micah. Micah ground against him, moaning silently, and deepened the kiss.

Dominic finally pulled back for air, and stopped dead.

Micah's face held that same detached emptiness he'd seen in the sale photo.

"Hey! Hey, where are you? You here with me?"

The light came back to Micah's eyes, and he stilled. And then it flickered, went out, and he pulled Dominic back toward him.

Dominic backpedaled so hard he nearly fell out of bed. "Whoa, hold up. What is that? What are you doing?"

Micah's eyes closed, his jaw clenched, and then that, too, was gone.

"Get your paper, man, we're talking about this."

Micah grabbed it off the nightstand. He was making a sign that Dom recognized as *sorry*.

"Don't be sorry. Just help me understand."

I wanted to do something for you.

"And I appreciate that, I do, you can do that whenever you want. I'm asking about the whole 'out of body experience' thing you had going on there. It's a bit freaky."

Micah looked at the ground. At the door. Anywhere but Dominic.

It's a meditation technique. For separating mind from body. It's to help indents get through difficult experiences.

"What's difficult?" Dom asked. He was so godsdamned confused. "If you wanted to . . . you know. What are you trying to get through?"

I wanted to use my mouth on you. I wasn't expecting you to want more.

Dom scrambled for something to say. "I was just gonna return the favor, man."

Micah nodded.

"That's what you didn't want to do?"

Micah nodded again.

Dominic sighed, ran his hands through his hair. "Okay. Hard rule. *Do not* fucking meditate yourself out of your body while we're, I dunno, 'being intimate' or whatever. If you don't like what I'm doing, you tell me to stop. Fucking punch me in the nose if you have to. You have my permission. Okay?"

Micah's face was indecipherable. Dominic sighed. "Look . . . you're good. That was awesome. Thank you. I was trying to say thank you. By returning the favor. I thought you'd like it. That's all."

Micah's jaw set. *I don't like it.*

"Like what?"

Getting touched. Like that.

Dominic's mind rewound with a screech as he tried to integrate that into his worldview. Micah was the most sexual person he'd ever met, *he* was the one who kept initiating . . .

"Okay. That's okay. We don't have to do that. It's fine." Dominic paused, trying to find the lines of the boundary Micah was setting. "The way we've been sleeping, though, that's okay?"

Micah nodded.

"And the kissing and stuff?"

Micah nodded again.

"So basically, I should just keep my hands off your junk and we'll be okay?"

Micah hesitated, then nodded again.

"Okay. That's okay. I can do that. I'm not gonna lie and say I understand it, like *at all*, but I can do it." Dominic paused. "Is there anything you *do* want?"

Micah leaned over and kissed him once, open and tender, and then he pulled away and left the room.

On the ninth day, Micah got a phone call.

On Dominic's phone, of course, because Micah didn't have one. He'd need one eventually, Dominic realized, and then a clipped British accent said, "Is he there or not?" and Dominic was pulled back into the moment.

"Sorry, who's this?"

"On what grounds are you asking?"

"The grounds that it's my phone. How did you even get this number?"

"A little birdie at the Selina police department. Now, please do put Micah on the line."

Micah was watching from his doorway. Dominic raised his eyebrows and held out the handset.

"It's for you."

Micah gave him a blank look. Dominic put the phone on speaker.

"He's here."

"Lovely. Hello Micah, my name is Mia Winters, and I've been informed that you might have a spot of legal intrigue. I'd like to offer my services."

"So you're, what, like a lawyer?" Dominic asked.

"Quite like one, yes, and if you don't mind, I'm speaking with Micah now."

"Did your little birdie mention that Micah can't talk?"

There was a pause on the line. "And why not?"

"His last holder had him devocalized."

"Oh, brilliant!"

Micah's jaw set, and Dominic did a ridiculous double take at the phone.

"I mean that's awful, of course, poor man, must be terribly difficult for him, but for my purposes that's quite good."

"Okay, it's gonna sound like I'm hanging up—"

"Oh don't pout, Dominic. This could work out well for you as well."

"I fail to see how."

"That's all right, we can't all be brilliant, it wouldn't be fair."

Micah let out a little laugh at that. Dominic was glad Mia couldn't hear.

"The report that I have here says that Micah's been sold to at least ten very wealthy holders. Can you verify that information?"

Dominic checked with Micah. Micah made a so-so gesture.

"Yeah, that's right."

"Micah's newfound freedom bodes badly for these holders. I'm sure you're aware of the difference between indentured and free men and the legal protections for each? Our friend Micah had quite a few more than they anticipated when they purchased him. Or thought they did. Minor details, not important. What *is* important is that each of these holders is now facing a veritable *cascade* of civil and possibly even criminal charges, the outcome of which will depend wholly on how ignorant they can pretend to be regarding the workings of their own households. It's going to be time-consuming, expensive, and *terribly* embarrassing for them," Mia explained, not sounding the least bit sorry for any of it. "My guess is that they'll be happy to pay a *substantial* remuneration to keep it out of the courts and, by extension, the papers. I'd like to help negotiate the proceedings, in exchange for a percentage, of course."

Dominic checked Micah. Micah had his arms crossed, worrying his lower lip with his thumb.

"I think he needs to think it over."

"Of course. One of my people is available at this number twenty-four seven, when you reach a decision. Just to help the deliberation process along, I can tell you that I've never settled a similar case for less than five hundred thousand."

Dominic gaped.

"Per holder," Mia clarified.

"We'll call you back," Dominic said, and hung up the phone. Micah was biting his lip, making tallies on a scrap of paper. Dom didn't need to do the math. "That's a lot of money."

I could tell.

"You want to take her up on it?"

I think I'd like to talk to Ian.

Ian was pissed.

"She shouldn't have been able to get your number," he snapped, his voice crackling over Dom's speakerphone. "If I find out who gave it to her, they're fired. I swear."

"But in the meantime," Dominic said. "Is she legit?"

Ian made a noncommittal noise. "If she's on your side," he admitted. "She's an evil conniving bitch, but she'll deliver you the world if you promise her a cut."

Micah wrote a question.

"Micah's asking if he should do it."

There was a long pause. "It's a gamble," Ian admitted. "Settling out of court means exactly what it sounds like. Out of court. If you press charges, I can't promise I can make any of them stick. To any of these guys. It's possible you could pay a lawyer and spend years fighting this and none of them will ever see a day in jail. Or you might get lucky and you might get a jury who throws the book at one or all of them. I'll help you as best I can, but Mia can promise results that I can't. Ultimately, the decision is yours."

Micah's brow was furrowed and his jaw was set. Dominic changed the subject. "Any news on Slate?"

"No. A couple indents were taken in during the estate raid, but they're not talking. Slate still holds their contracts; if they inform on him and nothing comes of it, he'll be able to take them back.

So naturally, they're reluctant to tell us anything. We're working on it. We've also pulled Arabelle in. She's a firecracker, lawyered up immediately, says she can't serve up any of her professional contacts without a subpoena. Once we get that, it'll be our best hope for finding Micah's original holders." Ian paused. "You should also know that Gerald's been brought up from Alabama. Slate has him. He's the registered holder, but technically, you have his title, Dominic. Do with that what you will."

Micah was pale. Dominic thanked Ian and hung up the phone.

"Lot to think about."

Micah nodded.

That evening, Micah came out of his room and helped Dominic make dinner. He got a bag of peas out of the freezer and microwaved them without being asked. Or asking.

The progress of the peas.

Dominic laughed a little too hard.

Afterward they curled up on opposite ends of the couch and watched *Fifth Element.*

"Do you know what state you were born in?" Dominic asked, trying to break the silence.

Micah gave him a questioning shrug. He'd relocated from the doorway to the couch, but he still spent most of his time reading or watching Dominic do things. Right now, Dominic was on the internet.

"If you want a driver's license, you need a social security card. If you want a social security card, you need a birth certificate. If you want a birth certificate, you need to put in a request to the vital records office in the state where you were born. So do you know?"

Nevada, Micah signed, spelling out each letter.

"Thanks."

Dominic made three phone calls to the Nevada Bureau of Vital Records and then started to seriously consider just getting Micah a fake identity. It would probably be easier.

After two weeks, Ian called to say that Slate had been officially charged with a number of indenturement abuses. He wanted to know if Micah was willing to testify.

Micah's expression didn't change as he listened, but when he nodded, his face was pale.

Ian wanted to know if they were working with Mia, and Dominic said Micah hadn't made a decision yet.

Ian had barely hung up before Dominic got a text from Garrett. Garrett wanted them to investigate a likely chupacabra picking off calves on a farm in Virginia. Dominic said he'd do it. He was getting stir-crazy sitting around the house this long. Micah heard them discussing the details, and disappeared into his room.

By the time Dominic was done packing, Micah was standing by the door, his crooked-stitched duffel over his shoulder.

"You *sure* you're up for this?" Dom asked.

Micah nodded.

From there, it was five hours of driving. They stopped four times to get gas or take a piss or just walk around. Every single time, Micah went into the gas station and walked up and down the aisles like he was searching for something. Whatever it was, he never found it.

Two twenties, a five, a single, and thirty-eight cents.

That was what Micah had in cash. That didn't count the four fifty-two in the bathroom, which he hadn't touched since the day he'd hidden it there.

He wasn't stupid, he thought, wandering down the aisles of the Circle K. He could add. Four fifty would buy him a couple of candy bars, or maybe a sandwich. He was capable of doing that math; he'd been capable of it the day he'd looked at the paltry sum and decided to steal it.

But Micah had always understood *money* as an abstract, something that free people used to get what they wanted. In the drowning chaos of the moment, he'd latched on to the idea that *money* might keep him safe.

It was the first choice Dominic had allowed him to make, albeit due to inattention rather than grace, and Micah had made the wrong one. It didn't bode well for his future as a free man.

Dominic finished paying for the gas, and Micah followed him outside, doing the math. Dominic had paid in twenties, filling a tank that had been half full to start with, so in a car like Dominic's (*Did it matter? How much?)*, Micah had enough money to get him four hundred and fifty miles.

He could buy eleven sandwiches, thirty-seven candy bars, or one prepaid phone with a gigabyte of data.

How long would a gigabyte last?

Micah slid into the front seat, letting his mind run headlong into this now-familiar wall. He didn't know anything about *anything*, which was a problem, because it was his responsibility now.

If there *was* anything Micah knew, it was that freedom was anything but free. Every slave, every indent, had a story about what they needed *the money* for, and why they hadn't had it. Freedom was a minefield he was navigating blind.

Micah glanced out the window, keeping his face blank so Dominic couldn't tell he was ready to scream.

Dominic would be unhappy about that, and Micah didn't know how long *that* would last either. And when Dominic finally—

Micah took a slow breath, counting backward, keeping those thoughts from coming. He didn't need to worry about how Dominic's displeasure would manifest, because there was nothing he could do about it. The master's discipline was the master's decision.

That had been a hard lesson to learn at first, after years of trying to predict and avoid his father's anger, and *they'd* never had money either, because—

Slow. Breathe. Don't go down that rabbit hole. Focus on what you can do.

"Do you know how to drive?" Dominic asked. Micah shook his head and made the sign for no.

"Oh. I know you don't have a driver's license, but I wasn't sure if they'd taught you off the books, or whatever."

Put another thing on the list, something else he was missing.

"I'll teach you when we get back home, yeah?" Dominic said, after a couple seconds of silence.

Micah nodded emphatically.

"So the goat thing is more of a generalization than an actual rule," Dominic explained, regarding the cows. Micah nodded. One of Dominic's textbooks was an encyclopedia of cryptids. Micah had read the chupacabra section before they left, and it was actually pretty robust, so he already knew a lot of what Dominic explained as they climbed up into the loft of the barn. He let Dominic explain it anyway. For one, it was difficult to sign *stop* to someone who was above him on a ladder. For another, he was painfully aware of how much he didn't *know* that he didn't know.

It was going to be a long, long time before he could assume he had all the information he needed.

"So the basic strategy here is that we set up containment around the perimeter of the barn with the trigger mechanism up here," Dominic explained, reaching the top and surveying the space. He turned back to give Micah a hand up. "You know how to activate a cantrip?"

Micah made a seesawing gesture with his hand. He'd had the basic intro to magic in school, but it had been a long time since he'd actually tried to *do* anything with it.

"Okay, that's fine. I'm gonna put you on the light, then, and if we can't get it working, we can just use flashlights."

Dominic knelt down, and Micah went to his knees beside him, watching as he drew a simplistic set of triangles on the dusty boards with a grease pencil.

"Once this is activated, it'll glow, and it'll keep glowing until it's released," Dominic explained. "It's just witchlight, so you really *can* do it with hand gestures, but I like having it down somewhere I can see it, you know?"

Micah nodded, mostly because he felt like he should. Dominic exhaled slowly, placing his hands on either side of the drawing. His fingertips pressed against the rough wood, and a moment later, the light in the loft began to change. The delineation between light and dark became sharper, the bright places blue, the shadows an unbroken black.

And then it snapped back, and the loft was once again bathed in the diffused orange glow of the sunset.

"Okay, now you try," Dominic said, setting back onto his heels. Micah studied the picture again, trying to remember how to put power *into* it. He leaned forward, resting his hands on either side, letting his fingertips dig into the wood.

Nothing.

Micah pushed harder against the floor, and Dominic shook his head.

"You can't *make* the power move. You just have to like . . . agree to share. Keep trying for a couple minutes, and I'll set up the trigger glyphs while you do that."

Micah scowled at the drawing. It was his power, part of his body, he *should* be able to *make* it move. It should do what he *told* it to.

But, no point bitching over it. He let his hands relax on the wood, trying to recall the feeling from the last time he'd had to activate an ikon. It had probably been ten years.

"The trap on this one isn't all that complicated," Dominic was explaining, and Micah tried to pay attention to both things. "We get some suppression ikons around the inner perimeter of the barn, and then we wait for our nasty little beasty to make its way inside. Once we spot it, we set off the trigger, and Bob's your uncle."

Dominic studied the new marks he'd made on the floor, and was Micah imagining it, or was it a little brighter in here?

No, the setting sun was coming through cracks between the boards, shining in his eyes and making it seem brighter. Damn it.

Micah stared at the triangles, willing them to glow. He had one job. *One job.*

"That ought to do it up here," Dominic said, rising to his feet and brushing his hands off on his jeans. "I'm gonna go back down the ladder and get started on the perimeter markings. You wanna come with me, or keep working on this?"

Micah indicated the floorboards with a tilt of his head.

"Cool. Don't force it. It'll go when it's ready."

And then Micah was alone, staring resolutely at the triangles that Dominic had worked instantly and willing them to so much as *spark*.

Below him, he could hear Dominic moving around, but he ignored it, focusing on the feel of his body. He tried to sense the energy inside himself, make it move, out through his hands and into the ikon that could turn it into something *useful*.

There was a rattling from below as Dominic shook a paint can, placing water-soluble sigils in the four corners and the cardinal directions. A door rumbled open on tracks, followed by the quiet lowing of the cows. The chupacabra had been focusing on the calves, so they'd be sleeping inside for the duration of the stakeout.

Micah balled his hands into fists, his knuckles digging into the rough wood with a satisfying sting.

"Hey, can you come give me a hand with this?" Dominic called from the bottom of the ladder, and Micah gave up, standing.

Instantly, the light changed. The warm amber of the sunset was replaced with blue—no, white. One of the cows made a confused noise. With his attention off the floor, Micah saw the darkness outside, heard the buzzing of the fluorescents overhead. Surrounded by the golden witchlight, he hadn't seen them turn on.

"I see you got the hang of it," Dominic said, popping into view. He heaved a coil of rope over the edge of the loft. "Help me tie this to something, and then we can deal with the rest of the gear. I've got a couple of the cages set up down here, in case there's more than one."

Micah couldn't resist touching the ikon one more time. Almost instantly, the light turned a warm orange, nothing at all like Dominic's sharp blue. This time, he could feel... something. Change. But he'd be damned if he could say what.

There wasn't much to haul up, just a cooler, a couple of blankets, and a duffel full of tools and protective gear. The duffel was almost a waste, because as soon as they got it onto the ledge, Dominic began to squirrel things into his pockets. He handed Micah a pair of plain Kevlar gauntlets, almost hesitantly.

"My dad wasn't much for finer details," he said, by way of explanation. Micah didn't understand what he meant until Dominic began strapping his own pair into place—worn, gouged leather, with a pattern of ikons burned along the outside edges. Dominic had pretty obviously done the detailing himself, and Micah found himself smiling at that.

By the time they'd gotten everything situated, it was fully dark outside. They turned off the fluorescents and settled in to wait.

Micah . . . actually kind of liked it. He and Dominic sat on the edge of the loft, the dim warm glow of the ikon behind them. Below them, the calves and their mothers settled into the hay to sleep.

Micah was doing a good job of holding the light, even without physically touching the ikon, and he chose to count that as an accomplishment. He was also manning the flashlight, an industrial thing the size of a car headlight, in case anything below needed a closer look.

Beside him, Dominic was using a felt-tipped marker to make a set of ikons along the length of a faux-leather collar. The marker left a trail of smoke behind it, as each ikon bound to the whole.

And despite the twenty-foot length of the ledge, they were sitting near enough to share a blanket, Dominic's thigh pressed easily along the length of his.

"These are the same sigils I used down below," Dominic was explaining. Long silences seemed to put him on edge, but unfortunately there was very little Micah could do about that. "Except, when we activate the perimeter down there, it's going to include, you know. All the cows."

Too much? Micah signed. Dominic's hands paused on the collar while he interpreted. Micah was considering getting his notebook out, but then—

"Yes and no? The runes suppress the will of lower life forms. It gets harder for smarter animals, and cows are like . . . a four? Out of ten? But there's like twenty of them down there, and that's a lot of threads to hold at once. It's more complicated than harmful. The spell really only draws power if I'm trying to get them to *do* something."

Dominic paused and frowned, counting off on his fingers. He did some kind of mental arithmetic in his head for a few seconds and then, almost to himself, "Yeah, I think I could make twenty cows do something they didn't want to do."

Micah laughed, nudging Dominic's shoulder with his own.

Dominic went back to marking the collar. "When you're a little better at this, one of us can hold the perimeter while the other goes in with the collar. Till then, the simplest way to do this is for me to hold everything still until I can get close enough to collar the chup, at which point I can drop the perimeter spell and use the collar to force it into its cage without getting bitten. The cows just have to not move, which is pretty much what they're doing anyway, so that doesn't really cost me anything."

Micah hugged his shoulders, peering past their dangling legs and over the edge. In the darkness below, nothing seemed suspicious yet.

It wasn't clear quite *how* the chupacabra was getting into the barn, but it had been kicking up a commotion on a near-nightly basis for two weeks now, no matter what traps or deterrents were put up outside. If possible, they were supposed to figure that out in the course of the stakeout.

Micah didn't know what would happen if they couldn't. Dominic had worked the terms of this job out via text, in conversations Micah hadn't been privy to. It put him on edge a bit.

With his previous owners, Micah was always given *exact* instructions, as well as the consequences for failure. Sometimes things were rocky right at the beginning, as he learned to adjust, but discipline helped him *do* that.

At the end, with Slate, sometimes the instructions had been impossible, because *being punished* was the real goal. But even then, Micah knew where he stood. When Slate was finished with him, Micah *knew* he'd taken what he'd needed.

Here, Micah was in the dark. Dominic had made an offhand comment about "when he was better," so clearly he needed to learn, and practice, and master . . . something. Somehow.

Does that work on people? Micah asked, going for his notebook rather than trying to sign.

"What?" Dominic asked. Then, when Micah gestured to the collar, "The suppression ikons? No. Higher intelligences are on pretty even footing, so the person suppressing and the person trying to resist just battle it out to no effect until they both exhaust their mana and die. Maybe you could use it on a vampire or werewolf for, like, *a minute*, but personally I wouldn't risk it."

Micah sighed. Too bad. For a moment he thought maybe he'd solved his dilemma, but that would be too easy.

Dominic probably wouldn't have gone for it anyway. He wanted Micah to enjoy being free, and wearing a collar like that didn't seem like the sort of thing free people enjoyed.

Well, he thought, remembering an owner he'd had when he was twenty or so, *not all the time, anyway.*

Something shifted down below, and both men froze, peering over the edge. But it was just a calf nudging closer to its mother. The night air was getting cool, making Micah glad for the blanket.

A cry broke the silence, definitely a sound of distress.

Something moved in the darkness. Something big.

"And there we go," Dominic said. He dropped the blanket and leaned over, pressing his palm against the perimeter trigger. His fingertips glowed blue for a moment, and blue sparks began circling the barn's perimeter lines. They were too dim, and moved too quickly, for Micah to see much of the creature.

"Careful now, don't spook it," Dominic whispered. He was down the ladder in a couple of seconds. Micah went more slowly, so he was behind Dominic when the creature noticed them.

It hissed once and then vanished.

Instantly.

"Oh, fuck," Micah heard, and the sparks moved faster. Dominic spun around, his hands resting on Micah's shoulders. "Look at me," Dominic said, and the usual levity was missing from his voice. "Keep your eyes on my face, okay?"

Micah nodded, keeping his gaze fixed on Dominic's. In the light, his blue eyes seemed to glow.

"This isn't just a wild cryptid. It's— *Fuck—*" He winced, dropping the collar, barely keeping his eyes open. "It's older, more complicated. A hidebehind. It's the thing that moves in the corner of your eye. And it is always . . . right . . . *behind you.*"

Ice slid down Micah's spine. He almost turned his head but remembered Dominic's instruction.

"I watch your back, you watch mine," Dominic said. "It won't attack when it can be seen. But the suppression spell won't buy us more than a couple seconds against something like this. I need—" He winced again. Something moved in the shadows behind him, or maybe it was just the weird blue lights moving slowly.

Micah remembered the sigil up in the loft, putting off its dim gold glow. Silently, he willed it brighter, bright enough to banish every dark corner, the shadows behind every crate and animal.

It got marginally brighter. Maybe.

"Get the flashlight up, we're going to lose the perimeter lighting," Dominic said before Micah could get frustrated with himself. He was holding something, a dark rectangle that Micah couldn't identify without looking away from Dominic's face.

"Okay," Dominic said, unsnapping his gun from its holster. "Sterling silver, so we just— *Ahh—*" He pressed his hand against one eye, the other still scanning the area behind Micah.

"It's made up its mind, *shit.*" Dominic abandoned the compulsion spell and the meager blue lights around them vanished, plunging the barn into near darkness. Micah shone the flashlight behind Dominic, the edge of the beam catching on the clip dropping from his gun, ignored in his haste to load the correct one.

The directional light turned every jumping shadow sharp, threatening, Micah's mind building each of them into a bloodthirsty nightmare ready to pounce. He didn't even know what the thing looked like, and that was his biggest problem until he realized that Dominic *didn't have a flashlight*.

Footsteps in the dark behind him, faster than he could have turned if he wanted to, and then Dominic was shoving past him with a curse.

Micah swung the light around and almost couldn't process what he saw. His first thought was *spider*, but that wasn't right. The long, spindly arms clawing at Dominic were humanoid. Eight of them, growing from a single legless torso, each of them as long as Dominic was tall.

Run, Micah thought, his heart hammering in his chest, but he was frozen to the spot. The creature bore Dominic to the ground, taloned fingers scoring deep gouges into his shoulder.

The gun went off, once, startling Micah back into action. He couldn't tell if the shot had hit its target, but Dominic wasn't getting another chance. One of the creature's arms pinned his wrist to the floor, and it was leaning in, too many sharp teeth in a face that would have set Micah screaming if he'd had the ability.

He didn't have a gun. He didn't even have a silver knife. And he didn't have time to experiment with iron.

He went for the collar Dominic had dropped, sliding one end through the metal ring to make a noose and yanking it over the monster's head without a second to spare. Its teeth snapped shut a millimeter short of Dominic's throat, and then Micah was on it, his arm joining the leather pulled tight around its neck, and he hoped to hell it had a humanoid difficulty in reaching its own back.

It let out a choked howl, scrabbling at Micah's arm, its claws scoring the Kevlar. It writhed, trying to dislodge him with the limbs it wasn't using to skitter backward.

Micah didn't mean to activate the collar's spell. He was just thinking about the witchlight and how he didn't want to die in darkness and then—

The ikons along the leather glowed gold, and for one fleeting second, Micah saw the will of this thing, how in a fraction of a second it would smash him to the floor, sink its venom into his body, and then go back for Dominic.

No, he told it, and with the command went all the heat in the room. His blood turned to ice, his bones were so cold they burned. The thing went rigid beneath him, the two of them locked in an impasse, and he couldn't hold, couldn't *hold*—

He needed to release the spell, but once he did he was dead, and Dominic was dead, the farmer and his family, and who knew how many after.

Micah held.

He could feel the vitality seeping from him, his life siphoned to power the spell, his body nothing but a grave in which his bones were already turning to dust—

And then he was falling backward, the broken halves of the collar coming apart in his hands. He hit the ground hard, the monster's body covering him, and he braced for the sting of teeth.

It didn't come.

The thing above him went still, and Micah didn't hesitate. He scrambled away in the split second before the creature collapsed to the floor. Above it, Dominic stood, panting, hand clasped over his wounded shoulder. Blood ran down his arm, mixing with the monster's where it dripped from the silver blade in his hand.

"Come on," he rasped. "I'll show you where I keep the first aid kit."

Micah's hands were shaky as he cut the sleeve of Dominic's shirt open. There was blood *everywhere*.

Dominic selected a foil package from the kit and tore it open with his teeth. Inside was a plastic flat pack, which he braced against his thigh until it gave off a series of cracks.

"The most important thing in here is actually the purification," he said, shaking it vigorously with his good hand. After a couple of seconds it began to glow a dull green. "It's mostly designed to avoid infection, but in this scenario, it also doubles as an antivenom. Grab some gauze, will you?"

Micah already had it, was pressing a handful to Dominic's still-bleeding shoulder. Blood was soaking through it at an alarming rate, bright red under the white fluorescent lights.

He pushed me out of the way, Micah thought. He couldn't tell if it was disbelief or exhaustion, but it echoed over and over in his mind. *He pushed me out of the way.*

He took the flat pack from Dominic and pressed it over the wound, securing it in place with medical tape.

By the time he'd wrapped the tape around Dominic's arm twice, the bleeding had stemmed.

"What do you think, doc?" Dominic asked a little weakly. "Am I gonna make it?"

Micah met his eyes and then, solemnly, shook his head once. Dominic laughed.

"How about you? If there's any broken skin anywhere, we should get you antivenom. The claws aren't venomous, but it's better to play it safe."

Micah took a quick inventory. Nothing. Not even a scratch.

Because he took the hit for you, he thought again, almost wildly. It felt like a mistake, but no.

"No antivenom, then, that's good." Dominic was lifting the gauze, trying to see the edge of the wound. It was already fading. "So. Ready to quit yet?"

Quit? The spell's residual chills were still trying to make his teeth chatter, but an even deeper cold came from the realization that if he hadn't been there, Dominic wouldn't be alive now.

With no instructions, no training, not even a plan, Micah had *saved his life.*

And Dominic thought he wanted to *quit*?

Not even close.

The Virginia Department of Fish and Wildlife showed up to collect the body.

The farmer paid in cash, four thousand for a job his insurance would never know about, and when Dominic handed Micah's share over, Micah tried to give it back. But Dominic was ready for him and dodged.

I owe you for buying me, Micah protested.

"You don't owe me for shit," Dominic answered. "I'd be dead if it weren't for you. Do you understand that? I decided to buy a contract because I knew this day was coming, and I was desperate. And Mic, I got every penny's worth today, so put that in your pocket and don't make me fight you."

Micah started to obey, then hesitated. He stared at the money. It *looked* like a lot, but . . . He did the math. The broken math that never squared because he had *no idea* what he actually needed, or how fast. And if Dominic was happy with him, this might be his best chance to ask. He got his paper. He didn't have the vocabulary to sign this.

Do you think I should take Mia up on her offer?

"Honestly?" Dominic said slowly, "I don't know. I've been thinking about it, and the guys who bought your contract, I mean, they definitely fucked up. It took me, what, like four days to figure out something was rotten in Denmark? It wasn't even that well hidden. You could have been free years ago, except that they weren't paying attention. Or didn't care. So Mia's whole 'settlement' thing seems like letting them buy their way out of trouble. Like they're above the law because they've got money."

Micah blinked. That hadn't been what he'd *meant* to ask, but. *Aren't they?*

Dominic looked at the paper a long time. "They're not supposed to be. Six months ago I would have said no. Not so sure now." He handed the notepad back. "But at the very least, you can make them *pay* for what they did. And with the kind of money Mia was talking about, you'd be pretty well set forever. Go to school, get your own place, whatever you want. So . . . I guess it's like trading your past for your future." Dominic shrugged. "You've just gotta figure out whether you want money or revenge."

Well, that clarified things. *I'm going to tell her yes, then.*

"Just like that? You sure?"

I don't need revenge.

Dom exhaled, hard, and Micah realized he'd said the wrong thing again. "You're a better man than me. I don't think I could ever forgive them."

They didn't do anything I need to forgive.

Dominic laughed incredulously. "Yeah, right. They treated you like you were a *thing*, Mic, some trophy they could buy and keep around as decoration because they felt like it."

Micah wrote his response but hesitated before handing the pad back. *You bought me too.*

Dominic was taken aback. "I *hired* you, man, there's a difference. I didn't just . . ." He searched Micah's face. Micah considered dropping it, but he had a creeping suspicion it was too late. "I bought your contract but for, like, an actual *job*. Not for like . . ." Dominic rubbed his face. "I never raped you."

Micah shrugged, hoping if he was nonchalant enough, then Dominic might understand. *Neither did they.*

"How can you even say that? Of course they did!"

Wrong tack. He was making it worse.

This time, Micah went slower, struggling to choose the words to make Dominic understand. *They didn't force me. It was my job, so I did it.*

"But you didn't choose it."

Did you choose yours?

Dominic blinked. "That's not the same. I can stop whenever I want. Nobody ever hit me with a strap because I wasn't *sitting* right."

Now it was Micah's turn to be taken aback. *That's not how it works, at all.* He wrote the next line very carefully, staring at it for several moments before handing over the pad, trying to decide whether this was something he really wanted to ask for. *Sometimes I wish you'd hold me to it.*

"You *miss* getting hit?"

Micah shook his head. This time he took longer, trying to explain in a way Dominic would understand. Dominic seemed to think that he'd spent his life in some mindless horror show, locked in a dungeon when he wasn't being tortured. Micah wasn't going to argue that his life had been *easy*, but it hadn't been the carnival of random violence that Dominic was imagining, either.

The training is based on obedience and trust. An indent is obedient because they trust their master. There are very clear expectations. I was rarely ever punished unless I deserved it.

"You never deserved it."

Micah rolled his eyes. They both knew the platitude was empty. *Of course I did. But I don't know what I deserve now. I don't know what's expected of me anymore. I don't know how to tell when I've done something wrong. I don't know how to make you happy.*

Dominic reread the words for a long time. "You're not responsible for making me happy, man. You just focus on you."

I don't know how, Micah wrote, and it twisted in his chest to admit it, because at the very least he should be able to *figure it out.*

"Well, you're gonna learn," Dominic said firmly. "I'll teach you. And if you do something wrong, I'll call you a dumbass. That's how you'll know."

Micah did one of his silent little laughs. *And if I do something right?*

"Then I'll give you a big sloppy kiss," Dominic joked, rolling his eyes.

Micah nodded. *Okay.*

Dominic's mouth opened, but apparently he didn't have a quip for that. He still didn't really *understand*, Micah knew. Maybe he couldn't. Maybe there was no way to explain the value of discipline to people who were good at being free.

But he'd done what he could. He'd told Dominic he needed directions. Whether he got them now wasn't up to him.

The knowledge felt like a weight off his shoulders.

CHAPTER NINETEEN

Micah eyed the storefront like the gates of hell.

"So here's what we do," Dominic was saying. "We're gonna go in there, and we're going to go up and down every aisle, and you pick whatever you like and put it in the cart. I'll do the same thing, but I'm going *behind* you. No cheating. And then whatever it all adds up to, we'll split it. Deal?"

You don't need to do this. I'm fine with whatever you want to get.

"I know you are. But you need to learn what *you* want."

Micah's diet, Dominic had learned, had been well-balanced but monotonous. In households with a large number of indentured staff, food preparation tended to be unspectacular and repetitive, focused more on mass production than flair.

Micah recognized prepackaged salad mixes, but he didn't know what a whole red cabbage looked like. He knew Italian and Ranch but was delighted to learn there were alternatives. He was equally excited to find that green beans could be bought fresh instead of canned. He recognized apples and oranges but not plums or grapefruit. Neither of them knew what a pomelo was.

The spice aisle held his interest for a while, but Dominic's knowledge of exotic spices began and ended with garlic salt, so he was no help there at all. He was equally useless in the foreign foods section, where they kept things like *wasabi* and *korma*. After studying the packages, Micah selected a bag of rice and some prepackaged meals with names like *satay* and *masala*.

What if they're bad? he asked.

"We'll toss 'em out and make something else. It's allowed."

Micah added them to the cart and they kept going. Micah wasn't a fan of frozen premade meals, but Dominic threw a couple of pizzas into the cart. He added a bag of chicken nuggets, and Micah raised an eyebrow.

"What? I'm a growing boy, Mic."

Micah wanted fresh chicken, and they had to get a glass pan because Dominic had never needed one before. He also learned that bread crumbs came in a cardboard tube. Then after that they had to go back to the pasta aisle to get alfredo sauce and spaghetti to go under the chicken. Dominic wouldn't let him buy Ragu. ("Sometimes you gotta splurge on the good stuff.")

By the deli there was a book rack with cookbooks, and Dominic put one of those in the cart too. He'd been living on the same five meals for the last year, and that was fine when it was just him, but he wasn't gonna do that to Micah.

They got distracted in the checkout line because Dominic wanted a PayDay and Micah didn't know what that was, prompting Dominic to investigate. Turned out Micah didn't remember Twix, either, or Snickers or Milky Way or just about anything else. Dominic ended up buying one of everything Micah didn't recognize.

"Having a favorite candy bar is an essential factor in developing an identity," he announced when the cashier smirked at them. Micah looked skeptical, but what did he know?

Micah was not as excited about his candy bar initiation as Dominic would have hoped. He googled a recipe for chicken alfredo while Dominic put the groceries away, and then he got to work slicing the chicken into thin strips. Dominic started a pot of water for the spaghetti, and then got out the candy bars, peeling back the wrappers and carefully cutting off bite-sized pieces. Micah wasn't even paying attention, which Dominic couldn't understand. If he were raring to learn about the varied bounty of the Mars corporation, he'd be riveted.

"I think the Snickers is a good solid place to start," Dominic announced, picking up a piece of the candy and holding it out to Micah. Micah grinned at him and shrugged, gesturing uselessly with his sticky hands.

"You're not getting out of this that easy—open up."

Micah did, giving every indication of nonchalance until Dominic reached forward with the candy, and then Micah leaned in, catching the tips of Dominic's fingers in his mouth. His eyes flicked upward, and he smirked. His mouth was hot and soft, sucking the chocolate off Dominic's fingers.

And then he went back to cutting up the chicken like he hadn't just treated Dominic to a porno-level come-on.

Dominic sat back, dumbfounded. "How is it?"

Micah chewed slowly, mulling over the taste. He shrugged.

"Want another one?"

That got Micah to grin.

"So, for all your later gargantuan-ness, you were a surprisingly small baby," Dominic said, waving a letter in Micah's direction. "Congratulations, partner, you're one step closer to being a real boy."

Micah snatched the paper, scanning the contents. It wasn't really that impressive: just an authorized copy of a birth certificate. It had Micah's parents' names, some illegible signatures, half a dozen stamps, and information about how big Micah had been. Or how small, as the case may be.

Micah was staring at it like it was the word of God.

"I've got a fireproof box in the closet. When you're done ogling it, you can keep it in there."

Micah grinned up at him. *I've never seen this.*

"Well, your dad didn't really seem the type to keep stuff like that around."

Micah's expression turned dark. The topic of his father was one they'd been avoiding, with some success, ever since Ian had called to say he'd been delivered to Slate.

"Mia's supposed to be coming by today, right?" Dominic asked.

Micah nodded.

Micah and Mia had been communicating through email, but there were things she insisted on doing in person, so they'd arranged a meeting.

Her voice matched her appearance perfectly. She pulled up the drive in a sleek black vehicle that looked like it had never driven on anything but clean asphalt. She stepped out of the car and surveyed the yard with an eyebrow raise that Dominic could practically *hear*. She was dressed in neat business attire: light ruffled shirt over a black pencil skirt, paired with the kind of makeup and glasses Dominic associated with naughty librarians in porn. As she made her way across the driveway, Dominic noted that her black heels were at least three inches high. And shiny. He grinned.

He opened the door before she could knock, and she walked in before he could invite her. She was carrying a heavy black briefcase, which she set on the kitchen table and opened with a *snap*.

She looked up at the two men, her attention switching between them.

"Which of you is Micah?"

Micah raised a hand, hesitantly, like he thought maybe he was going to get in trouble.

"Right. You're with me, then. Over here." She gestured to the other seat and began pulling stacks of paper out of the case. Dominic noted that she'd brought her own pens, sleek black things that probably had to be special ordered from Paris.

"So according to what I've found, you've actually had eleven separate holders, not counting the originals and your most recent. The authorities in Selina are already pursuing criminal charges against those two, so for our purposes they're out of reach. The others, though, have so far managed to avoid being entangled in this mess. My bet is that they will pay handsomely to keep it that way."

Mia pushed a stack of paper toward Micah. "Here you are, then. This is your agreement to never seek criminal or civil restitution against the holder named, in exchange for a substantial remuneration offered for services performed. This remuneration alters the contract between the two of you into one of mutual benefit, rendering null any future accusations of improper actions vis-à-vis the unfortunate circumstances of your, shall we say, *subjugation*. In addition, you agree not to speak publicly about actions taken while under their employ, up to and including actions which may violate local, state, or federal laws." Mia gave him a thin smile. "Barring legal compulsion, of course."

Micah nodded and wrote something down.

"Backtrack for the morons in the room?" Dominic interjected.

Mia peered over her glasses at him. "Micah agrees to reframe the relationship with his clients as one of employment rather than indenturement. His previous holders render appropriate back pay, and in exchange, Micah agrees not to drag their reputations through the mud. I'm assuming some of the details of his experiences are rather sordid."

"And you get a cut of that back pay."

"In exchange for negotiating the appropriate fees for Micah's caliber of service, naturally." Mia's smile was distressingly perfect.

Micah tapped the notebook with his pen, drawing Mia's attention back to him. Her eyes widened marginally as she read.

"My, my, we have done our homework, haven't we?"

Micah nodded.

"As noted, these are eleven distinct cases. I'm proposing a sliding percentage based on the number I'm able to win. It's quite standard for this sort of case. I'll also be negotiating payment plans and setting up escrow accounts. You know, the standard rider services."

Micah started writing again.

It took them four hours to go through Mia's ream of contracts. Dominic lost the thread of the conversation about ten minutes in, both because he was missing Micah's half and because he had no idea what Mia was saying. He tried googling phrases he was able to catch, but the legal terminology led him down rabbit holes of Wikipedia links that got very deep, very fast.

What did interest him was how many links were already purple.

He knew Micah had been spending time on the laptop, but he'd assumed he'd been doing normal internet stuff, like reading news or looking at pictures of cats.

He opened the search history and scrolled through. And scrolled, and scrolled, and scrolled.

Mia wasn't kidding. Micah *had* been doing his homework.

Contract law, indenturement law, employment types, labor laws, tort types, wage guidelines, court records . . . Micah had been reading into all of it. And now he and Mia were working through about a billion contingencies and, by the sounds of it, Micah was holding his own.

Dominic was impressed.

He clicked through onto a page of court cases regarding freed indents, and was in over his head before he even got through the third paragraph. One thing was for sure, though: There was money at stake here. A lot of it.

He was spared the indignity of the remainder by the sound of his phone buzzing. The caller ID said Ian. He ducked into his room before answering. "Yeah?"

"Hey, Dom. Is Micah around?"

"Yeah. He and Mia are in the kitchen discussing terms." Dominic dropped his voice. "Ian, that woman is terrifying."

Ian laughed. "It works to her benefit, in her line of work. She's not an enemy I'd want to have."

"Well, hopefully it works out for Micah. What's new on your side, anything?"

The mirth dropped out of Ian's voice. "Can you bring him in tomorrow?"

Dominic's blood ran cold. He'd gotten Micah home; he wasn't giving him up again. Not without a fight. "Why?"

"We have someone here who wants to see him."

"Who is it, Ian." His voice had an edge of steel.

Ian sighed. "We got Slate's financial records, and we've pinned down the doctor he was using to have his slaves altered."

Slaves. The word caught like a fish hook. If Dominic had heard it the day before he'd met Micah, he might have assumed it was political rhetoric. Not anymore.

"We've pulled him in and charged him," Ian was saying, "and he's agreed to cooperate with us, but not until he's seen Micah."

"Why Micah?"

"As far as we can tell, Micah is the only, uh, *patient* that we can directly connect to him. The others have all been transferred or are otherwise out of our reach."

"Which doesn't explain why the doc wants to see him."

"That I can't explain. All I can say is, he's clammed up tight and won't tell us anything else until he sees Micah. So can you bring him in?"

Dominic cracked the door, making sure Micah and Mia were still seated at the kitchen table. "I'll ask him if he'll go. I'm not promising anything. I'm not his holder anymore; if he doesn't want to talk to this quack, he doesn't have to."

"I know that, Dom."

Dominic sighed. "Sorry, Ian. I don't mean to take it out on you. It's just . . . there's a lot of shit happening. He's, uh . . . I don't know if he's gonna be okay."

"He's in good hands."

Dominic scoffed. Like those hands weren't the problem.

He hung up the phone and made himself scarce, heading back to the bedroom under the pretense of sorting laundry. By the time he worked up the nerve to brave the living room again, Mia was gone.

Micah had retreated to his place on the couch, taking the laptop with him. More Wikipedia, by the looks of it.

Dominic gestured to the lake of purple links. "You read all that stuff? Like in the last week?"

Micah nodded.

"And it made sense to you?"

Micah nodded again.

Dominic collapsed onto the other side of the couch. "Tell you what, you're a lot smarter than me. You're way too smart to stay an exterminator. You should go to school and be, like, a doctor or president or something."

Micah smiled, just a little smirk, but there was a twinge of sadness in it.

Dominic didn't say anything further.

"So tomorrow, I'm thinking we should go back to Selina."

It was late, and dark, because Micah couldn't talk in the dark and Dominic was a coward.

He'd been lying there long enough for his eyes to adjust, and even still, all he could see was a vague outline of Micah's body next to him.

"We should still see about getting you a social security card. And, uh, Ian called today."

Micah didn't respond, because of course he didn't, because he couldn't.

"They've got the doctor. The one who, uh, who worked on you. On your voice. And he wants to see you. Says he'll cooperate with the police if he can talk with you. You don't have to. But think about it? Ian thinks it would be helpful. If he . . . helped. I guess."

Micah didn't react, not for a long time, and Dominic wondered if he'd fallen asleep. "You awake?"

Micah shuddered, and Dominic reached for him. His fingertips brushed the edge of Micah's shoulder, and Micah curled in on himself. His whole body was tense.

Dominic pulled his hand back. "Hey, hey, you don't have to go. You don't have to. It's fine. You don't have to."

And in that moment, Dominic felt nothing but his hate for the man who'd done this. The man who'd left Micah shaking and terrified and unable to even ask for help.

He didn't know how to fix this. He wanted to reach for Micah, to hold him close and tell him he was safe, but he couldn't predict how Micah would react and he didn't want to make it worse.

"I'm here," he said finally, uselessly. "And I'll be there, tomorrow. If you want me to be."

Eventually Micah relaxed. His breathing evened out, and finally slowed into sleep.

Dominic listened for a long time.

Dominic woke up late, morning sun already streaming in from the hallway. Micah was gone, and his half of the bed was cold.

Dominic wasn't surprised to find the other man up and dressed, sitting cross-legged on the corner of the couch with the computer on his lap. His hair was wet, which meant he'd been up long enough to go for his run and take a shower.

Dominic's phone buzzed.

When he picked it up, he saw one new text message. The caller ID was listed as Micah's email address. The message read simply, *Good morning.*

Dominic grinned at Micah. "Aren't you clever?"

Micah gave him a thumbs-up, then went back to typing. Dominic's phone buzzed again.

I'll go.

Micah was much faster with a keyboard than he was with a pen or his limited ASL, and Dominic's phone buzzed all morning as Micah fired off message after message. Micah had always seemed like the strong, stoic type, but apparently that had more to do with the difficulty of communication than any part of Micah's personality. So far this morning they'd discussed Mia's visit, the weather, what to have for breakfast, what route to take to Selina, and a dozen other topics all carefully unrelated to Micah's upcoming meeting.

"What did you do outside?" Dominic asked when the conversation lulled. "That day when you came back all muddy."

Micah grinned and attacked the keyboard.

Bzzz.

I built a dam.

Bzzz.

There's a stream out back and there was a place where the water was all caught up behind some debris. I cleared it out and the pool drained and the water carved all kinds of new pathways, downstream.

Bzzz.

And it was interesting the way the sudden flood of water did all kinds of unpredictable things, so I built a better dam, upstream.

Bzzz.

It was really big. I think the water got to be about two feet deep and I had to move some rocks to make a C shape because the water kept escaping around the sides of the dam.

Bzzz.

And finally I couldn't keep it together anymore so I just pushed the whole thing over and let the water escape all at once. And I followed it down the hill to see what it would do.

Dominic read the slew of messages with a little grin. He knew exactly the creek Micah was talking about, and he'd built a fair share of dams himself there over the years. Not recently, though. The last time he'd played in a creek he'd been about twelve.

Sixteen years. How time flies.

They were in the car by the time it occurred to Dominic to call Ian and tell him they were coming. But Ian already knew. Apparently Dominic wasn't the only one getting text messages this morning.

He'd gotten so used to the buzzing that the car seemed unusually quiet. The laptop needed wi-fi to send messages, and Dominic couldn't read them while he was driving anyway. So the conversation halted and they made do with Barenaked Ladies's "Play the Game."

Dominic made a mental note to check for wi-fi when they stopped for lunch. He liked talking to Micah. He liked that Micah's messages were getting longer. He didn't know if it was the ease of typing, or some change happening inside Micah, but Micah was getting more descriptive. Less formal. Less apologetic.

"You know, we should get you a tablet," Dominic remarked after a while. "They connect to the cell network so you can send messages anywhere there's cell service. And the keyboard's pretty big, so it'll be easier to type than with a phone."

Micah was smiling—a real one, not tinged with sadness or cynicism—and suddenly Dominic wanted to grab his face and kiss him.

In the name of not driving off the road, he resisted.

They got to Selina too early to even pretend either of them was hungry, so they ended up in front of the police station before they went anywhere else.

"We don't have to go to see Ian yet," Dominic said after a minute passed and Micah had made no move to get out of the car. "The federal building is right over there. We can go spend a couple riveting hours trying to prove your identity to the government."

Micah smirked, rolling his eyes, and reached for the door handle.

He didn't walk toward the federal building. He walked toward the police station.

Dominic shoved his hands into his pockets.

Time to face the demons.

The interrogation room was exactly like every interrogation room Dominic had ever pictured. The guy sitting at the table, not so much.

Dominic had envisioned the doctor as a young professional, sleek, calculating, sarcastic. You know. Evil. The kind of person who would stroke his goatee while negotiating his fees for building clones.

Doctor William Godfrey came off more like somebody who would misplace his stethoscope and then give you a lollipop to take home even though you were pushing thirty.

"He wanted me to take the tongue out," Godfrey was saying to Ian. "The whole tongue. Do you have any idea the kind of recovery time that takes?"

Micah looked like he wanted to deck the man in the face and then throw up. Dominic felt like he shouldn't be here. Once again, the worst shadows of Micah's life were getting dragged into the light, and *none* of it was Dom's business.

He stepped back, silently moving toward the door. Micah's hand shot out, taking ahold of his sleeve. Dominic froze. Micah glanced over, like he was surprised to see what his hand had done. He let go like he'd been burned.

"You want me to stay?" Dom asked.

Micah barely hesitated before nodding.

So here he was. Face-to-face with a monster who acted way too much like somebody's uncle. Some sick bastard who was still telling Ian the finer points of tongue-removal.

Dom shoved his hands into his pockets and resolved to be civil.

Micah swallowed, suddenly far too aware of the feeling of the tongue stud against the roof of his mouth. He had no trouble believing that Slate would have ordered such a thing.

"It takes *months* to learn to eat properly," Godfrey was saying. "Those muscles are all interconnected, and they go all the way down the throat. Ideally, you'd have to feed the patient with a tube, and even then the chances of infection are *massive*."

Ian was not impressed. "Your point?"

"Other than talking Slate out of that procedure *more than once*? Stroke of genius on my part, seriously. I mean, who wants a sex slave without a tongue? Reduces their usefulness significantly, as I'm sure you can imagine."

"You're a paragon of altruism," Ian growled before Micah could nod. "Is there a point you're arriving at?"

The doctor scowled, fixing his gaze on Micah. "The *point* is, I've had nothing but *your* very best interests in mind this whole time."

Micah hadn't even begun to express his doubt before Dominic beat him to it. "Yeah, you did great, you didn't hurt him as bad as you *could* have. And so this is, what, an apology?"

The doctor pinned Dominic with a level stare. "You have no idea the money my customers pay to make this happen. It's illegal, I know that. But if I hadn't done it, someone else would have, and Micah was much better off in my hands than in theirs."

"Tell it to the devil and he'll put you in a smaller fire," Dominic snapped.

"You know, I'm thinking I'll change my mind about this whole 'cooperation' thing if that's how you're going to treat me."

Micah leaped over the table, pulled Godfrey up by his lapels, and slammed him into the far wall. Air tore through his throat as he screamed, but of course no sound came out. Thanks to the man in front of him, nothing ever would. He slammed Godfrey into the wall again.

"Stop it, Micah," Ian said, but there was no anger in his voice. It occurred to Micah to wonder how far Ian would go to hinder him, if he decided to inflict an injury onto the doctor.

His face was an inch from Godfrey's, and it was impossible not to realize how much of an upper hand he had now, how easy it would be to turn the tables, how *quickly* he could—

"Please put me down," the doctor squeaked.

Micah dropped him. He didn't want to test Ian's limits just yet. He stalked back across the room, kicking the table as he passed.

Dominic was eyeing him warily, but Micah didn't look back.

"You can't cough, can you?" the doctor asked after he'd regained his feet. "I mean, you can, but it's silent, right?"

Micah shrugged.

"So?" Dominic translated.

"So I'm guessing none of you went to medical school and so you don't know how *wrong* that is. Through all of this, did any of you crack a book to try to figure out what I *did*?"

"You sliced him open and took his voice away," Dom snapped. "Who cares how you did it?"

"Well, apparently no one, which is why I wanted him *here* for this." The doctor made a *come here* gesture at Micah, who did no such thing. "Fine. Pout. Do me a favor, though. Say 'check please.'"

Micah glanced to Dominic, then did as he was asked. As he expected, there was nothing.

The doctor grinned at them like he'd finished proving something very important. When all he got was blank stares, he rolled his eyes. "Say it again. And officer, put your hand on his throat when he does it."

Micah pulled away so fast he would've knocked the table over if it weren't bolted to the floor. Ian raised his hands, as if in surrender. The doctor rolled his eyes.

"Oh my *god*, you slaves are twitchy. Look, it's an important demonstration that's going to knock years off my sentence, so suck it up and do it."

Micah looked to Ian, then Dominic. They hadn't let him bring the laptop in, or any phones, so he picked up his notepad.

Why?

"Because it's the fastest way to prove what I'm trying to tell you."

Micah was frozen. In the back of his mind, the little voice hissed that he was *ignoring an order*, a direct order, and not a difficult one, all he had to do was lift his chin and let Ian touch him. He shoved it down and mustered his courage, writing out a new line.

Can Dominic do it?

The doctor shrugged. "Sure, whoever, I don't care."

Micah met Dominic's eyes and then raised his chin, baring his throat.

Dominic hesitated before reaching out and gingerly taking hold. His hand was warm and not as rough as Micah expected.

"You might have to squeeze a little harder to make it work," Godfrey said, and Micah felt Dominic hesitate. Micah set his jaw, giving him a little nod. Fractionally, Dominic tightened his grip. He was miles from anything that would cause discomfort, let alone harm, and his caution made something warm bloom in Micah's chest.

Dominic glared at the doctor. "What am I supposed to be feeling?"

"Micah, say something. Anything."

Micah murmured words that no one would hear, feeling them against the pressure of Dominic's hand.

"See what I mean?" Godfrey exclaimed.

Dominic dropped his hand. "You have five seconds to stop being cryptic, and then I'm gonna hit you till you puke."

"I'm surrounded by morons," Godfrey lamented, rubbing his eyes. "I told Slate I'd burn out his vocal cords, and if I had done that, he would be *hoarse*. His voice isn't muted, it's *gone*."

"And that's *better*?" Dominic demanded.

"Yes!" the doctor said, looking over Dominic's shoulder at Micah. "Cluck your tongue. Whistle. Make a 't' sound. Or a 'k.' Or an 'f.' You can't."

Micah was thinking he might need to introduce the doctor to the wall again, and he didn't get the idea that Dominic would try to stop him.

"So?" Ian asked, before either of them could move. "All you've done is prove the extent of what you did to him. Congratulations, you're the scum of the earth, are you done taunting him now?"

"You aren't paying *attention*," the doctor said. "Do you know how to whistle? You blow air past your lips. All there is to it. So explain to me, please, what I did to his *throat* that interferes with his *lips*." The doctor rounded on Dominic. "When he was talking. You felt it in his throat, right?"

"Yeah? So?"

"*So*, humans vocalize by making vibrations in their vocal cords. The vibrations create sound waves. It's not magic. *So*, if the vibration is there, then *where is the sound*?"

Micah flipped his notepad up to face the doctor. *What did you do?*

"And there's the million dollar question!" Godfrey leaned back in his chair, crossing his legs. "I didn't take your tongue, and I didn't take your vocal cords, so why can't you talk?" The doctor was grinning. "It's a sigil. That's all. Simple little silencing sigil incised on the back of your throat. You're quiet, Slate's happy, and best of all, it's totally reversible in the event that it ever gets back to me. See? Not a monster after all. Told you I was looking out for you."

Micah collapsed into the chair. A sigil. Not a horrific mutilation beyond the help of magic or medicine, just . . . one more little scar.

Godfrey cackled.

To no one's surprise, Micah was unwilling to let Godfrey do the reversal. Not that he could have, anyway; Ian was one hundred percent certain that Godfrey was going to lose his medical license.

After Micah left, Godfrey sang like a canary, giving up the names of dozens of holders who had come to him for his alteration services.

Verification of Godfrey's story required photography a little beyond Ronnie's abilities, which is how Dominic ended up in the waiting room of an ENT while Micah got a camera stuck down his throat.

Micah might have wanted him there for that. He wasn't sure. Ian had called in a favor with the doc, and Dominic had agreed to drive Micah over. Then a nurse had come out and called Micah's name (Micah Sawyer, his full name, which caused a number of confused looks from patients who had noticed his barcode), and Micah had gone alone. Just before the door closed, he'd turned back toward Dominic, eyes wide, but then he was gone and Dominic was left . . . waiting.

It took a long time, longer than he thought it should take to snap a couple of pictures, and then the nurse was back. Without Micah. Her face was pinched, like she'd tasted something bad.

"He's asking for you."

CHAPTER TWENTY

The office had a white board, which Micah had co-opted for his own purposes.

TAKE IT OFF.

The doctor raised his hands placatingly. "Mr. Sawyer, I understand this is frustrating for you—"

Micah almost hurled the marker across the room, but fortunately the nurse returned with Dominic just in time to stop the doctor from blabbing about what he *did not at all understand.*

Dominic took in the room, and Micah slapped the whiteboard to get him up to speed. Dominic nodded. "Gonna need some more details, there, buddy."

Micah rolled his eyes, then turned to scribble wet black letters on the board. *They can break the sigil, but they're saying not for weeks.*

"We'll need to put you under anesthesia," the doctor explained. "Which means an operating room, and they're booked. We can try to refer you to our witch, remove the scar magically, but we'd need to do some blood tests to make sure there wouldn't be a reaction to the tincture."

Micah wiped his hand across the board, making room. *So don't put me out.*

The doctor set his jaw. "Mr. Sawyer, I don't think you understand quite how painful this sort of thing can be."

Micah stared at the doctor for a moment, ice in his eyes, and then he pulled his shirt over his head and turned back to the whiteboard.

The marks from the whip were healing well, but Micah knew they still stood out in bright straight lines on his skin.

The doctor coughed a little, as if not sure what to do with this new information.

Micah sighed. *I can handle the pain. I just want to talk again.*

He turned to Dominic for support, begging him to back Micah up. The medical team had seen his barcode. They knew what it meant. They weren't going to take his word on anything, no matter what Ian had said. They'd look to Dominic to make Micah's decisions, and Micah knew it. He stared at Dominic, willing the other man to meet his eyes.

Dominic addressed the doctor. "Don't you have a sorcerer on staff? Someone who can take curses off people?"

"This isn't a curse," the doctor insisted, speaking only to Dominic now. "It's a glyph carved directly into his flesh. We have a sorcery student, but she's going to tell you the same thing I am."

"Let me see the sigil," Dominic said after a pause.

Micah's shoulders dropped.

The nurse brought Dominic a printout of the photo they'd taken. It showed a white, twisted scar wiggling across the pink, wet flesh of Micah's throat.

"That's all? How big is it?"

"About two inches wide. On the back of the throat, low enough to be hidden. We think it was burned in. The tissue damage to the surrounding area is minimal, and the scar itself is shallow but clear."

"It would have to be," Dominic remarked. "If the sigil is altered, it won't work. In theory, all you'd need to do is nick any of these white lines, and it would break the sigil."

Micah turned hopefully to the doctor. One cut, less than an inch long? That was *nothing*.

"It's not a matter of ease," the doctor protested. "I can't just start cutting into people and hope it'll go fine. I need a paralytic agent and some painkillers. If your indent flinches with a scalpel down his throat, I could end up causing more problems than I solve."

Micah started to protest that he *could* hold still, but Dominic was ahead of him. "He won't flinch. And he's not mine. He's a free man and he wants his voice back."

"I respect that, but I can't do it."

Dominic rubbed his temples. Micah's stomach dropped as he realized Dominic was giving up. "Fine. How soon can we come back?"

"You'll have to talk to the woman at the desk about that. At least a week, though."

A week. Another week of silence. Micah swallowed hard, feeling the sore lump the camera had left. A week wasn't that long. He could handle it.

It had been months. He hadn't spoken in *months*.

The notepad and the laptop and the ASL were helping, but they were recent. Before that, at Slate's, he'd had nothing. And he'd handled that just fine.

He could do another week.

Micah glanced up at the doctor, at Dominic and the nurse, and nodded. He tried to smile and failed, miserably.

Can I have a minute?

"Sure," Dominic said.

The doctor patted Micah's arm condescendingly. "Take as long as you need."

Micah nodded, keeping his eyes respectfully low.

And then they left him alone.

Micah turned his attention to the far wall, the desk with its row of drawers. The doctor had opened the far one to get the marker, and Micah had seen the baskets of supplies inside. Cotton balls, Q-tips, empty syringes, and there, in the back, scalpels.

Micah put his shirt back on, expecting that this would end quickly and he might not be able to grab it later. He hesitated as he reached for the drawer. This was direct disobedience. He was going to get in trouble for this. Maybe a lot.

He didn't care. He wanted to talk.

It was just another week, but he couldn't do another week.

The drawer slid open, and there they were, right where he'd thought. A set of four, each wrapped in sterile plastic. It was really going to be that simple.

The camera hadn't gone too deep. It would be easy to feel when the blade reached the same place—but he had to do it now, before they decided he'd had enough time to cope.

Body relaxed, eyes closed, Micah slid the blade along the back of his tongue. He didn't gag, just like he'd known he wouldn't. And then he pushed, unflinching, and a line of fire opened inside him. He withdrew the scalpel and coughed. Blood dripped down his throat and it was *weird* and he tried to swallow, which lit up the line of fire again.

He groaned.

And then he laughed. It hurt, but he didn't care because he could *hear* it.

The scalpel dropped into the sink, and he spat a mouthful of blood onto the stainless steel next to it. He could hear himself panting.

It hurt a *lot*.

He laughed again.

It was that easy. All this time, it was that easy.

The laughter wouldn't stop. He'd forgotten what it sounded like, couldn't remember the last time he'd laughed—not faking it, not being polite, but because he was *happy*.

There was a knock at the door, but Micah couldn't stop laughing long enough to answer. He spat into the sink again, then sank to the floor. There was a stitch in his side and he couldn't breathe.

The door opened and Dominic stood there frowning, and his confusion sobered Micah somewhat. He stopped laughing and caught his breath.

"Do I have blood on my face?" he asked, and Dominic's shocked expression was enough to set him off all over again.

To make a long story short, the doctor asked them not to come back. Apparently that was what happened when you slit your own throat in someone's office.

Micah giggled again. Dominic was starting to give him weird looks, but he didn't care. *So* many things were funny today.

His throat hurt, a lot actually, but the doc had determined that the cut was superficial. Micah, to his credit, did not say *I told you so*, even though he was now completely capable of it.

They sent him away with an antiseptic gargle and little bottle of painkillers, which served the dual purpose of lessening the ache in his throat and making everything funnier.

He and Dominic were planning to go to the social security office, but by the time they got outside, Dominic had decided it was probably best to head home.

Micah was okay with that. He'd probably be okay going to the social security office too. Actually, he was up for going just about anywhere.

And he could. He could go wherever he wanted.

He waited for the mantle of terror that usually settled in with that realization. It didn't come . . . but it wasn't gone. It was still right there at the back of his mind, waiting for him to slip up.

He glanced over at Dominic. Dominic was playing an imaginary drum solo on the steering wheel, but Micah wasn't fooled. He saw the nervous side-eye Dominic was giving him. He had to do something about that.

It might be time to suck it up and tell Dominic he wanted to fuck.

He'd have to do it eventually. Dominic was new to this and it made him patient, but Micah wasn't stupid enough to believe he'd wait forever, especially if Micah kept earning the wariness Dominic had now. Dominic could hire any indent to help him work; if Micah wanted to keep his place, he needed to be *more*. And it would be worth it, if it meant not being cast out into the world alone.

It certainly wouldn't be the worst thing he'd done to keep himself safe.

The truth was, Micah liked Dominic. He liked the calm assurance with which Dominic navigated his world. He liked the way Dominic sprawled out in his sleep. He liked the way Dominic had breakfast cereal for dinner sometimes, because meal schedules weren't a thing that existed for free men. He liked the way Dominic would get distracted in the middle of a task and just go *do something else* because if the task wasn't done, Dominic had no one to answer to but Dominic. He liked that Dominic picked his own jobs and got in his own car and went wherever he wanted. Dominic lived a life completely free of the fear that paralyzed every one of Micah's own thoughts. Dominic could have that, because he was *good* at it.

Micah knew that following Dominic around was cheating, a way of pirating secondhand freedom, but he didn't care. It was close enough for him, and he wanted every second he could scavenge.

"Earth to Micah. Earth to Micah. Anyone home?"

Micah snapped out of it. "What?" His voice was raspy and harsh, from disuse as much as his recent adventure with the scalpel.

"I wanna get some grub before we get out of town. What do you want?"

"You know I'm fine with whatever you pick."

"Yeah, I know you are. Think about it, though. Do you have a preference?"

Micah thought for a moment and concluded that he did not. Another time, he might have lied and chosen something, because Dominic liked to think he was making progress. Right now, though, his throat was throbbing and the painkillers were making him sick, and he honestly wanted nothing to do with food. He shook his head.

Dominic picked the closest fast-food joint, and they ate drive-thru in the front seat of the car. Dominic got a chicken sandwich. Micah got a chocolate frosty and, because Dominic insisted, french fries.

"Ice cream is not a meal. You need a vegetable."

"I just want something cold," Micah explained.

After a minute, Dominic said, "It's so weird to hear you talking."

Micah froze. "I can be quiet again if you want."

Dominic winced. "Not how I meant it. It's weird, not bad. Don't be quiet. I like hearing you talk."

"Wait till I start singing."

Dominic laughed out loud. Dominic laughed with his whole body, and Micah was glad to be the cause of it. He mashed a fry into his ice cream, then swallowed it whole. Something outside caught his attention.

"I thought of something I want to do."

"Finally," Dominic said, tension gone for the first time since they'd gotten into the car. "Name it."

Micah inclined his head toward a neon sign across the street. "I want to get a tattoo."

Dominic nodded. "Let's do it."

As it turned out, they wouldn't do a tattoo without some kind of ID, but the artist was happy to talk about the design he wanted.

Her name was Alex, and she could draw like nobody's business.

She hesitated when Micah told her he wanted his barcode covered up. Her eyes flicked to Dominic, who nodded his approval. "His contract's not mine."

"Whose is it?"

"Mine," Micah said.

She turned back to him. "Shift over, then? That's cool, never seen that before. So, any ideas?"

"I want it covered. Totally. And the number too."

"It's pretty big. To have it covered up you're probably looking at almost a half-sleeve."

"That's fine. As long as it doesn't look like a code."

She took his arm in her hands, turning it back and forth to see the way the ink moved with the skin. Micah let her do it. He was used to being looked at this way: Practically. With intent.

"What about trees?" He gestured across the thick lines of the barcode. "Birch trees. Change the lines to be the edges of the trunks, use the white space to add knots and cracks in the bark. And then use cross-branches to break up the parallels."

Alex released his arm. "It could work. I can do some drawings and get back to you. Do you mind if I take a photo?"

Micah shook his head. Of course he didn't mind.

He realized this was the second time he'd been asked for permission. He'd been photographed a ton of times, but normally they just told him how to stand and where to look.

"Not surprised you want it off," Alex said, snapping a photo with her phone. "People come in wanting 'em sometimes. I don't do them, personally; they usually end up causing too much trouble and the client regrets it. Yours looks good, at least. Who'd you get to do it?"

"I don't know. My holder had it done when I was sixteen."

Alex blinked at him. "You can't have a holder when you're sixteen."

"No one told him."

Alex stared at him incredulously for a second, then started laughing. "Dude, that is *fucked*! That blows, really. Don't worry. I'll get you taken care of."

He met her gaze, looking right into the violet of her eyes, and grinned.

CHAPTER TWENTY-ONE

"You can just get it removed, you know," Dominic said. "That's what most people do. You don't have to cover it up with another tattoo."

Micah looked up from the laptop, where he'd been chatting with Mia about her first two cases. They were going well. The first holder had put their attorney in charge of the suit, and it was now a matter of agreeing on a number. The second holder was dealing with Mia himself, trying to bully her into dropping the suit and walking away. Micah remembered that holder. He liked to have Micah fuck his wife while he hid in the closet and watched.

Mia found this extremely amusing.

"There's, like, lasers or whatever," Dominic carried on. "That'll take it off. Or you can probably get it magicked off."

Micah frowned. "I'd rather cover it. There's no point pretending it was never there. I'd rather change it into something I actually like."

Dominic let out a little laugh. "That's fuckin' deep. Did you just think of that?"

Micah shrugged. "I guess. I just want to get rid of the barcode. I don't like how people look at it."

"What, like how people keep thinking your contract belongs to me?"

Micah shook his head. "No, not exactly. As long as it's there, I'll have people turning to you to double-check my decisions. It's too easy. I have to be able to stand on my own."

Dominic didn't say anything. Micah dropped his gaze. "Sorry. I shouldn't put that on you. It's not your problem."

"No, it's just, I've never thought of it like that." Dominic chewed his lip. "I used to rely on my dad. He taught me everything I know. Half the stuff I learned, I did just to try to impress him. Make him proud, you know? We worked together my whole life, and the whole time, I was trying to convince him that he could depend on me."

Micah searched his face. It occurred to him that he didn't know anything about Dominic's father. "What happened?"

Dominic paused for a moment. "Cancer. He kept getting headaches, but we got beat to shit so often he figured it was nothing. Wouldn't go to the doctor, you know? Then one day he passed out in the middle of breakfast, and they did an MRI and hey, brain tumor. He died about two months later. Forty-nine years old. Just like that." Dominic ran a hand through his hair. "So I guess I know what it's like to suddenly be stuck with your own decisions."

Micah almost reached out but thought better of it. "You're doing a good job. From what I've seen, you've got your life very well managed."

Dom's laugh had a touch of cynicism. "I guess. I just kept doing everything that I'd *been* doing, you know, before. There were things Dad did that I took for granted, but I learned to do them myself. Except it's more dangerous to do them on my own. I can't be two pairs of eyes, no matter how hard I try." He sighed. "Honestly? I don't know what I'm gonna do when you leave."

Micah dropped his gaze to the floor. He'd been trying not to mention it. "I don't know either."

"Well yeah, no, I know. But, dude, you're friggin' *smart*, the way you've been going through my books so fast, and then the way you learned all that legal shit Mia was talking about? Nah, man, leave creature control to the meatheads like me. You can do whatever you want. Especially once Mia gets you the money. You're gonna be great, man."

Micah kept his eyes on the laptop, willing his body to stay relaxed despite the fear. Dominic didn't think he should stay. Dominic wanted him to go do something else. And he said it so casually, like he didn't realize that Micah could barely even get through a single day on his own. He wore the clothes that Dominic had picked out for him, and sat on the couch where Dominic gestured, and went to the places that Dominic took him in the car that Dominic drove. The one decision he'd made on his own was to *attack* somebody, and only then because he was pretty sure it was what Dominic had wanted.

Maybe he should just *keep* the goddamn barcode.

"Can you teach me to drive?" he asked.

Dominic nodded. "Sure. Once you're off the painkillers, yeah? No offense, but I'm kinda fond of my car."

"Thank you."

"Hey, no big deal."

Micah wanted to protest and say that it *was* a big deal, and that *everything* Dominic had done for him was a big deal. He wanted to tell Dominic how much he *had* done and what it meant, but even with his voice back, the words weren't there.

Living with Dominic was educational in a number of ways. For instance: the various circumstances that called for celebratory pie.

Garrett messaged Dominic about some kind of forest spirit picking off hikers in West Virginia. After a couple days of investigating, they concluded that the spirit was a holdover from a clear-cut operation that had gone down back in the seventies. The company had been responsible and replanted, but that kind of disruption, Dominic explained, left a scar on the energy of a place.

In this case, the forest had developed a sort of immune reaction, viciously rejecting any humans who ventured too far from the paths. It hadn't been much of a problem until a nearby university had begun creating a new set of walking paths straight through the area. The school had gotten enough witches together for a wide-scale healing of the forest's energy, but they couldn't start until it was safe to travel through the forest. So Dominic and Micah headed off into the woods.

There was nothing to do but wait for the thing to take the bait. They passed the time holed up in an abandoned logging cabin, sitting on the rickety porch furniture and playing twenty questions until it showed up. Dominic took point and it managed to throw him to the ground twice before Micah tackled it into a containment circle.

Vanquished forest spirit called for lemon meringue, which they got from a diner boasting "mile high" pies. Micah liked that Dominic had a mental roadmap of these sorts of places.

His world was so *big.*

When Micah got a social security card and a photo ID and a bank account, those meant cherry pie, sweet and flaky. They bought slices from a bakery and ate them with plastic forks, sitting on the curb and watching people pass.

"You're a real boy now, Pinocchio," Dominic said, leveling a fork at him. "You want to go to Disneyland?"

Micah shrugged.

"Yeah, Florida sucks," Dominic agreed, going back to his pie. "All they've got down there is seafood and alligators. They say they've got swamp creatures, but they're lying. *Every* time, it's an alligator."

"You can't take down an alligator?"

"Of course I can, that's not the point."

Dominic went off on a tangent about specialization and the shortage of creature controllers in the first place. Micah listened, smiling, and finished his pie.

When Mia reached a settlement with Micah's second owner, she deposited the settlement in Micah's brand-new bank account. Micah showed the balance to Dominic, wondering if they'd need to discuss the subject of rent. Instead, Dominic declared that it was time for "pecan cream," and Micah was treating. Micah wondered if Dom was finally initiating some kind of sex with him, but this turned out to be another kind of pie. It came from a diner that Dominic detoured twenty minutes to get to. The silverware didn't match and the place was full of children, and the pie was delicious.

When Micah and Alex agreed on a design for Micah's tattoo, Dominic went with him to get it done. He extolled the benefits of moral support, but Micah suspected he might have been there for a bit of good-natured schadenfreude, as well.

Alex kept up the banter as she worked, claiming that a tattoo was as much about good vibes as art. She and Dominic traded opinions on modern rock, speaking over the buzzing of her tools. Under her gun, a pattern of branches and bark appeared, covering Micah's arm from the wrist nearly to his elbow. The barcode vanished as though it had never been there.

It took almost all day, but she eventually declared the piece complete. Micah raised his hand, watching the perspective of the forest change as he moved his arm. Alex had put her own mana into the work, infusing the art with magic.

"Like this," Alex said, taking his hand. She placed his thumb against the pad of his smallest finger and then rotated his wrist. A small black-and-white chickadee appeared, hopping amiably along a twig. "Free as a bird," she said with a wink.

She wrapped Micah's arm in black plastic and told him not to touch it for at least six hours. Afterward, they got peach cobbler and vanilla ice cream from a place off the side of route 281.

A week after getting the tattoo, there was a knock on Dominic's front door.

They both turned as one, staring at the front of the house.

"You expecting company?" Micah asked.

Dominic shook his head and slipped a knife into the waistband of his jeans before crossing the room to answer.

It was a man with a clipboard. Behind him, a large truck rumbled in the driveway. "Dominic Blackburn?"

"Yeah?"

"You gotta sign for this."

"What is it?"

The man rolled his eyes. "It's a big heavy friggin' box. You're not expecting a delivery?"

"Nope. Though I sometimes order stuff online and forget. How big and heavy are we talking?"

"Sign the slip and I'll show you."

Dominic signed. Micah peered over his shoulder. The delivery man turned and waved to someone out of sight, and together they dragged a large wooden crate off the back of their truck. It was marked *fragile* and *express* and was at least four feet to a side. Micah could not help but notice that neither the box nor the truck bore the logo of a delivery company.

"What the fuck?" Dominic muttered. "I definitely did not forget ordering anything like that."

"You signed for it, it's yours now," the man said, shrugging.

"Do you have a crowbar?" Micah asked, and Dominic nodded and went to fetch it.

The truck was gone by the time they worked the tool into the seam of the lid. Dominic hauled down on the bar, and the lid rose, the nails screaming. Micah shoved it the rest of the way off, and sunlight streamed into the box.

"Oh, *really*?" Dominic groaned. "He couldn't have called?"

Micah stared inside, eyes wide, voice once again frozen.

From underneath shaggy hair streaked with gray, his father stared back at him.

Micah heard ringing.

"Hey, Mikey," Gerald said. He tried climbing to his feet, but was quickly stymied by the chains connecting him to the floor of the soundproofed crate.

Transport bindings, of course. Slate was a big fan.

"There's no fucking way this is legal," Dominic was saying, and he was right, but that was the *point*. Slate didn't worry about things like *laws*; Slate knew it and Micah knew it and now he wanted Dominic to know it too.

"Put the fucking lid back on," Micah hissed. He hoped Dominic could hear him, but couldn't look away to check. "He's not staying."

"Uh, I get where you're coming from," Dominic said, peering into the box, "but the truck's gone and this box isn't gonna fit in my car."

"Then we'll roll it into the *fucking river*," Micah snapped. Under the familiar terror of his childhood, he was *livid*. A detached part of his mind wondered where it was coming from; it wasn't like he'd spent the last thirteen years planning revenge.

He'd barely thought about his father at all, really. Their situation hadn't been complicated; Micah had been too much trouble to keep, and so Gerald had given him away. And Micah had gone to live somewhere new, somewhere where the violence was predictable and served a purpose. If he'd felt anything about his missing father, it was relief at no longer having to live under his shadow.

For fifteen years he'd taken that safety for granted, only to have it shatter in an instant.

"Don't be like that, Mikey. Get these damn chains off me, we can talk about this."

Mikey. That was right. His father used to call him Mikey.

Micah's vision shook. His body was frozen with some awful internal pressure that threatened to tear him apart. He couldn't breathe.

For the first time in his life, Micah turned his back on his father and walked away.

The problem they had was that Gerald's paperwork was valid. Slate had authorized Megan to transfer a contract of his, and Megan had, *arguably*, transferred it to Dominic. Slate had apparently decided to recognize that purchase and had forwarded Gerald along to him, just like he'd promised to do in the police station.

In short, Gerald's contract legally belonged to Dominic, and there was nothing to be done about it.

"Don't look at me like that," Dominic said, once he got off the phone with Slate's secretary. "I didn't ask for him. They just sent him."

"So get *rid* of him." Micah's hands tightened on the edge of the kitchen table. He didn't know where he was supposed to be. What he was supposed to be doing. His father was in a wooden crate in the front yard, and while a logical part of his mind knew they couldn't just *leave* him there, another small but loud part was terrified to be near him. There was no way to know what would set Gerald off, make him angry, make him violent—

Micah shook his head.

He wasn't a little kid anymore, cowering in the corner and hoping he could avoid his father's attention. He was a grown man, as big as Gerald had ever been, and stronger and more skilled to boot. There was no rational reason for him to be afraid. Yet, somehow, his heart raced at the thought of Gerald coming into the house.

He hadn't realized until this moment that he thought of this place as *home*.

"Micah. Calm down." Dominic's hands were on his shoulders, steadying him, bringing him back into the moment. Dominic's eyes were *so* blue, he thought, taking in every fleck of light and dark, making them his focus. He bit the inside of his cheek, letting the pain ground him. He was better than this. He had to be.

"Okay," he said, and then, because it came out too weak for his liking, "It's okay. I'm okay."

"Breathe. You're gonna get past this. He's not staying. Okay? He's not staying. But I need some time to figure out what to do with him. And I can't leave him outside forever."

"Yeah. Okay."

"Okay? I've gotta put him somewhere. I'm guessing you don't want him in the living room."

Micah shook his head.

"Okay. So, move your stuff into my room. We'll share for now and keep him shut up in the guest room. Sound like a plan?"

"Yeah, okay."

Dominic released him, slowly, like he thought Micah might lose his balance and fall. Micah didn't fall. He wasn't going to fall. He was upset, *too* upset, but he wasn't some Victorian lady waiting to swoon.

He went alone into his room—the room he didn't sleep in. Most of his stuff was still in the duffel bag he'd used to carry it inside. It didn't take long to move into Dominic's room. He put his clothes in the corner, folded and stacked to take up as little space as possible.

The least he could do was be unobtrusive.

He did a once-over of the guest room, ensuring he hadn't left anything, and then he went outside to face his father.

Dominic had found the key to the chains in with the shipping documents, and now Gerald was sitting on the edge of the crate while Dominic unlocked him.

"Lookit you, kid!" Gerald said when their eyes met. "You got tall! I told 'em you'd grow up big, just like your dad."

"You were right," Micah said woodenly. His father's face was lined and worn, but the resemblance was there, plain as day. Micah didn't want to look at him.

"So what's the plan?" Gerald asked, slapping his palms against his knees. "How are we going to fix this?"

"Haven't figured that out yet," Dominic muttered.

"Well, you've got the title, right? That's what the other guy said." Gerald wrinkled his nose. "He was a bit weird, right? Bet you're glad to be out from under him, eh, Micah?"

Micah clenched his teeth. "Tomorrow. We're going to Selina *tomorrow*."

"Right. So we'll go into town, do the switch, and you can carry on the way you planned."

"Sorry, what?" Dominic asked. "What switch?"

"The paperwork thing," Gerald explained. "Couldn't do it before, he was too young, sorry about the bait and switch with the title there. The guys I was working with *swore* no one would ever notice. But it's all square now that he's grown. Buy off my contract with his. We just need to get it registered and then you're good to go."

"Why," Micah started, "would I *ever*—"

"Because you're doing well, right? In the rings? I told them you would. And some of the guys I've seen come out of there. Wow. Fucking mess. But you're doing great, right?" Gerald turned back to Dominic. "Did he tell you he started training when he was eleven? And it all paid off—look at him, not a scratch. That's my boy."

"I've never been in the ring," Micah said hollowly. It wasn't technically true, he'd been in plenty, but never as a real contestant.

Gerald blinked at him. "What do you mean? They said they were going to train you to be a fighter."

Micah crossed his arms. "They did. But they couldn't make me brutal enough, so they switched me over to hospitality instead."

Gerald's expression flickered. "Oh. Well, that explains the . . ." He gestured vaguely at his own face. Micah assumed he was talking about the piercing. Then Gerald grinned. "So that's what you've been doing since I left? Tending to trophy wives and widowers?" He waggled his eyebrows. "That's my boy." He turned to Dominic again. "So he's what, a present for your wife?"

Micah's anger was gone, replaced with a simple emptiness. His voice was flat. "Most of my owners have been men."

A warm sort of satisfaction flooded Micah's stomach as he watched the blood drain out of his father's face.

Gerald looked back at Dominic. "You—"

"Not married," Dominic remarked, raising his bare left hand and wiggling his fingers.

"You mother*fucker*!" Gerald shouted at him. "How *dare* you!"

"How dare he?" Micah said incredulously. There was something tugging at the back of his mind, something he hadn't let himself think yet. "Of course they *dare*, they *own* me. That's what I'm *for*. Did you think you were dropping me off at summer camp? Did you think you'd get a permission slip to sign? You handed me over and *left* me!"

But no, that wasn't right, Micah realized. The errant itch at the back of his mind had become a full thought, the first domino of implications he'd carefully avoided examining.

"You *sold* me," he said out loud. He was too high, he wanted to curl into a ball and let these thoughts *have* him, but not in front of Gerald. "It never had anything to do with *me*. You left me because they *paid* you."

Gerald's jaw set, and Micah saw the indignation there. "It's not like I didn't think of you. I thought it would be better for you—"

Micah hit him. The blow sent Gerald sprawling to the ground.

"You thought it would be better for *you*," Micah hissed, looming over him. He'd spent his whole life avoiding this man's anger, and suddenly he wanted nothing more than to provoke it. "*You* should have been the one in chains. Not me."

"And what if I was?" Gerald's lip was split and there was blood on his teeth. "What if I *had* been the one with the contract? What happens to you then? You end up in some state-run foster home—"

"And they'd what?" Micah asked. His voice was horrifyingly flat. From the corner of his eye, he could see Dominic's worried expression. "Beat me? Drug me? Or maybe I'd just get passed around like a party favor. Yeah, Gerald, that would have been a *much worse* way for me to grow up."

"That wasn't how it was supposed to go," Gerald said quietly. "They said they'd teach you a skill. Make something of you."

"Well, they did."

Gerald had nothing to say to that. Dominic waited a second, and when Gerald didn't speak, Dominic hauled him up by the shoulders and frog-marched him into the house.

Micah watched them go.

He stared at the front door for a while, trying to decide what to do.

He should go inside. Dominic might need something.

But he *really* didn't want to be around his father. The thought of being trapped inside with him . . .

What Micah wanted to do was go build a dam.

It wasn't in any way a practical use of his time. But he'd enjoyed it before and, fuck it, he wanted to do it again.

A free person would just go, he realized as he headed for the woods. Wouldn't even think about it. Free people knew what they wanted and made it happen.

But what freedom meant for him, *really* meant, was uncertainty. He hadn't had to make a real choice since before his first owners, and those had been terrifying, uncertain times. He didn't remember where he and his father had lived before he was indentured. They'd moved a lot. He'd learned not to leave things in his locker in case he got home from school and his dad moved them before he got the chance to go back.

He'd spent a lot of time wondering what was going to happen next. Where they were going to sleep. What they were going to eat.

What his dad was going to do.

And then he'd been sold and things had become wonderfully, *beautifully* stable.

Hard, sure. They were training him to fight, and they didn't waste their time having him pretend-spar with other little boys. He went to bed with his fair share of bruises, but that was nothing new, and at least they always made sure to feed him afterward. And unlike his father, after they hit him, they showed him how to block. When he learned to block, he didn't get hit. Simple. The sparring room was, ironically, the first place in his life he'd ever felt safe.

He'd stopped worrying about his future. He'd learned, he'd adapted, and he'd worked toward being worth keeping. Being useful. Pleasing his masters. Always.

He grew up, he grew out, he got strong. After a couple of years, he was almost as big as his father had been, and nobody landed hits on him. Not anymore.

Only problem was, Micah hadn't grown up into the fighter they'd hoped for. In the competitions they whispered about—not the ones on ESPN, but the ones on private estates like Slate's—people got killed. They weren't supposed to, but they did. And Micah wasn't willing to kill. It made him a bad bet in the ring, and his owners were unhappy.

Micah pressed the heels of his hands against his eyes, old memories dredging up again. The uncertainty worming its way back in. He'd tried to be what they'd wanted, but he just . . . couldn't.

And now his future was uncertain again.

Micah reached the stream, sinking to his knees in the loamy soil and focusing on the sounds of running water. He took deep breaths, in through his nose, out through his mouth, calming himself the way Arabelle had taught him.

He couldn't have been much more than sixteen the first time he'd met her. They said she was going to train him, and he went in expecting a fight. Instead, she told him to take his clothes off. He had, blushing as she looked him over. Then she told him to touch himself while she watched.

It was fun at first. Arabelle taught him about the human body, hers and those of the slaves she owned. Micah lost his virginity to a pretty blonde whose name he didn't know. He learned how to sooth and tease and fondle and massage, rarely ever the same woman twice.

Sometimes Arabelle had him learn on men too, straddling their buttocks and working his fingers deep into the muscle of their backs. He didn't like them as much as the women, but he learned all the same. He learned how to make his partners come with his hands, then his mouth. He learned to please two partners at once.

And then one day Arabelle was waiting for him with a pair of leather cuffs. They hung from the ceiling and held him still while a man took him from behind. A blonde woman sucked him off while it happened, keeping him relaxed.

He thought the woman might have been the one from before. He never saw the man.

That night Micah had lain awake, staring at the ceiling of his cell. He couldn't stop thinking about it. The warm burn of the man *inside* him. Pushing into him, holding him back with fingers digging into his hips. Micah had tried to focus on the woman, on what she was doing with her mouth. It was good, but not enough to distract him completely.

The next day, Micah was fucked again, this time on his knees, his arms braced against the headboard. This man was bigger than the first, and he kept telling Micah how well he was doing. He urged Micah to relax, rubbing little circles into his back while tears formed in Micah's eyes.

Arabelle had reached between Micah's legs and stroked at his cock, making approving noises when he began to harden. She liked it when he could get hard and stay that way. She said his masters would like it too.

So he learned to do it.

He learned about the things he'd be expected to do, to take, to know. He learned about canes and manacles and blindfolds and gags. He learned to breathe around a face-fucking and that it didn't hurt if he relaxed.

And he learned it perfectly because, in amongst all the confusing, burning pleasure, he found absolute stability. When Micah wasn't being used, he knew he should be at his master's side, hands on his knees, waiting. He knew how to offer, how to display, how to please, how to present. After a few years, he didn't even need to think about it. He slipped into his life, let it happen, gave up action in favor of reaction.

And now it was all gone. Everything weighed on his shoulders again. *Everything* required a decision. Decision after decision after decision.

He picked up a rock and threw it into the water. It flowed easily around this new obstacle, carrying on as though nothing had changed.

Micah watched the water tumble downstream.

He could be like that, he knew. He could adapt to any obstacle put in his way; he just needed to know where he was going. He needed to choose something to head toward. Some vessel for him to mold himself into and fill.

He thought of Dominic's car, every one of Dominic's tools in its own place, ready to be needed.

Micah smiled to himself, gritting his teeth. He could fit into that tool set. He could. He just had to learn how. Dominic couldn't teach him with Arabelle's surety or Slate's adamance, but that was all right. Micah would learn anyway.

And the first step was going back to the house.

True to his word, Dominic had confined Gerald to the guest bedroom. For the first time, Micah was able to climb into Dom's bed knowing that he was meant to be there. It should have felt nice, but he was too focused on the task he'd set for himself.

Dominic could tell there was something wrong, but he was resolutely pretending everything was normal, probably for Micah's sake.

Just tell him. Admit it, Micah snapped at himself, when Dominic turned out the light.

"There's four dollars in the bathroom," he finally said.

Dominic rolled over, facing him in the darkness. "What?"

"In the medicine cabinet. The bottom of the box of bandages. Four dollars and fifty-two cents."

"Okay . . . what? I'm sorry, this isn't making sense to me."

Micah sighed, letting out the confession he'd been avoiding. "The day you bought me. You gave me money for food, and you never asked me for change. So I kept it." Micah paused. "I hid it."

Dominic rubbed his eyes. "God, that seems like ages ago. How do you even remember that?"

"Because for several hours, it was the most important thing in my life." Micah paused, not wanting to admit the next part, but knowing he had to. "I wasn't sure whether Slate had sent me to you. If he had . . . If he had, I thought maybe you were going to kill me."

There was a beat, while Dominic processed. "Oh."

"Dominic . . ." Micah reached out, trailing his fingertips over Dominic's ribs, over his side, letting them rest on his hip. Micah hesitated, choosing his words carefully. "You can't understand how small my world was. How focused. How utterly limited to the things my master asked of me." Micah bit his lip. "Gerald said he thought about me. He's lying, but I didn't think about him, either. I didn't think of revenge or escape or the future or what I wanted to do with my life. I didn't think about what to wear, or what to eat, or what to say, or where to go. I waited for orders, and then I followed them."

He leaned in, pressing his lips to Dominic's. His hand tightened on Dominic's hip. Dominic kissed him back, hesitantly.

"You think I'm smart, but I'm not. I can't make basic, stupid decisions for myself, and I don't want to leave." He kissed Dominic again, deeper, his hand sliding under the waistband of Dominic's pants. "Please don't make me go. I know you don't want to own me, but I can make it *so* worth it."

He kissed Dominic again, but Dominic caught his wrist, pulling away. "Don't. You don't have to sleep with me to stay."

Micah pressed his body up against the length of Dominic's, rolling his hips against him. "I want to. You've been good to me. Let me."

"Micah, *stop*."

Micah had never had this much trouble getting someone to fuck him. The occasional guest had been hesitant to take a slave, but once Micah reassured them, their reservations dissipated. And Dominic *wanted* him, that much was obvious several times over. So what the hell was going wrong here?

"Let me," Micah murmured. "It's what I'm good for."

"Then let me touch you back."

Micah paused. "If that's what you want."

"Is that what *you* want?"

"I want to give you what you want," Micah said, trying not to sound desperate. This situation could be so *simple* if Dominic would just *let* it. "Does it matter whether I want it too?"

"Yes!" Dominic insisted, pressing his lips to Micah's knuckles. "Of course it matters."

"*Why*?"

"Because sex isn't payment. Nothing I've done means that you owe me this."

Micah bit his lip, trying to find an explanation that Dominic would understand. "But I do owe you *something*. I don't have anything else to give."

"What's your middle name?"

Micah blinked. "What?"

"Your middle name. Or are you one of those freaks who only has one?"

"It's Frederick."

"Micah Frederick Sawyer." Dom pronounced it carefully, then smirked. "Also known as Mikey."

Micah scowled. "No."

"All right. What's your favorite color?"

"I don't . . . green? I guess."

"Mine's blue. Dark blue, like the sky gets in summer when the sun never really goes all the way down. Sweet or salty?"

"Salty. Why are you asking me this?"

Dominic released Micah's hand, letting it settle back across his waist. "You think you owe me something? Then I want to know about you."

"What good is that?"

Dominic leaned in and kissed him, a soft press of lips against his. Micah tried to deepen it, and Dominic pulled away. "I don't want you doing anything to me unless you'd want me to do it back to you. I don't think I can explain it to you, but it's disturbing to me. Call it a free man thing."

Micah frowned. He didn't want Dominic touching him sexually. He didn't even touch *himself* that way. His owners had always wanted him hard, wanted him to "enjoy" it. He could do it, of course. It was all part of the performance. But it was a lie.

He didn't want to lie to Dominic. And it was pretty clear that Dominic didn't want to be lied to. "I might never want anything back," Micah warned.

He thought that would be the end of it. Dominic would realize there was no point in waiting and use him. Like he was meant to be used.

Dominic kissed him again. "That's okay. You don't have to."

Micah's breath caught. *That doesn't make sense.* "Then what's the point of keeping me?"

"Would you rather be hot or cold?"

Micah tried and failed to fit the question to the context. "Hot."

"Why?"

"Slave quarters are usually underground and it's cold. Being hot would be a nice change of pace. Why do you care?"

Dominic let out a breath. "Because I care about you."

Micah could feel Dominic's smile against his cheek. He shook his head. "But there's nothing *to* me, that's what I'm trying to tell you!" Tears pricked at his eyes, and he willed them back. "I'm whoever I'm *told* to be, but you won't *tell* me, you—"

Dominic cupped his face, and this was it, he'd finally gone too far, been too contrary, and this was going to be the end—

"There's more to you than that, and I'm going to prove it to you," Dominic insisted. "I don't care if it takes a week, or a month, or years. And if you want to give me what I want, then *believe* me." He leaned in, kissing Micah again. "So. Apples or oranges?"

That one was easy, far easier than trying to convince Dominic that this was pointless. "Oranges."

"Why?"

"They give me something to do with my hands."

"Who told you that?"

Micah frowned. "No one."

"Didn't think so," Dominic said, nuzzling against his cheek.

Micah blinked. Was that really all there was to it? What Dominic thought he should be made of? Dominic moved through life with the fortitude of a free man, a virtue that Micah had always thought he simply *lacked*. But was it possible that, without an owner's discipline, the foundation of Dominic's assurance was simply the ability to fearlessly choose *wrong*?

That was fine for little things, an apple or an orange, but . . .

"Have you ever been to the beach?" Dominic asked, and Micah realized he'd drifted.

"No," he answered, shaking his head.

"Me neither," Dominic said, a little wistfully. It seemed he hadn't noticed Micah's lapse in attention. "Sour or bitter?"

"Sweet."

"That's cheating."

"Why have you never been to the beach?" Micah asked. He felt Dominic shrug.

"Never had anybody to go with, I guess. You wanna go?"

"Sure," Micah answered without thinking, agreeing because Dominic had asked him to. But Dominic was giving him a knowing smile. "Would you *actually*, really want to go?"

Micah had to stop and consider it. "I don't know how to swim," he admitted at last. "So if you'd want to—"

"Even without me," Dominic clarified, and Micah had to think again. He fought back the suspicion that this was a test, motives buried in so many layers that the correct answer could never be deduced. So he pictured it, standing on the sand and watching the waves, smelling the salt, the sound of gulls . . .

"I'd want to go," he said, and it was the truth. "But I'd want you to go with me," he added, and that was also the truth, and the smile on Dominic's face told him he'd answered right.

CHAPTER TWENTY-TWO

When Micah woke up the next morning, his father was standing in their bedroom doorway. Dominic was still sleeping, his back pressed against Micah's chest, their fingers intertwined over the sheet. Gerald was regarding them silently, his expression dark.

"And here I was," Gerald said quietly, "all broken up about that sob story of yours. And you let me feel guilty."

Micah tried to come up with a response, but Gerald was already gone, walking down the hall to the front room. Micah shifted a little, checking to make sure Dom was still asleep. He was, and Micah took the opportunity to shower.

When he got out, Dominic and Gerald were shouting at each other in the kitchen.

"*It's none of your goddamn business*!"

"Of course it's my business, he's my son!"

Micah stepped into the main room, towel around his waist, staying close to the hallway. He didn't like the idea of planning a retreat, but that was exactly what he was doing.

"You *can't* think he wants that," Gerald was saying. The rage in his voice made Micah's skin crawl. "Not my son. Whatever you've done, you've tricked him."

"I haven't done *anything*, and you don't know anything about what he wants. You just met him yesterday!"

"I *raised* him!"

"You didn't," Micah interjected, before Dominic could reply. Gerald was momentarily speechless. "A lot of people brought me up, but you weren't one of them."

Gerald's jaw set. "Is that where I went wrong? Turning you over to a bunch of freaks who raised you to think you were . . . *this*?" Gerald gestured to Dominic.

Micah laughed. It wasn't a good laugh. "No. You went wrong a long time before that."

Gerald sneered. "Maybe I wasn't the best father. I might have made mistakes, but at least I'm not the one *fucking* you."

Dominic gaped. Micah shrugged, too wrung out to be offended on Dominic's behalf. "I'd be nicer to him. He owns you."

And with that, he headed back to the bedroom to get dressed. Immediately, he heard Dominic's footsteps in the hall behind him. For a moment, Micah considered ignoring him, but his training won out.

"What can I do for you, Dominic." He lacked the energy to make it a question.

"He's yours," Dominic said.

"What?"

Dominic was fidgeting. "He's yours. I bought him, technically, I hold his title, but I have no right to him. He's yours. So I'm giving him to you."

Micah paused. "I don't *want* him. What am I going to do with him?"

"I don't know. But you should figure it out, because he's yours."

The floor was dropping out from under him, and it was all Micah could do not to kneel just for stability. "Then I want you to sell him. I owe you for my contract." Dominic took a breath to protest, but Micah didn't give him the chance. "You want me to make decisions, this is the one I'm making. I want you to sell him. I don't care who to, as long as it's *soon*."

Dominic hesitated. "I know a place. But he'll probably end up in a work camp."

Micah sighed, rubbing his eyes. "I cannot explain to you how little I care."

"He might die. The conditions in those places aren't great."

For the first time, Micah met Dominic's eyes. "And wasn't that where I was headed, when you found me? While he was off living his life with my name? He left when I was a child; he has *nothing* to do with the life I have here, now."

Dominic regarded him for a long moment. "Okay. If you're sure."

Micah nodded. "I'm sure."

They ended up going back to the same dealership where Dominic had bought Micah, though this time the sale took place indoors. Gerald spent the whole drive sitting in the back seat and lamenting the state of America's ungrateful and morally bereft youth. Micah, to his credit, did not hit him.

After making it absolutely clear he was there for a cash sale and not a trade-in, Dominic signed the transfer paperwork. Micah didn't ask Dominic what they gave him for the contract. He didn't want to know. If Dominic thought they were square, then they were square.

Micah didn't respond when Gerald said goodbye. And that was the end of it.

He asked Dominic what kind of pie that called for, and Dominic just rubbed his face and didn't answer.

CHAPTER TWENTY-THREE

∞

Ian called with Slate's court date. Godfrey's testimony had implicated two other doctors, and one of them linked one of the murdered slaves to Slate. Three more holders were being investigated in relation to statements from the doctors. Ian said there might be enough to qualify as a ring, and he was working with other departments out of state to see if any other cases might be related. Micah asked what kind of pie they should get. Dominic said he thought maybe Micah didn't understand the point of pie.

In between all of it, Micah somehow never got around to moving his things back into the guest room.

It wasn't that he didn't mean to. It just . . . never really seemed to matter. Dominic didn't mind having him there, or if he did, he didn't mention it.

Meanwhile, Micah cherished the little things, like how their feet touched under the table, or the way they always ended up sitting on the same side of the couch. They'd pass in the hall and brush hands—not stopping, just reaching out and knowing the other was reaching too. Micah got used to the feeling of Dominic's hands on him. Not like before, with the others; Dominic wasn't groping or fondling him, just feeling, like he wanted to make sure Micah was still there. The touches were soft, lingering, but never demanding more.

And through it all, Dominic kept asking questions.

It was at night, usually, when they'd settled into bed together. Sometimes Micah didn't understand the question (Kirk or Picard?), and Dominic would get very excited and start making plans to introduce Micah to the things Dominic loved.

Other times Micah understood, but didn't know the answer (What was your favorite class?), and Dominic would get quiet and that would be the end of questions for the night. Micah tried to always have an answer, but sometimes even that seemed to make Dominic upset, like when Dominic had asked for his greatest childhood accomplishment, and Micah told him about the time he'd pinned a training partner even with a dislocated shoulder. Dominic stuck to yes-or-nos for a while after that.

Between rounds of questions, they watched a lot of movies, making up for a "lifetime of pop culture deprivation," as Dominic termed it. Micah enjoyed most of them. Some of them he didn't understand. But he watched them anyway, because while he watched the actors, Dominic would watch him. Micah's reactions seemed to mean a lot to him, and that made something warm and soft and unfamiliar settle into Micah's chest.

"I want to kiss you," Micah said.

"Awesome. Do it." Dominic leaned in, making a ridiculous puckered-up face.

Micah pushed him away, laughing. "Shut up. I'm serious."

"So'm I." Dominic propped himself up onto one elbow and met his eyes. Morning sunlight trickled in from outside, bathing the bedroom in a golden glow.

"This is . . . different. From before." Micah swallowed. "Before, I had a reason. Like I was trying to calm you down, or turn you on, or . . . do what I was supposed to. But now I just . . . want to. For no reason." Dominic's face didn't hold half the judgment Micah had feared. "Does that make sense?"

Dom gave him a smile, but there was sadness at the edges. "That's how it's supposed to be, Micah."

"This isn't going anywhere," Micah warned when Dominic leaned in.

"It doesn't need to."

Dominic's voice was soft, honest. He meant it.

Micah laid his hand against the side of Dominic's face. His fingers mapped the contours of Dominic's cheek, his forehead, his hair, his ear, his jawline, his mouth. And Dominic let him, not pushing for more, not touching back, just, letting him.

"Can you . . . Would you take your shirt off?"

He worried Dominic might make some stupid joke, play it off like a stripper, and that would have shattered the whole thing. Micah would have punched him in the shoulder and called him an idiot and they would have gotten up and had breakfast.

But Dominic didn't do that. He sat up slowly, pulling his shirt over his head, and lay back down without a word.

Micah had never picked his partners. Whether they were attractive didn't matter, and so he had never paid attention. But now, with Dominic, there was something he liked. Something he *wanted*, even if he wasn't sure exactly what it *was*.

Micah knelt at Dominic's side. Not straddling him—that was too close to what he'd done before. He paused before reaching out, then steeled himself and let his hands settle on Dominic's chest.

He'd touched a lot of people in his life. Of every kind. Always for them. The focus had always been on whether his hands felt good to *them*. Now, Micah let himself focus on how Dominic felt to *him*.

His skin was warm, and the hair on his body was wiry and rough. Micah traced his chest, his belly, his arms, the familiar textures of muscle and bone and tendons. He took his time, mapping Dominic out inch by inch. All the things that made up Dominic's body, and in there, somewhere, the thing that made the *want*.

Dominic didn't resist, submitting to Micah's curiosity with uncharacteristic gravitas. Micah took Dominic's hand in his own, drawing his fingers across Dominic's wrist and palm. He stroked up each finger, watching the way the muscles and tendons flexed all the way to the elbow. Dominic's arms were covered in shallow scars, a lifetime of fighting and fixing and spellwork. Each of those scars held a story, one tiny fragment of *Dominic*, and suddenly Micah wanted to know them *all*.

"What's your middle name?"

"James," Dominic answered softly, and Micah leaned down and kissed him. Dominic opened for him, but Micah didn't deepen it any further. He just lost himself in the feel and taste and texture of Dominic's mouth, until there was nothing more than that in the world. That was all Micah wanted, and Dominic didn't ask him for more.

When they finally roused out of bed, Dominic went to take an extra-long shower, and Micah didn't begrudge him that.

Micah ducked into the bathroom when Dominic was finished, locking the door and stripping off his clothes. He turned the shower handle to hot and waited. His reflection caught his eye in the mirror.

He'd only been with Dom a few months, but he was already losing the sharp, hunted look he'd picked up while living with Slate. It wasn't just that the food was better. He still did the bodyweight exercises and stretches he always had, but he did more now too. He went *outside*.

He leaned in, meeting his own eyes in the glass. His hair fell across his vision, and he remembered that Dominic wanted him to cut it. He didn't want to. He liked it long. He knew that much.

He pulled away from the glass, taking in more of his reflection. The hair on his body was mostly grown back. Some of his previous owners had liked it; others, like Slate, had wanted it removed. He didn't know which one he preferred. He'd probably let it grow.

The shower ran hot and the mirror fogged, so Micah stepped into the water, closing his eyes and letting the tension drain out of his body.

He wondered which parts of him Dominic liked.

Dominic wanted him to get off, which Micah was used to. But he wanted Micah to *want* it, and that, Micah would have to work on.

He thought about it as he washed his hair, finishing off with the conditioner he'd bought. What sex would he *want*? If he came up with an agreeable fantasy, maybe he could think about it in bed. He'd just have to be careful not to get too removed.

Dom didn't like it when he distanced himself too much.

He'd have to work on it, he decided.

He shut off the water.

CHAPTER TWENTY-FOUR

"Your phone rang," Micah said when Dominic shuffled into the kitchen for breakfast. "It's Ian."

"You can answer it, you know."

Micah shook his head. "It's not mine."

"We'll have to get you one, then. Now that you're all loud again."

"Who would I call?"

"Ian, apparently." Dominic picked up his phone. Ian had called half a dozen times in the last half an hour. He punched the redial.

"What's the emergency?"

"Anyone ever tell you you should answer your fucking phone?" Ian's voice came over the speaker filled with static. "What do you know about wards?"

"What, like, magic barriers? Lots, why?"

"Because we've got something weird out here. Can you come? We'll get you your normal consulting fee."

"For you?" Dominic said with a grin. "Always."

Ian gave him an address, and Dominic marked it down on a scrap of notepaper. It was a cabin on the shores of Milgram Lake, which the map had tagged as some sort of resort.

As Dominic plotted a route, Micah came out of the bedroom with a pair of duffels slung over his shoulder. His was already packed. It didn't take Dom long to catch up. "You want to drive?" Dominic asked.

"Aren't we in a hurry?"

"It's a straight shot down 91 to Franklinburg. Then you turn left. I think you can handle it."

Micah smirked. "Yeah, all right."

The other upshot to Micah driving was that Dominic could call Ian back. "We're on our way. What are we walking into?"

"Remember the other holders we were investigating? They all have a connection to this resort. Them, Slate, the doctors, and a half-dozen other shady individuals. We finally got the authorization to search it, and when we show up— I'm not gonna lie. I've never seen anything like this, and I have a feeling it's only going to get worse. A couple of the doors are warded, and we've got no idea what might be behind them. I'm hoping you can get through."

"I can't promise anything, but I can certainly try."

"Well if you can't, I'm not sure who to call. I talked to Garrett over at creacon dispatch, and he didn't have anybody in the area other than you. This is some serious hoodoo. Our witch is working on it right now, and she's got nothing."

"You've got a witch? Can I talk to her?"

Ian said something to someone, and then a woman's voice came over the phone. "Amanda Montgomery."

"Hi, Amanda, this is Dominic Blackburn. I hear you've got some wards?"

"Yeah. Weird stuff. I'm pretty good with ikons and runes, but nothing I've got will touch it."

"You try Dobb's decryption ritual?"

He could almost hear her eyes roll. "I don't *specialize* in warding, but this isn't my first day. I've tried standard and inverse, no effect. I'm setting up for a Nilsson and Rye, but honestly, I'm not optimistic. Whatever this is, it's all interlocking circles. A circle of interlocking circles. You break one and the rest hold firm, and by the time you pick off a second, the first one's regenerated."

Dominic considered. "I've seen circles. Can you send me pictures? I'll get you a list of stuff I'll need."

They pulled up the pristine driveway to the cabin—more like a rustic manor—a little before dark, passing a line of police cruisers on their way in.

Light spilled across the lawn from inside, and the grass was dotted with spotlights. Ian was waiting for them by the front door.

"Follow me and don't touch anything."

"Yes, sir," Dom said, giving him a salute.

"What did you find here?" Micah asked, taking in the baroque décor.

"Slaves," Ian said grimly. Dominic almost asked him to clarify, but the grim expression on Micah's face made him think better of it.

The main room was mostly circular, with staircases on either side curving up toward a balcony. The warded door was between the two staircases, and hidden well enough that Dominic had to focus to be able to see it. It was covered in intricate wood inlays, circular, just like Amanda had said. Dominic tried to analyze them and found his eyes slipping off.

"Okay, I need a space to work. At least four feet wide. Can you do that?"

"Yep!" came a chipper voice from beside him. Dominic turned to see a purple-haired woman wearing a name tag that said *Amanda*. "You're standing right in the middle of it."

Amanda didn't need her magic spelled out on the floor, but she had chalk and string and the two of them made short work of a new summoning circle for Dominic's sake. Amanda laid out a seven-pointed star while Dominic set up small mirrors Micah fetched from the car. A mirror at each point would prevent their magic from bleeding out into the air. Dominic's hands glowed almost imperceptibly as he set a clear crystal sphere in the center of the circle.

"What are you thinking?" Amanda asked.

"The thing about a circle," Dominic answered, "is that all parts are equal. Round Table and all that."

"That's the problem." Amanda crossed her arms. "Regeneration's weak spot is always the master molecule, but this setup doesn't have one. And with everything I've got, I can't knock individual sections out fast enough to make a hole."

"Well, I've got enough power to jump a car, on a good day," Dominic said. "But I think I might have something for this."

He went back to his bag, pulling out a tapered wax candle and a couple of different oils to smear along its length: cinnamon, clove, peppermint, orange. One on each side. He lit the candle and held the end over the sphere, murmuring a blessing as the wax dripped onto the crystal. That done, he planted it at one corner of the star.

"I already tried this," Amanda said. "A Banri dispersion? I focused on the first section, and it knocked out fine, but I couldn't reset for a second before it regenerated."

"What I'm thinking," Dominic said, pointing Micah toward the candles remaining in the bag, "is that we *don't* reset. I'm guessing you set your focuses up in tandem?"

"Sure, you get the most hit points that way."

"But you only focused them on one section."

"It's the only way to do it. If you attack the whole circle at once, it's not enough to break it anywhere. You trade one problem for another."

Micah's candle was ready, and he lit it, dropping a few splotches of wax onto the sphere. Dominic took it from him, setting it at the second point of the star.

"I came up with this on the drive over," he admitted, "but using candles as the focuses, we could set them out of sync. Put each one at a seventh of a rotation from the one before it. But since they're still, technically, a circle—"

"It forms an iterative loop." Amanda socked Dom lightly in the arm. "Weakening the whole circle without resetting. You might be onto something, Blackburn."

Dominic tried not to look too pleased. He might not have the aptitude to work his magic without a circle, the way Amanda could, but sometimes there were benefits to mapping it out in a physical space. The three of them finished the other five candles, and Dominic carefully positioned one at each remaining point of the star.

"You're going to have to power it," Dom admitted. "It's definitely not going to work with just me."

"No problem." Amanda turned to the assorted officers milling around curiously. "Make a hole, folks!"

They quickly cleared out, and she closed her eyes and spread her hands, concentrating on the spell. One after another, the candle flames began to flare, chasing each other around the circle like carnival lights. In the center of the circle, the crystal ball binding them together began to heat, melting the wax covering its surface.

"Now what?" Ian asked Dominic.

"Now we wait and see if it worked."

They didn't have to wait long. After a minute, the smell of burning wood began to fill the room, and Dominic found it easier to look at the door. The interlocking circles were smoking, the wood charring and blurring the sigils.

"You might want a fire extinguisher," Dominic remarked, and then the wood burst into flame.

The door went up in a flash—common with sigil breaking and usually not dangerous unless there was something flammable nearby. There wasn't, but one of Ian's men hit it with a powder extinguisher anyway.

Dominic stripped off his overshirt, wrapping the flannel around his forearm to protect it, then pushed the smoldering door open.

The smell of burning wood and chemical retardant was replaced with the reek of blood.

"Fuck me," Dominic muttered.

"Let me go in," Amanda said, slipping past him into the darkness. She had a mag light and a drawn gun, so Dominic let her take the lead.

Ian stepped past him too, motioning for Dominic to follow. "There might be some more protective warding down there, and I don't want Amanda running across it alone."

Micah found his place at Dominic's shoulder. "Do you want me to wait up here?"

"If you want," Dominic said, starting down the stairs. "Or come be my bodyguard."

Lights flickered on, illuminating the staircase. It was narrow, and wood-paneled to match the décor upstairs.

"There's a switch down here," Amanda called out, her voice hollow.

Dominic reached the bottom and saw why.

The stairs opened into a wide round space set under the room upstairs. The floor was concrete, etched and stained into an elaborate pattern.

The space was filled with cages. The cages were filled with animals. And the animals were dead. Blood spilled out of the wire and metal enclosures, obscuring the ornate designs.

"That's a leopard," Amanda said, pointing to a ball of fur huddled in the corner of a nearby cage. The fur didn't move.

More officers were coming down the stairs, pausing on the landing and surveying the scene.

"I want this all cataloged," Ian instructed, gesturing at everything. "If you find a dead *ant* I want to know about it."

"You've got some supernatural stuff in here," Dom told him, his attention fixed on the surrounding carnage. "You've got a chupacabra there, and, uh, those three are phoenixes, and that, um . . . that dog's got three heads, so it probably falls into the supernatural category too."

Ian's jaw set. "Go with the photographers and tell them what you know."

There was no point trying to avoid the blood. It was everywhere. It lay in a sheen over the entire floor. Some of the officers went upstairs to retrieve plastic shoe covers, but Dominic didn't bother. His soles were thick. He'd walked through worse.

He stepped out into the maze of cages and got to work.

It went back, and back, and back into the dark. Some of the creatures were clearly monsters, but some were humanoid. Some looked like normal people, but their wrists and ankles and throats were wrapped in warded leather or metal cuffs. Some of the sigils Dominic recognized. Some he didn't. Slowly, he made his way between the cages, giving identifications as best he could. Micah stayed at his shoulder, listening. Ostensibly, he was there to keep things from sneaking up on Dominic while he worked. In practice, there was nothing to protect against.

There were harpies and kitsune and a curupira, werewolves and vampires, all of them dead. These kinds of creatures could heal fast, and superficial wounds rarely left scars or marks of any kind. The ones he saw must have been starved, though, because the marks on their naked bodies had barely healed at all.

They all showed signs of torture. They'd been whipped, or pierced, or bitten, or tattooed. Dark, bruised handprints stood out on throats, on hips, on thighs, on breasts. Everywhere he looked, there were marks of cruelty and pain.

Dominic wasn't innocent. He knew that. He'd killed creatures like this before. But he'd never done anything like this. Never had. Never would.

This was *senseless*.

Micah made a sound behind him. Dominic didn't turn. He didn't think he could look Micah in the eye. All he could think of was the bruises and scars, and how Micah's body had borne the same.

"This is the man who owned you?"

"Yes," Micah said simply.

"And he did . . . this? To the people he owned?"

"Sometimes." Micah's voice was empty, and Dominic knew that those hazel eyes would be as blank as a mirror.

In a way, he envied Micah's ability to escape.

Micah listened to the dark. Anything dangerous that came at them would make a sound long before he could see it. Dead things did not pose a threat, and so he didn't need to look. Didn't need to see.

The body of a human was slumped, motionless, in the space between two cages. It wouldn't make them any safer for Micah to recognize the uniform, or the face, so he didn't. It was that simple.

He would *make* it that simple.

He *had* to, because he had a job to do. He didn't need to see the roster of the dead; he just needed to make sure Dominic stayed off it.

That was his job.

Dominic stopped suddenly, his attention drawn to something on the near wall. Micah didn't follow his gaze, just continued focusing on the dark around them. Farther away, he could hear the voices of the officers. Their flashlight beams swept across the walls, the high ceiling, revealing nothing of note.

"There," Dominic said, and Micah looked to see what he'd been focused on. In the center of Dominic's light was a door, unwarded and partly ajar. "Come on," Dominic said, and pushed it the rest of the way open. The room was red, plastic red, from the smooth linoleum to the leather couches to the vinyl pads on the various machines positioned throughout the space.

Light poured through the doorway into the darkened room, and for a moment, Micah thought it was illuminating a painting. Some sick parody of a crucifixion.

The creature on the far wall had been a man, before they'd gotten hold of him. He hung limply from his arms, which were spread wide and bound to a crossbar. His throat had been slit, and his naked skin was crisscrossed with deep slashes, streaks and drips of dried blood painting his emaciated body. The silver bands around his throat and wrists and ankles were caked in it, and the skin beneath was chafed and burned. But that wasn't what drew Micah's attention.

Emerging from his back were a pair of gargantuan black wings, spread wide and mounted to the wall with spikes, like pins through a massive butterfly.

In the light of the room's single spotlight, the feathers glinted with blue and red and purple. Watching them, Micah saw sunsets and fireworks and bonfires and lightning.

It was abhorrent and terrifying and the most beautiful thing he'd ever seen.

"Get him down," Dominic whispered, and then lunged forward, grabbing one of the spikes in both hands and *yanking*. The spike didn't move. It was too high, the wing easily two feet above Dominic's head. The angle was wrong.

"Get him *down*!" he shouted. His movements were frantic, almost desperate. "Help me. Micah, *help me*!"

Micah didn't want to go near the body, but Dominic had given him an order. He tried not to touch it as he wrapped his hands around Dominic's, and together they yanked the spike from the wall.

The wing collapsed, folding in on itself in a thousand intricate places, flopping into the blood on the floor. From this angle, the mottling on each feather aligned into a pattern of overlapping circles. Micah's heart sank. He'd seen that pattern before.

Dominic was already moving, hauling at the other spike as hard as he could, but he still needed Micah's help to pull it free. The second wing collapsed like its twin, and the creature's shoulders slumped further against the crossbar.

Micah carefully didn't look at its face, but Dom had no such qualms, staring at the corpse with something like despair. He pulled his knife from its sheath and used it to saw through the ropes binding the thing's arms.

"Support him," he ordered.

Micah couldn't find an unharmed place to put his hands. His best option was a ladder of shallow cuts that ran up one flank, new and bloody at the top but near healed at the bottom.

He desperately did not want to touch them.

"I think we should wait for the photographers," he started to say, but didn't get to finish because several things happened at once.

The rope snapped and the creature started to fall, but Dominic caught it. The creature's head fell back, and as Micah got his first look, its eyes opened. They were dark, and clear, and focused immediately on Dominic's face.

He's alive, Micah had time to think, and then the thing seized Dominic's arm with a strength Micah wouldn't have predicted.

For a moment, Micah stood frozen, unsure of what to do. Dominic didn't react, or at least, he didn't move.

The creature began to *glow*, a purple so deep it was almost ultraviolet. It spread across the creature's face and then down its chest, engulfing it in a moment that seemed like slow motion.

Then the glow spread further, enveloping Dominic in a blinding radiance.

"*Dominic*!"

Dominic still didn't react; Micah grabbed his collar and hauled him up and away from the creature. It crashed to the floor, the light vanishing.

"No!" Dominic lunged for the fallen thing, but Micah's arms locked around his chest. Behind him, Micah heard someone come through the door. He glanced back, verifying that the new arrival wasn't a threat. It was just Amanda. Micah ignored her.

"Stop it! Dominic— *Dominic*! *Stop it*!"

"Let me—he's dying!" Dominic screamed, but Micah held fast. "He's— Shit . . . what *is* he?"

People were coming faster now: Ian and a couple of others Micah didn't recognize. Amanda had her gun drawn and leveled on the creature.

"With those wings?" she answered, not taking her eyes off the still form. "Don't know. I've never seen anything like it."

"Don't shoot him, Amanda," Dom said. "He's not dangerous."

"Are you serious?" Micah asked. "He just *attacked* you while you were trying to help him! You're lucky I was here."

Dom's thrashing no longer seemed frantic, so when he shrugged out of Micah's grip, Micah let him go.

"No, he . . . he asked. I let him."

"Yeah, no, he didn't. I was right here, Dominic. I saw the whole thing."

Dominic's brow furrowed. "In my head. I heard him asking."

"It's psychic?" Ian backed away from the creature.

Dominic rubbed at his scalp. "Maybe? I got this kind of impression we were . . . somewhere else? I'm not sure. It was weird. But he wasn't trying to hurt me. I know that for sure."

"Then what's this?" Micah pressed gently against Dominic's forearm, where the creature had grabbed him. It had left a handprint, the outline of each finger already bruising.

"What in the hells?" Dom twisted his arm to get a better look. Micah winced. How could he not have noticed? That should hurt like a bastard.

"I had to," a rough voice intoned. Amanda twitched and almost shot the thing as its wings shifted, folding in on themselves. The being pushed itself up. It was clearly taking all its strength just to look around at the assembled group, eyes defiant as it regarded them. "I will *not* die in this place."

Dominic moved toward the creature again, but Micah snagged one arm, holding him back.

"What do you need?" Dominic asked, at the same time Ian asked "What are you?"

"Let me make the bond again," the creature responded, eyes locked on Dominic. Its voice was raspy.

"Dom, don't," Micah warned, not taking his attention off those dark, otherworldly eyes.

"Share your toys, Micah," Dominic muttered, trying to pull out of his grip and failing. "Micah, really. It's okay."

"He'll kill you," Micah protested.

Dominic shook his head. "No, he won't."

The creature's gaze flicked to Micah. "He will suffer no lasting damage. You have my word."

Its word meant less than nothing to Micah, who was still thinking of the bruising on Dominic's arm.

"What *is* it?" someone asked nervously.

The creature fixed them with an angry stare. "*He* is a daiyura."

Micah glanced to Amanda, but it appeared that she'd never heard of it before, either. The daiyura scowled. "We do not occupy this plane. Whatever your purpose here, I have no reason to hinder you. If I had strength, I would already be on my way."

"See? Totally safe," Dominic announced, and tried pulling away from Micah again. Micah did not let go.

"That's not enough to risk your life on," he hissed.

"Look at the bands," Dominic insisted. He'd stopped pulling, for the time being. "Look at the ikons."

Micah obeyed. Blood had seeped into the engravings on the cuffs, making them stand out against the silver. And sure enough, he *did* recognize them. At least, some of them. "Suppression bands," he said softly.

Dominic nodded.

"Well," Amanda said hesitantly. She was frowning at the dirty bangles. "No, I think there's more. For that kind of magic to work on a *person* . . ."

Surprise flickered across the creature's face. It was quickly replaced by a dark scowl—but not too quickly for Micah to notice.

"You'd need some stronger power source to break the stalemate," Dominic finished. "Someone with a Gift, maybe?"

Amanda shook her head. "That might buy you a couple hours, but . . ."

"It's the blood," Micah blurted. He gestured to the creature's wounds. "The cuts on his side. They've been made over time, by people using blood magic to bolster the spell." He turned to the creature for verification. "Right?"

The daiyura stared daggers at him. "Don't play stupid. Too many humans have marked me for your pretense of innocence."

Micah nodded, satisfied. "As long as his blood is used when activating the bands, he can't fight them without draining his own life force. He'd be harmless."

The creature groaned, collapsing back against the bloody wall. He offered Dominic his forearm. "If that's what it *takes*," he muttered. "Mark me, then."

"Um . . . mark you how?" Dominic asked.

The creature shrugged his shoulders in a surprisingly human gesture. "However you'd like. It doesn't seem to matter. Knives or burns, usually. One man bit me. It seemed to work."

Ian sent a sharp look in Dominic's direction. Dominic held up his hands defensively. "No way I'm biting you, man. Not on the first date."

"Any mark should work. A small cut would be sufficient." He paused. "I will not fight you."

"I'll shoot him if he tries," Amanda piped up.

"You don't need to do this—" Micah started, but Dominic took advantage of his distraction to drop out of his grip, twisting away from Micah's attempt to recapture him.

"Seriously, Micah, knock it off."

Micah set his jaw, then turned his attention to the figure on the floor. "If you hurt him, I will kill you myself. Do you understand?"

The creature met his eyes with an unyielding stare.

Dominic approached him again, crouching down so they were on the same level.

"I trust you."

"Dominic, I'm not sure this is a good idea," Ian started, but Dominic raised his knife and nicked the creature's arm. The silver bands brightened, small blue sparks winding lazily along the surface.

"The spell has sealed to you," the creature said. "You are safe. May I make a bond?"

"Dom, you have no idea if—"

"Yes," Dominic answered before Micah could talk some sense into him. He focused on the cut he'd made, watched the daiyura's blood trickle along the silver cuff. The spell on it was *complicated*, using almost twice as many ikons as the ones Dominic made for random ghoulies. He really had no idea whether the magic would protect him at all, and his gut was screaming at him to *run*—

And then the blood dripped onto the floor, the floor that was already soaked from the slaughter they'd been too slow to stop. Dom glanced at Micah, trying not to think of how easily it could have been him here, and Dom would have been too late, too late, *too late*—

The last survivor reached out to him, fingers trembling, and laid his hand on the bruised impression he'd made before. The violet light returned, searing into Dominic's skin, filling his entire body with tingling warmth. Dominic began to unfold, his body losing the solid presence he'd never realized he had always felt. He was weightless, formless, warm. Something nudged him, keeping him centered. Slowly, he began to slip toward the daiyura, threads and trickles of himself seeping into the other being.

Thank you, he heard, and then his body snapped back into its usual form. He staggered.

"Dominic!" Micah called, reaching for him again.

Dominic waved him off. "I'm fine. I'm fine. It just feels a little weird."

"Holy shit," Ian murmured, gaping down at the creature. He'd pulled himself into a sitting position, cross-legged, his wings splayed to the sides. The backs of his hands were resting on his knees, and his head had fallen against the wall.

And he was glowing.

Across his chest and limbs, his skin was knitting itself together, the blood seeping into the flesh like a sponge. The silver bands were sparking with power, and his face was contorted in pain, but he was healing. The dark bruises on his throat and hips and arms faded, growing mottled before disappearing completely.

His head fell forward, his body spasmed, and then he turned his head and spat out a bullet. It hit the ground with a faint *ping* that drove home exactly how *quietly* this was all happening.

"Holy *shit*," Ian said again, staring at the little blob of metal.

The light began to fade, starting at his fingers and toes and working its way down his limbs. The last of it gathered in the hollow of his throat, flickering brightly before finally going out.

He slumped forward, apparently unconscious.

The room was utterly silent.

And then it burst into sound: everyone had questions, half of them directed at Dominic, half of them rhetorical.

"Let me see your arm," Micah demanded, cutting past the others. Dominic blinked and shook his head, his focus returning. He raised his arm for Micah's inspection.

The fingerprints were gone, nothing but a faint flush to the skin. "It doesn't even hurt," Dominic said quietly.

Micah's jaw set. "He said you'd have no damage."

"I'm not sure this qualifies as damage. It's barely even a mark. And anyway, whatever he did, it saved his life."

"Took him back to mint, by the looks of it," Ian remarked, crouching down to examine the slumped creature. "The blood's gone, the wounds are gone. All but this one."

He pointed to the creature's arm, showing them the tiny nick Dominic had made with his knife. It had healed, but unlike the others, there was still an obvious mark.

"He said 'diurnal,' right?" one of the other officers asked, keeping his distance.

Amanda and Dominic exchanged glances. "Daiyura. Yeah. From 'another plane.'"

The officer stepped forward, his eyes wide as he took in the creature's wings. "He's an angel. That's what he is. Brought here from Heaven."

Dominic shrugged, too tired to debate the likelihood. "Maybe? I've never run across anything like him. And I've never heard of anyone with a legitimate claim of having found an angel."

"He could be one of the fae folk," Amanda speculated. "They're supposed to have wings, and they're associated with lights and magic."

"We'll ask him when he wakes back up," Micah said.

"He's already—" Dominic was interrupted by a growl. The creature was up, fast, pushing past Ian with no sign of his earlier weakness. His wings spread wide, beating once and taking him over the heads of the gathered spectators, and then he was through the door and gone.

"Wait!" Dominic shouted, scrambling out the door after him.

"He has to—" Amanda started, but Dom was too far away, and her words got lost in the commotion.

Dominic rushed across the main room, past the photographers and officers staring at him with wide eyes. He didn't need to ask which way the creature had gone. They pointed anyway.

The angel was paused at the base of the stairs. His wings were wrapped around his body, and he was trembling like staying upright was taking some monumental effort.

"Hey, we're not gonna hurt you," Dominic said, in what he hoped was a reassuring voice. "We're just trying to figure out what happened here. The people who did this—we're not with them. We're trying to bring them to justice. But we could really use your help."

The daiyura rounded on him, and Dominic lurched at the hate in those fiery eyes.

"You are *all* the same," the creature spat. "You are *all* in this together."

"That's not really fair, man. I just saved your life. I trusted you. Trust me."

Blue sparks flickered along the silver bands, and the creature winced. His eyes cut to the side, and Dominic didn't need to turn to know that Micah had come up behind him.

"Why'd you stop?" Micah demanded. "It's a clear shot to the outside."

The creature scowled but didn't answer.

"Is it the bindings?" Dominic asked. "Holding you in?"

"In a way," the daiyura answered.

"We're trying to help. Work with me here." The silver flickered again, and again, the creature winced. Dominic kept his voice soft and reassuring. "Are the bindings holding you in the building?"

"No." The daiyura's jaw was clenched so tight Dominic could almost hear teeth cracking.

"So why didn't you leave?"

"You . . . told me to wait."

The words came out forced, like he was trying not to breathe while he spoke. Anger burned in his eyes, and Dominic suddenly realized what he'd said.

"That's part of the binding spell. You can't hurt me, but you also have to obey me."

"Yes," the creature rasped, tendons straining in his throat. His voice sounded like it was being dragged over glass.

"That's what Amanda was trying to tell you," Micah said. "He didn't mention it and hoped he'd be gone before you found out."

"Your pet is smarter than he looks," the daiyura sneered.

"He's not my pet. He's my—" *Friend, just say friend.*

Yeah, he's my friend who sleeps in my bed and sometimes wakes me up with blowjobs and sometimes looks at me like I'm the only person he's ever really seen.

"—friend," he finished, looking away. He didn't have time to worry about that right now.

"Clearly," the creature deadpanned, and Dominic glared at him, because he was *so* not in the mood to take sass from an angel.

"We're not talking about him. We're talking about you. Can you tell me your name?"

"No," the angel said, and Dom thought he was just being obstinate, but then he waved a dismissive hand. "My identifier would best be translated into your understanding as . . . I don't know. A color." He paused. "But the humans who brought me here referred to me as 'the Gestalt.'"

"Okay. Gestalt. Did you see what happened here? Before the slaughter?"

"Yes."

"Did you see the people who did all this?"

"Some of them."

"Could you identify them?" Micah asked, coming up beside Dom.

Gestalt nodded.

"Good. Then you can go with Ian back to the station and look at some mugshots," Micah concluded. He turned toward where Ian was standing just out of earshot. The lightshow earlier seemed to have spooked him enough to give Gestalt a wide berth.

Gestalt eyed the detective coldly, then nodded. "I can do that."

"Good," Dominic said, beckoning to Ian. "That's all settled, then."

"You should mark him," Micah said the moment Ian got close. "He'll obey Dominic, but there's nothing protecting you."

The glare he got from the angel was pure ice.

"I'm not sure I'm comfortable with that," Ian said.

Micah scowled. "You want his help, right? And he's clearly not going to cooperate of his own free will. Seems like a pretty easy decision to me."

"Except that he *has* free will, and I'm not sure it's ethically permissible to circumvent that. Even assuming I was personally open to the suggestion—which, frankly, I'm not—I'm not sure a subjugated testimony would hold up in court."

Dominic rounded on Micah. "I'm actually surprised at how okay *you* are with that. Especially considering it hasn't been that long since you were in his place."

Gestalt perked up, honing in on Micah, who ignored him.

"I *was* in his place," Micah said evenly. "And maybe that's why I'm the only one paying attention here. This is what Slate and his friends will do to cover their tracks. You think this is the only menagerie they're liquidating? The only witnesses they need to get rid of? Don't be naïve. This ends when they're in jail. And this thing might be the key to making that happen."

Dominic wrinkled his nose. "He's not a *thing*, Micah, be nice."

Micah rolled his eyes.

"I know that name," Gestalt said slowly. "Slate. I have met this man. He was . . . forceful."

"Yeah, I know," Micah snapped. "Been there, done that, got the scars." Micah pulled his shirt collar down, exposing the scarred edge of a whip mark.

The angel reached out, his fingertips grazing Micah's throat. A purple flame passed to Micah's skin, flickering under his shirt. It blazed across Micah's back like St. Elmo's fire, splitting and reforming, stingingly bright even through the cloth. Dominic closed his eyes, but it was already done—a stygian echo of Micah's scars appeared in the darkness like a firework.

"The fuck—" Micah started, but Gestalt cut him off. "His marks are gone from you. You are freed."

Micah gaped for a moment, then wrinkled his nose. "It doesn't work that way for humans. Don't touch me."

Dominic didn't miss the way Micah rolled his shoulders. "Are they really all gone?"

"Yeah," Micah muttered.

Dominic resisted the urge to roll his eyes. Talk about looking a gift horse in the mouth. He addressed Gestalt on Micah's behalf. "Micah's being a little bitch right now, but he means 'thank you.'"

"I do not," Micah snapped. "Are we done here?"

Dominic shrugged, pointing Ian out to the daiyura. "If I send you with Ian, are you going to attack him? Tell the truth."

"I will make every attempt to escape," Gestalt confirmed, nodding.

Dominic crossed his arms, tilting his head. This wasn't the first creature he'd had to negotiate with. Their motivations could be bizarre, but they usually weren't too complicated. It was just a matter of finding an in. "You aren't at all interested in getting justice?"

"Not so interested that I am willing to become a captive again."

"But you told me how to work the binding."

Gestalt sighed. "Without your mana, I would have died. You—"

"Hold up, *mana*? As in, his *life* force?" Amanda interrupted; Dominic hadn't even noticed her catching up with them. "What did you *do* to him?"

The creature focused on Dominic. "Humans have a near *limitless* ability to regenerate," he said, and Dom thought he detected a hint of apology there. "You won't even notice that it happened."

"I believe you," Dom said. Then, to the rest of the group, "I feel fine. Really."

"You seem fine," Micah begrudgingly admitted.

"See? No enemies here," Dom said to the daiyura. "Let me get you out of those cuffs, and we'll work something out." The silver sparked again. Dom frowned. "Why is it doing that?"

"You gave me an order," Gestalt answered in a clipped voice.

Dom played the last minute back in his head. "What? No I didn't."

"You said 'let me.' That's close enough to count."

"But that's just a figure of speech."

"Apparently the spell doesn't make exceptions for *idioms*," Gestalt snapped.

Dominic held up his hands. "Okay, I'm sorry. *Will you* let Amanda take a look at you? She won't hurt you, and I think she might be able to help."

The angel considered, then nodded. Amanda fished an emergency blanket out of her kit, which Gestalt was eventually convinced to wrap around his waist.

She couldn't do much else. She had never seen anything like a daiyura, or the extra ikons on the bands used to contain him.

Dominic was starting to get a tension headache. Probably just from the smell of blood. "I'm gonna go get some air," he told the assembled group.

Micah, predictably, followed him.

"I don't trust him," Micah said once they were up the stairs. The foyer was mostly empty, only a couple of people making their way in or out of the basement.

"That's pretty obvious, man." Dominic's head was pounding. "Maybe tone down the bulldog act a bit? I can take care of myself, you know."

Micah pushed a burned woodchip across the floor with his boot. "I know you can. He just—there was this light, and I thought he'd vaporized you or something and I . . . I'm supposed to be your bodyguard."

Dom laughed. "I was kidding about that."

"Yeah. But I like the idea of protecting you."

"Oh my *god*. Come here, you giant sap." Dominic pulled him into a one-armed hug, but Micah wrapped both arms around him and held him tight, which ended up being a good decision because Dom's head was practically *reverberating* and his vision was getting fuzzy and he had just enough time to hear Micah say, "Knock it off, I can't hold you—" before everything went black.

CHAPTER TWENTY-FIVE

"*What did you do*?" Micah demanded, storming back into the basement.

It was loud enough to turn the creature's attention away from Amanda, his brow furrowed in a mixture of confusion and concern.

"*What are you doing to him*?" Micah roared, seizing the thing by the arms and slamming him into the wall. "Fix him, or I swear to god I will kill you with my own two hands!"

"I'm not doing anything to him," the monster protested. It was a good impression of remorse. "He's sleeping off the effects of the transfer. I may have . . . overestimated earlier. I took too much. I was desperate and I apologize."

"You apolo—?" Micah slammed him into the wall again. He didn't have time to negotiate this. "Give it back to him! Whatever you took, give it back!"

The creature fixed him with a glare. "I cannot transfer the energy back. Healing him would weaken me beyond even my earlier state."

"What part of '*I will kill you*' led you to believe I care?"

The daiyura bared his teeth. "He will be fine, and it is out of gratitude to *him* that I have not killed you for touching me. My patience is wearing thin."

Stupid, Micah realized. He'd been desperate and it had made him stupid.

Micah dropped him, and before Gestalt could catch his balance, Micah had pulled his knife from its sheath and sliced Gestalt across his chest.

Gestalt hissed, staring daggers up at Micah.

Micah held his ground. "That's my mark now, yeah? You've got to do what I say, and I say *fix him.*"

Those dark eyes went wide with a mix of hate and fear. When he spoke, the bravado of a moment ago was gone. "Please, human, your master will be fine. I swear to you. Make me do this and I will die for nothing. Please." His voice tremored. "I do not beg lightly."

"Why would I believe you?"

The creature reached for him. Micah withdrew. Sparks danced across the bangle, and the skin beneath was turning an angry red. "Please. Let me show you."

He shouldn't. He knew that.

But Dominic would never forgive him if he didn't at least try.

Micah inched back toward the creature on the floor. "Don't hurt me," he ordered as Gestalt reached out again, pressing fingertips against Micah's forearm.

Color spilled from the contact, a dark purple flowing over him and expanding until it filled his entire world. The angel spoke to him, though his lips weren't moving and there was no sound. Because even though he had a voice, and a mouth, and a body, that wasn't him. He was dim, flickering, an ultraviolet so rich it was almost dark. Micah sank deeper into it and saw the bright sapphire stream of *Dominic* threading through the almost-darkness, binding the creature tight. The blue faded at the edges, and where it ended, the purple was a little bit brighter.

As the light mixed and churned, Micah saw desperation there. And fear, and anger, and regret, and sadness, and even hate. But no malice. No deception.

He drew back with a gasp.

"Gods," he whispered. "How are you alive? You're *shattered.*" Micah didn't know how a color could possibly be *broken*, but he knew what he'd seen. "I mean, I'm no expert at . . . judging people's soul-health or whatever, but there's nothing *left* of you. Dominic's the only thing holding you together."

Gestalt withdrew his hand, saying nothing, waiting for Micah's judgment. Something twisted in Micah's stomach. He didn't fully trust Gestalt, but that didn't mean he wanted the guy to *die*.

And Gestalt *would* die. He wasn't lying about that.

"Do you still order me to heal him?" Gestalt asked, trembling with the effort of resisting the command.

Micah paused, instincts screaming at him not to *hesitate,* Dominic might not have time for him to *waste* like this. "Not if you *swear* he'll be fine."

Gestalt nodded, slow and serious, not taking his eyes off Micah's face. "Your master will wake within the hour. I swear it."

"He's not my master."

"So you say."

The daiyura was very expressive, Micah realized with a hint of annoyance. He was saying all kinds of sarcastic, demeaning things, and he was doing it with nothing but his facial expressions. It made it very hard to argue, even when he was *wrong.*

"I'm a free man. Got the papers and everything."

"I've seen your soul, human."

"What's *that* supposed to mean?"

Gestalt was saved by a voice from above: "Micah? You down here?"

Micah whirled to the stairs, where Dominic was looking a little pale, but otherwise okay. Gestalt's weird goading was forgotten in a heartbeat.

"Careful on the stairs. Don't pass out again."

"Yeah, okay, *mom.* I'll be careful on the stairs. What's with you today?"

Micah rolled his eyes, scowling. "I have a limit on how many times I can watch you almost die."

Dominic gestured to Gestalt. "So did he manage to convince you that he wasn't killing me telepathically from all the way down here?"

Micah set his jaw. "Yeah, I'm convinced. But it *is* his fault you fainted."

"I didn't *faint.*" Dominic's gaze fell on the angel. "Wait, did you—Micah, did you *cut him*?"

Micah crossed his arms and raised his chin. "I thought you were dying. I thought he was *killing* you."

"So you marked him?"

"I was only *half wrong*," Micah snapped. "How are *you* not more pissed about this? He drained you until you passed out."

"Because I told him he could. And I'm awake now. No autopsy, no foul."

"Not to interrupt your lovers' spat," Amanda interrupted, "but can you have it later? I need to get some more photos."

For what seemed like the first time, Micah realized the room was full of people. They were shuttling between the cages, categorizing and documenting and photographing and more than a few were shooting glances in his direction.

"We're not having a spat," Dominic said, turning his attention wholly to Amanda. "We're done. Do you need help with identification?"

"Yeah, there's like, an entire block of weird chimera-looking things over there. If you could take a look, I'd appreciate it."

Dominic nodded and set off in that direction.

Micah suddenly didn't know where he should be. It seemed evident that whatever Dominic was doing, he didn't want or need Micah there with him. And Gestalt was probably one measly containment spell away from literally murdering him.

"Can I . . . do anything?" he asked Amanda.

"Other than not beating the crap out of my witness?" Her tone wasn't entirely serious. "Maybe. By the sounds of it, you guys knew a lot of the same people. Ges, are there any other names you can give me?"

Gestalt blinked, as if unsure as to whether he was being addressed. "Coffey. He's the one who shot me. I assume he was responsible for a good deal of the bloodshed out here. There were two others helping him, but I do not know their names."

"Coffey," Micah asked. "Tall guy with a scar?" Gestalt nodded. "Yeah, I know him. Lucas Coffey. He and Slate went to a lot of the same . . . parties."

"That's where Slate marked you. You were his slave," Gestalt said, connecting the pieces. He tilted his head at Micah. "You said you were a free man. How did you escape?"

"Dominic and Ian," Micah said shortly. "What about Arabelle, do you know a Arabelle? Or a doctor by the name of Godfrey?"

Gestalt shook his head. "None of these are familiar to me. Do you have a photograph? Many of the people I saw were not formally introduced."

Micah snorted. Gestalt seemed unaware he'd said anything funny.

"We've got pictures back at the station," Amanda said. "And we arrested a lot of people when we came in today. I'd like you to look through the photos and tell me if you can place any of them in the basement here." Amanda's face turned a little bit red. "It would be really helpful if we could get . . . details. Of what happened. If you're comfortable talking about it. We have a couple counselors on staff, if that helps?"

Gestalt blinked. "Why would that help?"

"Some people are just more comfortable describing their . . . experiences. With a counselor. Instead of a cop."

"Why?"

Amanda shrugged. "Not sure. Maybe they feel less like they're in trouble?"

"Why would they be in trouble for something that someone else did to them?"

Micah was with Gestalt on this one. Amanda held her hands out. "I dunno, Ges, that's just how they feel."

"Hmm."

Ian appeared before they could continue the conversation, a pair of bolt cutters slung over his shoulder. "You get pictures of those cuffs yet?" he asked Amanda.

She nodded. "I don't recognize *everything*, but they should be safe to cut off."

"Wait," Micah protested. "Those bands are the only thing keeping him here. For all you know, the second you've cut through them, he'll be back in his own dimension. We still need him. He's the *only* witness to this."

"I'm not having this conversation with you, Micah," Ian said shortly. "If he wants to help, that's *his choice*. Understood?"

Micah dropped his gaze, nodding once. "Yes, sir."

Ian turned his attention to Gestalt, but the angel was still watching Micah. "All right, let's see what we can do with these."

The metal around Gestalt's wrists looked like sterling silver. It even had the tarnish that silver got. But silver was soft and malleable. This, not so much. The bolt cutters had no effect. An EMT produced a ring cutter, which was equally useless.

"It's the spell," Amanda declared at last. "Whatever's protecting this, it's magic. And it'll need to be magicked off."

She took some pictures with her phone. "My coven meets on Thursdays for drum circle and cosplay appreciation," she told Gestalt. "Hopefully at least one of them will recognize these."

Gestalt turned to Micah in confusion, and Micah shrugged. He didn't understand her any more than the angel did.

The grounds of the manor were actually quite nice. Dominic stood with Gestalt and Micah on the shore of the lake, watching the fog roll over the water.

"Kinda sucks that a place like this gets filled up with shitty people doing shitty stuff," he mused after a minute. "There should be, like, kids playing here or something."

No one had anything to say to that. The water lapped softly onto the beach. Somewhere behind them, a sprinkler kicked on, disturbing a flock of birds.

"I'm not gonna order you," Dominic said, turning to Gestalt. "But we do need your help. Everybody else down there is dead. You're the only one who can say what happened."

"I would assume that the corpses speak for themselves," the daiyura said, not taking his eyes off the water. The waves were barely visible in the predawn light.

"But they don't say who did it," Dominic argued. "We need you for that."

"And what do I get out of it?" Gestalt asked almost idly.

Micah snorted. "What, angels don't believe in revenge?"

Gestalt turned his head slowly. "What makes you think I need your help to exact my revenge?"

"I'll figure out how to get the cuffs off," Dominic offered. "If you help Ian with the investigation, I'll work on breaking the spell. I'll get my friend Garrett to take a look at it. He might recognize the sigils and have an idea."

The daiyura's brow furrowed.

"Plus, you can crash at my place," Dominic added.

Micah made a strangled little sound. "Can I talk to you for a second, Dominic?"

"I'll do it," Gestalt said.

"Dominic? A second?"

"Yeah?" Dom said to Gestalt.

"I'm being serious," Micah said, grabbing Dominic by the arm and pulling him further down the bank. "What do you mean he can crash at your place? This is the same guy who tried to drain your soul like an hour ago."

Dom sighed. "He *asked*, Micah. I don't know how many times I'm going to have to tell you this. When he touched me, it was like he was in my mind. And I knew he was dying, and he asked me for help. And I helped him. And so what if he took a little too much? Who cares? I'm fine, look at me. And I don't know how to explain it, but it was like . . . I *saw* him, you know?"

"I saw it too," Micah murmured.

Dominic's eyebrows rose. "Is that what you did while I was out? Mind-melded?"

"Don't call it that," Micah said, wrinkling his nose.

Dominic stared at him for a long second. "Sounds like you saw what I saw. We can trust him. He's not gonna murder us in our sleep."

"What if what we saw was a front? What if he can lie, show us what he wants?"

Dominic didn't buy it. "Do you really think he can?"

Micah's shoulders slumped. "No," he admitted.

"I didn't think so. So what's the real problem?"

"I don't know. There's just something about him."

Dominic waited to see if he would say more, then broke out into a grin. He threw his arm around Micah's shoulders, drawing him in. "Aww, don't worry, Mic. You're still my favorite."

Micah looked up a little too quickly.

Dom gave him a squeeze. "And hey, look. Now we've been to the beach."

Micah scowled. "This beach sucks."

"Yeah, I know," Dominic said, tone turning serious. He pulled Micah closer, the arm around his shoulders dropping to his waist. "But we've got time to do something better. You know that, right?"

"Not if you get yourself killed." Micah turned, pulling Dominic into a full embrace, his forehead resting against Dom's shoulder. "I told you, I want you to come with me."

"I will," Dom promised. "Do you trust me? Can you trust me on this?"

Micah exhaled, reminding Dom of his silent laughs. "What are my choices?"

"That's the spirit," Dom said brightly. Micah didn't reply, just stared out over the lightening water. Dom sobered. "You do have a choice, but . . . does he really bother you that much?"

"I know we need him," Micah acknowledged. "It's just . . . Does he really need to come *home* with us?"

Dominic grinned.

Micah squinted at him "What?"

"You called our place 'home.'"

"Yeah, well, you just called it 'our place.' And sorry if I don't want a monster camping in the spare bedroom."

"I didn't invite him because I thought it would be fun. He doesn't have anywhere else to go."

"The police can find him somewhere."

"Yeah, the police," Dominic said, running a hand through his hair. "Slate shipped me a human being in a *box*. That's not a guy who's afraid of the police. And that basement, all those bodies . . . those people were alive when the sun went down. Their killers didn't have enough time to clean the place out, but they weren't taken by surprise, either."

"You think there's someone on the inside."

"I think there has to be. So if we've only got one witness, I think it's probably safest to keep an eye on him ourselves."

Micah's head fell back, and he groaned up at the sky. "I don't *want* him coming home with us—"

"If you're dead set on this, fine, I'll get Ian to—"

"—but fine, you have a point," Micah finished. "If putting up with him for a couple weeks is what it takes to stop all this, then that's what we'll do."

Dominic squeezed him tighter, a silent thank-you. "You want to take him home with us."

Micah grinned. "Yes, Dom. I'll let you take him *home* with us."

"To *our place*," Dominic started to say, but Micah had already leaned in, pressing one of his soft kisses to Dom's mouth. Dom hugged him close. It was going to take a week to wash the smell of blood out of his hair, but that was later's problem. They were safe for now, and Micah was kissing him again because he *wanted* to, and—

"Is this going to take very long?"

Fuck. Gestalt.

Micah let his forehead drop onto Dom's shoulder, laughing a little. "You ready?"

"Yeah," Dom murmured into his hair. "Let's go home."

Explore more of *The Powers That Be* series at:
riptidepublishing.com/collections/series-the-powers-that-be

Dear Reader,

Thank you for reading Hazel Domain's *Any Price*!

We know your time is precious and you have many, many entertainment options, so it means a lot that you've chosen to spend your time reading. We really hope you enjoyed it.

We'd be honored if you'd consider posting a review—good or bad—on sites like **Amazon, Barnes & Noble, Kobo, Goodreads, Twitter, Facebook, Tumblr,** and your blog or website. We'd also be honored if you told your friends and family about this book. Word of mouth is a book's lifeblood!

For more information on upcoming releases, author interviews, blog tours, contests, giveaways, and more, please sign up for our weekly, spam-free newsletter and visit us around the web:

Newsletter: riptidepublishing.com/newsletter
Twitter: twitter.com/RiptideBooks
Facebook: facebook.com/RiptidePublishing
Goodreads: tinyurl.com/RiptideOnGoodreads
Tumblr: riptidepublishing.tumblr.com

Thank you so much for Reading the Rainbow!

RiptidePublishing.com

ACKNOWLEDGMENTS

I cannot properly acknowledge all the people to whom *Any Price* and *Any Cost* owe their existence.

Some are obvious, like Rachel, who agreed to look over a manuscript on the brink of being self-published, and then messaged me at 3 a.m. to say "I'm still reading." Or Alex, Grace, and Caz at Riptide, who went through it line by line and made it clear that I have never paid attention to one (1) detail in my entire life.

Others are more indirect, like Matt, who told me I was a writer. I didn't remember—after a traumatic brain injury in 2019, I didn't remember very much at all, actually. I don't remember writing this book, and as such, have had the rare pleasure of being able to read my own writing the way a stranger would. I liked it enough to finish editing it, albeit a few years behind schedule.

There are dozens more who I can't acknowledge the way they deserve. There are comments and encouragements on faded paper, taped to the wall above my desk, whose receipt I don't remember and whose usernames are those of strangers. For all I know, they've forgotten as well; it *has* been nearly a decade. But if that's not the case, if they've remembered this story all these years and somehow found their way here, despite everything? Well. I hope they know I never could have done it without them.

ALSO BY HAZEL DOMAIN

The Powers That Be
Any Cost
Broken Contracts

ABOUT THE AUTHOR

Hazel Domain is a cryptid who escaped Ohio and can now be found roaming the woods of eastern Maine. Hazel spends their time fixing computers, fiddling with databases, making renaissance faire costumes and, when all alternatives have been exhausted, writing.

Hazel has five Nanowrimo certificates, a doctorate in parapsychology, and a cat.

Tumblr: .tumblr.com/hazeldomain
Twitter: twitter.com/HazelDomain
TikTok: tiktok.com/@theehazeldomain

Enjoy more stories like *Any Price* at RiptidePublishing.com!

Deal in Divinity

Lots of people have demons, but they're not usually literal.

ISBN: 978-1-62649-990-4

Surreal Estate

Houses just want to be homes. These guys just want to be together.

ISBN: 978-1-62649-855-6

www.ingramcontent.com/pod-product-compliance
Lightning Source LLC
LaVergne TN
LVHW091124080826
845145LV00008B/2037